Luca

NIKKI J SUMMERS

Copyrighted Material
LUCA

This book is a work of fiction. Names, characters,
businesses, places, events and incidents are either the
product of the author's imagination or used in a fictitious
manner. Any resemblance to actual events or persons living
or dead is purely coincidental. Any trademarks, product
names or named features are assumed to be the property of
their respective owners and are used for reference only.

Copyright 2019 by Nikki J Summers
All rights reserved. No part of this work may be reproduced,
scanned or distribute in any printed or electronic form
without the express, written consent of the author.
A CIP record of this book is available from the British
Library.

Cover Design: Sarah Paige at Opium House Creatives
Editing: Lindsey Powell

Other Books
by NIKKI J SUMMERS

STAND-ALONE:

This Cruel Love
(Jackson's Story)

Hurt to Love
(Cillian's Story)

JOE AND ELLA SERIES:

Obsessively Yours
Forever Mine

All available on Amazon Kindle Unlimited.
Only suitable for 18+ due to adult content.

Trigger Warning
A MESSAGE FROM THE AUTHOR

This story is intended for readers of 18 years and upwards, due to the sexually explicit content. It also deals with issues which some may find difficult to read and may cause distress.

This includes sexual violence, kidnap, and scenes of violence and murder.

Prologue
CHLOE

14 years ago…

I heard the faint, low rumbling sound of the removal van in the distance, way before it wound its way around the corner of our cosy little neighbourhood. I'd been beyond excited for days now. Ever since Mrs Price, from two doors down, had told me that the old Lanson's house had finally been sold to a family. I prayed hard every night after that, hoping they'd have kids that were the same age as me. Being an only child was lonely enough, but being an only child, with no extended family, cousins or other children around, was downright depressing.

Our little road housed mostly old people. That was great when they passed you sweets, because they just loved watching you playing out in the street on your own, or gave you ice cream on a hot day, because they wanted to bring a smile to your 'pretty little face', but not much use when you needed another person in your game. In those instances, I usually deferred to my cat, Tilly, or my toys to play those parts. But now, with the possibility of another little boy or girl coming to live next door, I might not have to do that ever again.

I slumped down on the dusty kerb outside our house. My denim dungarees had gotten really muddy that morning from playing armies, and crawling through the dirt like the commandos my Dad liked to watch on TV, but I didn't care.

'Our Chloe, is a take me as you find me kind of girl. She can give any boy in her class a run for his money.' My Dad always liked to tell people. I had no idea what he meant by that, but he always followed it up with a proud smile aimed my way, so I guessed it was a good thing.

My wayward brown, curly hair was tied back into a ponytail. I liked to keep it long. I liked how it felt down my back, and when I twirled the curls around my fingers, but I always wished it could be straight, like the pretty girls at school. Their ponytails hung sleek and neat. Mine was big and bushy, and hung to the bottom of my back, with curly ringlets breaking free out of the sides by my ears because it was so unruly, just like me. That's what my Mum said, anyway.

I watched, as the removal van pulled up outside the house next door, but I couldn't see who was inside. They were all up too high in the drivers' cab. I started to feel butterflies in my tummy, so I held Bow-wow, my threadbare cuddly dog, up to my face to smell his comforting homely smell. I'd had Bow-wow since I was born, and even though Mum was always trying to get rid of him, I always found him in time. Often in the trash, usually just before the men came to take all of the rubbish away. He was always meant to be with me, that's why I always saved him just in time. He was mine.

A man stomped out of the van first. He must've been the Dad, I thought, as he grumbled and muttered under his breath. He was dressed casually in jeans, old trainers and a dirty T-shirt, and had a big fat belly that stuck out underneath. His dark hair was cut very short to his head and he had tanned skin, with a teardrop tattooed on his cheek. Why anyone would want to have a tattoo that made them look like they were crying baffled me. He gazed up at the house, but didn't crack a smile. Not even a hint of a grin graced his sour face. I wondered why he seemed so angry. Wasn't this the house he'd wanted? He didn't wait for anyone else to get out, just marched up the path like a disgruntled ogre, and without saying a word he disappeared inside. I never saw him again that day. I was glad really, because he didn't look too friendly.

I turned my attention back to the van, and saw a lady hop down from the open door. She was tanned like the man, but unlike him, she looked kind and had a gentle serene smile on her face. She looked like the friendly Mums I'd seen hanging around the school gates. The ones who took the time to look at their kids art work at the end of the day, and *hugged them, telling them it'd go up on the fridge or on the wall at home. Mine always went back into my bag or in the bin, but I was used to that. It didn't bother me anymore. I kept the best pieces for myself and didn't even show Mum, in case she threw it out.*

This Mum looked around the neighbourhood with a nod of approval, then her green eyes settled on me, and I felt a warm buzz go through my body. She waved and I waved back, letting Bow-wow drop into my lap, as I gave her my best and most polite smile. The one I'd always been told to give to adults.

She turned and called out to someone in the van, and I tensed up with nerves. This was it, the moment I'd meet my new best friend. A boy, around my age, came out of the same door she'd exited, and grinned a huge, silly grin at me as his Mum pointed me out. I felt embarrassed all of a sudden, and clutched Bow-wow to my face again, so only my eyes could be seen. Bow-wow was always my protector, when I got scared. But when the boy waved, I waved back. He was slightly chubby, but not fat, like his Dad. Just cuddly, with a round face and friendly, laughing eyes. He wore shorts and a T-shirt, and his trainers were old and scruffy, but I didn't care. He looked like the type of boy that liked getting into mischief, and that was something I was extra good at.

I heard another door bang closed, and then a second boy walked around the back of the van, and stood to join the Mum and her son on the pavement. The Mum had her arm around the chubby boy, but this new boy didn't go to stand on her other side, for her to hold him. He stood slightly apart from them, his eyes glazed over like a zombie, as if he wanted to be anywhere but here on our little road.

I couldn't take my eyes off him, though. I'd never seen a boy who looked as pretty as he did before. He was beautiful, so striking. I felt mesmerised by him. He wasn't chubby like his brother, he was taller and leaner. His skin was tanned and his hair was jet black, and although it was short at the side, it was long on top and flopped into his eyes. He had cheekbones like a girl. I think my Mum would've called them chiselled or defined.

His Mum nodded over to where I sat, and he turned to look at me, but he didn't smile and wave. He just scowled and looked away. I felt hurt by the way he ignored me, and his eyes made me feel a sadness I hadn't felt before. Why was he so sad? His stormy eyes were green, just like his Mum's, but they didn't glow like hers. Instead, they seemed to hold dark secrets, maybe fears? The way he stood made him look tired, weary, as if he'd already given up on the world. I should've shunned him then and there, for being so moody and unfriendly, but I didn't. Something about him intrigued me. I wanted so badly for him to like me. To change the look in his eyes. But also, I wanted to be his friend, so that I could stare at his pretty face whenever I wanted.

-

I spent the rest of the afternoon watching avidly from

the kerb, as Mother and sons lugged box after heavy box into the house. When they stopped for a rest, the Mum came over to me with an ice lolly, and sat down next to me.

"Hi! I'm Maria. What's your name?" Her smile was dazzling and infectious, making me feel instantly comfortable in her presence.

"Chloe. Chloe Ellis. I live next door," I announced as politely as I could, pointing to my house behind me. "Thank you for the ice-pop."

"You're very welcome, Chloe. Is it fun living here?"

"It's a nice neighbourhood, but I'm the only kid. So it can get lonely sometimes," I said, giving away more information than she probably wanted.

"Well, I hope you won't have that problem now that we're here. How old are you, Chloe?"

"I'm eight. I'll be nine in eight months." I was already counting down the weeks.

She laughed at my response, but not cruelly like my Mum, or the girls at school might have. Her laugh was kind, and held a hint of endearment.

"My son, Freddie, he's nine. That's him over there in the shorts," she said, pointing out the chubby boy who was bouncing a ball on the front lawn. "And my eldest boy is called Luca. He's twelve."

I looked round to where Luca was sitting. He wasn't playing like Freddie, or eating an ice-lolly like me. He just sat on the porch, fiddling nervously with his hands, and *looking thoroughly fed up.*

"Luca is a quiet boy, but once you get to know him, you'll see he's just as fun as Freddie. Luca is just sensitive, more...closed off." She sighed, and smiled shyly at him. Then she stood up, as if she'd just remembered she had work to do.

"Well, these boxes won't move themselves." She ran her hand down my cheek affectionately, before saying goodbye. Then she hauled another box into her tiny arms, and went puffing and panting back up the path.

Luca stood, and took the box from her to carry it inside. All I could think was, why wasn't the big, strong Daddy helping them out? My Mum would never lift anything if my Dad was around to do it instead. She'd always nag him too, if he ever forgot.

I didn't see Maria again after that day. What happened to her? We never did find out. But, Federico, 'Freddie' and Luca Marquez... they became my whole world.

Chapter One
CHLOE

Present Day

Why did nothing ever go right when you were in a hurry? It was like an unwritten law.

'Thou shalt fuck everything up, whilst trying to be on time.'

I made one last effort to fix my bouncing curls into a style that could be let down in an instant. You know, to add that extra turn-on to the guys who loved the whole secretary letting her hair down, and shaking it out fantasy. Thankfully, I just about managed to pin a messy bun up on my head. My curls were more defined now, less unruly, thanks to decent hair serum and styling products. But I still struggled with them.

"Five minutes, Chloe. Get a move on," Ron shouted, giving me his countdown.

Ron was one of the security guys here at the club. Jack's Kitty Kat gentleman's club, a far less seedy title than calling it what it actually was; a strip joint for old, bald guys and perverts. I still had no idea who Jack was, and neither did anyone else who worked here.

It was only my second shift at this dive, but the money was okay and the tips were awesome, so I just sucked it up and got on with it. It was just dancing, but with less clothes on than a normal Saturday night. That's how I'd reasoned with myself, when I'd debated over taking the job. Plus, I needed the money to pay my tuition fees through medical school. I was getting pretty good at zoning out the crowd and the hecklers, and focusing on with the job at hand. Also, I was slightly less nervous tonight than I had been last night. Last night, I'd panicked that I'd stumble, or struggle to get my clothes off in a seductive way. I needn't have worried. I could've stood on the stage in my sweats and stripped, and they'd have loved it. The audience weren't picky, as long as they got what they wanted at the end.

Jack's had a strict no touching policy, which the patrons usually stuck to. The burly security guys pacing the room kept the more outrageous guests in check. It was a blessing for us girls that they took their job so seriously, as some of the guests could get quite rowdy. The stage wasn't that high. It was easily accessible for the guests to reach up and stick money where they wanted; which unashamedly, they did. Tonight, I wasn't going out wearing that much to start with. I was doing a pole dance tonight. I liked the underwear I had on for it though. Black and lacy, with tiny red roses in the middle of the bra, running along the edge of each cup and at the back of the thong, just above my ass. I was borrowing a pair of black Louboutin's from one of the other girls. The red soles set the look off perfectly, and the stockings I wore were the icing on the cake. I looked like every guys' wet dream, or so Ron had told me when he checked in on me ten minutes ago.

I was just debating over whether to take a whip out with me, when Ron called out. "You're on, Chloe."

I left it behind. I didn't have the experience to introduce props to my act yet.

"Break a leg, kid." One of the older dancers called out. I gave her a wave, as I left the communal dressing room and 'Chloe' behind me, to assume the role of my alter-ego.

The bass of the music, that was vibrating from the floor and up through my body, along with the sound of the audience's chattering laughter, made my stomach clench with nerves. I took a deep breath, and reminded myself that I was dancing for me, no one else. The butterflies soon flew away, replaced by adrenaline, and the determination to get this done and do it well, then get home.

I strutted confidently onto the stage to a howl of cat-calls, wolf-whistles and shouts. Blocking them out, I focused my eyes on the bright spotlight ahead of me, and stood in front of the pole. My legs were slightly apart, and my eyes were hooded with faked desire. Red lighting was piped around the edge of the stage, adding to the whole black and red theme I had going on. I prowled seductively around the pole. In my head, I was in control of every man and woman in this room. Then with a wink and a sway of my hips, I held onto the pole to do my first twirl. I bent down in time to the beat, and let the pole skim along the crack of my ass. It sent the left side of the club into a frenzy, and the right side calling out to see more. Some random guy reached forward to try and grab my leg, but I smirked down at him, and shook my finger to indicate no touching. Then I squatted down in front of him, and ran my long, red nails suggestively along the inside of my thighs, as if to say, 'look what I've got, but you can't get at it.' His friends next to him groaned, and he fell back in his chair moaning and grabbed his crotch, shouting, "You can slide up and down my pole anytime gorgeous." Dream on loser.

I spun around some more on the pole, rhythmically bumping and grinding seductively to the music. Then I reached up and pulled my hair out of the bun, shaking the chocolate curls loose and sending the room crazy. I was just about to showcase some of the more acrobatic pole dancing moves that the girls had taught me, when I heard a commotion coming from the left side of the stage. I didn't look down, intent on keeping my focus on that magic spotlight and staying professional, but I could've sworn I heard someone say Chloe. That was strange, because I never danced under my real name. I was like the rest of the dancers here, I'd been given a stage name from the start. I was Kiki the Kitty Kat. Not the best stage name, I knew that. But then, if I had my choice, I wouldn't be spending my nights anywhere near a dive of a club like this. Whenever we were front of house, we only ever used our Kitty Kat code names. It helped to keep the creepier clients from trying to invade our real lives.

I turned away from the bustle unfurling behind me, and yelped as an oversized men's suit jacket was suddenly thrown over my shoulders. Startled, I turned around, but I couldn't see who had covered me up, because I was immediately disorientated from being thrown over a muscly shoulder. What the hell was going on? I screamed for this guy to put me down and banged on his back, but I didn't get the response I was expecting.

"Shut the fuck up, Chloe. I don't know what you think you're doing, but you don't belong here."

How did he know my name? And why on earth were the security guys just standing around watching, not coming to help me out? I was being kidnapped and they didn't seem to give two shits.

The crowd booed and heckled angrily as some other 'suit' held the door open for my kidnapper, and before I knew it my exposed ass met the biting cold night air, as he marched us towards the car park.

"Let me go. Put me down you asshole."

I wriggled in his hold, trying to kick my legs free, but he was too strong for me.

"Calm down, Chloe. I'm not gonna hurt you, okay?" He

sighed.

"How the hell do you know my name?" I snapped, ready to use every ounce of power in my five-foot-four frame to kick the shit out of him and make a run for it.

He threw me into the back seat of what looked like a Range Rover. Then he held both of his tree trunk arms on either side of the car to fence me in, and stepped back slightly, so I could see his face.

"Don't you recognise me, Chloe? It's me. Freddie."

My mouth dropped open and I stared at him for what must've been a long time, because he reached up and shut my mouth for me.

Federico 'Freddie' Marquez.

He hadn't changed a bit, not really. He still had a round, friendly face, but he wasn't over weight anymore, he was muscly and strong. The white shirt he was wearing stretched tightly over his broad shoulders, and I could see tattoos on his arms and neck, hidden just under his collar. Those hadn't been there the last time I'd seen him. They looked good on him.

"Freddie? What the fuck are you doing here? And why have you kidnapped me?" I said, still scanning the car park behind him for an escape route.

He seemed disappointed that I wasn't throwing my arms around him in gratitude, or hugging him like some long lost relative. But I hadn't forgotten how he'd left me all those years ago. I never forgot what that hurt felt like, even to this day.

"I'm saving you, Chloe."

I thought I detected remorse in his eyes, but I couldn't tell for sure.

"Chloe, you can't work there, not for that guy. Do you have any idea who your boss is?"

I was just about to argue that of course I knew my boss, and I had every right to work where I damn well pleased. I was an adult now. But some thug from the driver's seat piped up.

"Enough with the reunion Fred, we need to get out of here before shit goes off."

Freddie nodded and pushed me across the leather seat. Then he climbed in next to me and we sped off, as he locked the door beside him.

"Where are you taking me? They aren't gonna like you stealing me from the club you know. My roommate, Teresa, she'll be calling the cops if I'm not home in the morning," I said, glancing sideways at Freddie, as he bit his fingernails and fidgeted beside me. I couldn't stop myself from pulling his arm down. Old habits die hard, I guess.

"I still bite them when I'm nervous." He shrugged.

"Why are you nervous? And why didn't the security at the club stop you taking me and beat your ass?"

I was getting pissed off with the lack of information coming from him right now.

He turned to me and glared. "Because I'm Luca

Marquez's brother, and that fucking means something where those guys come from."

At that precise moment a mobile phone rang, and the driver answered by saying, "You're on speaker phone..."

"What the fuck did you do Freddie?" A familiar voice, only deeper and gravellier than I remembered, roared through the car stereo system.

"My phone is ringing off the hook, God damn it. I have enough shit going on without you adding Sanchez to the list, little bro."

Sanchez. That was the name of my boss. Eduardo Sanchez, or Ed, as most of the girls called him. The men called him Mr Sanchez, out of respect, but he liked the girls to call him Ed, well the ones he'd probably fucked. I'd only met him once and he scared the hell out of me. I didn't call him anything other than scary boss man, when I was talking about him in the dressing room, which wasn't often, believe me.

"You'll understand what's going on when I get to you, Luca. You'll see why I did what I did." Freddie replied, and I looked across to him with my eyebrows raised. If he thought for one minute he was taking me to Luca, he had another thing coming.

"I think I understand well enough. You've busted some stripper from Sanchez's club, and now you want my protection. Shit Fred, are you really that desperate to get pussy that you have to kidnap it?"

"Fuck you, Luca. I'm not talking about this over the

phone anymore," Freddie spat out. Anger I'd never seen in him before came radiating over to my side of the car.

"Fine. Take the back stairs. Leo and Dan will meet you there. Don't let anyone see you and don't talk to anyone. Are we clear?" He shouted down the phone.

"Crystal," Freddie replied and the call was shut down.

I went to speak and was met with Freddie's hand in the air in front of my face.

"Don't, Chloe. I don't have the energy or the patience for your independent, argumentative bullshit."

I huffed and folded my arms over my chest. If he thought I was causing shit now, he hadn't seen anything yet.

Chapter Two
CHLOE

12 years ago…

I crouched down by our back door listening, and terrified of the angry shouts coming from next door. The bangs and crashes that always followed the hollering made me jump in fear. I knew I'd need to spring into action in a few minutes, when the shouting subsided and the dust started to settle. Luckily, Dad was engrossed in his army T.V program. The voiceover, telling him how the D-Day landings had started, helped to mask any noises I made in the kitchen getting my provisions ready. Mum was out on a girls' night with her friends and wouldn't be back for ages, so I had the perfect opportunity to do what I always did.

The noises finally began to wane, and I checked my bags for the twentieth time, making sure I was well stocked. Then I crept out of the back door and down to the bottom of our garden, where the fencing had become rotten. One of the panels was loose, and I pushed it aside to stealthily make my *way into the Marquez's back yard. I knew exactly where I'd find Freddie. I always went to him first because he was the closest. Sure enough, he was sitting under the oak tree at the bottom of the yard with his head in his hands.*

"What was it this time, Freddie?" I whispered.

"The usual. Dad's drunk and he said he's tired of paying for two fucked up sons. Said we were a waste of his time and money." He was crying big, fat tears and sniffling.

"Well, I love you. Don't listen to him. He's a mean old man."

I wished Mr Marquez was the one who'd disappeared, not their Mum, Maria. He was a violent, nasty drunk, who treated his sons like punching bags, when they weren't acting as his personal slaves that is.

"I can't wait to leave this house when we're older."

I knew that was for the best, but hearing Freddie say it out loud made my heart twinge and my stomach churn.

"Where are you hurt?" I asked, giving him my warmest smile.

"He hit my head and caught me on my arm, but I didn't get it half as bad as Luca. I never get it as bad as Luca."

I knew Luca always protected Freddie. He took the hardest beatings, and worst knocks to save Freddie from harm. He really was the best big brother in the world.

"Here, rub this wipe over where it hurts and then stay here until Luca tells you it's safe, okay?" I said, handing Freddie an alcohol wipe. I'd no idea if it'd help, but my

nursing skills as a ten-year-old were somewhat limited, and Freddie always seemed grateful.

"Thanks, Chloe. You're my favourite little sister." He winked at me and I laughed quietly.

"I'm your only little sister, Freddie. No dropping me for another one, okay?"

"Never." He smiled, and I crawled away from him over the grass, using my best commando moves, with my first-aid bag secured safely on my back.

I found Luca in his usual spot on the porch at the back of the house, sitting guarding his back door. I knew he was keeping watch, so that if his Dad came back out to start on them again, he would only find Luca. It made my chest ache to see him sitting there with a split lip. His teeth were clenched together, and his knees were bent to his chest, arms wrapped around them protectively.

"What're you doing here, Chloe? You should be asleep in bed."

He hissed at me in irritation, but I knew he wasn't really that mad. He liked me comforting Freddie. He wasn't so keen on the comfort himself, though.

"You're hurt, and my Dad says I'm good at healing, so here I am," I said matter of fact.

"I don't need your help." He didn't make eye contact with me and spoke gruffly, as if he wanted to scare me away, or make me mad enough to leave.

"Everyone needs help, Luca, even you." I reached out to

touch his arm, but he flinched and pulled away from me.

"I don't. I can manage just fine on my own."

He looked down at the dirt and started making circle patterns on the floor with his grubby fingers. It didn't matter to me if he refused my help. I'd always come over to him, no matter how many times he tried to turn me away.

"Is it your head that hurts, like Freddie? Or your arm?" I started to rifle through my bag and Luca shot his hand out to cover mine, stopping my movement.

"You need to be quiet, Chloe. If he comes out and finds you, he might hurt you too." He stared at me for a few seconds then sighed. "Fine. If it'll make you go away quicker, it was my chest, my back, my head and my lip, look." He pointed at his split lip.

"I have wipes you can use, but I don't think wipes or band aids will help your lip, will they?"

"No."

He broke my heart. He was so beautiful. I hated to see the bitter, painful storms raging in his eyes. It reached out to me and held my heart in a vice. Any pain Luca felt, I felt it too.

On impulse, I leant forward and put my lips gently against his, giving him a delicate kiss, so as not to hurt him anymore than he already was. Being so close to him, feeling his warm breath mingle with mine, made me faint and giddy.

"What're you doing, Chloe?" He screwed his face up and

pulled away from me sharply. "You can't kiss me."

"Why not? My Dad kisses me when I hurt myself. He says a kiss makes anything feel better."

"He says that because he's your Dad, and he's kind, not like ours. He loves you, Chloe. But kisses don't make anything better."

"They make me feel better. Anyway, I wanted to kiss you, Luca. You're mine." I told him this most days, but it still hadn't sunk in yet. Boys were stupid.

"I can't be yours, Chloe, I'm too old for you. You need to find a boy your own age." He said that most days too, but I never listened.

"You're only fourteen, Luca, and I'll be eleven soon."

"I'm fifteen next month. Anyway, a fourteen-year-old boy can't kiss a ten-year-old girl, it's not allowed." His rules were rubbish.

"That's a silly rule and I don't like it. If I want to kiss you, I will."

"Chloe Ellis, you're a stubborn little girl who never does as she's told. You need to go home now before you get caught. I have enough to do protecting Freddie. I can't protect you both."

I huffed in protest, but he was right. So I sneaked back to my warm, safe house in record time and slinked up the stairs, making sure to miss the parts where the floorboards creaked, and headed into my pink, princess bedroom. Out of my window I could see the Marquez's back yard and the *shadow of Luca, sitting as still as a statue on the porch. His head was bowed in sorrow, and I couldn't stop myself from blowing him a secret kiss and praying it'd touch his heart of stone.*

Chapter Three
CHLOE

Present Day

We drove on in uncomfortable silence for another twenty or so minutes, before we pulled into a secluded car park surrounded by buildings and totally deserted, apart from a few cars scattered around. This must've been the back entrance to wherever Freddie was taking me. I'd no idea what I was going to walk into, but I had my badass attitude gauge cranked up to maximum, and I wasn't about to show any weakness.

Freddie opened his door, then grabbed my arm and pulled me along the back seat of the car with him, to exit on his side.

"You don't have to dislocate my arm you know, Jesus." I whined like a kid.

"I can't afford to let you run, Chloe. I need to keep you safe, now more than ever." His eyes bored into mine, but I just rolled mine in a blasé way to show him he wasn't scaring me.

"I think you're over exaggerating how valuable a stripper, and an average one at that, could mean to a club like Jack's."

"It's the boss I'm worried about, not the club," he replied, yanking my arm again to get me to walk towards a dark alley in-between two buildings.

I stumbled along reluctantly. I could hear the familiar noise of club music, bass thumping and reverberating off the walls around us. It was biting cold out, so I pulled the lapels of Freddie's jacket tighter round me, to give my scantily clad body some form of protection from the imminent bout of pneumonia that I was sure to develop tomorrow. Freddie stopped at a door and knocked. He was growing anxious, I could tell. He wasn't just biting his nails, he was tapping his foot too. A nervous habit he'd had since he was nine.

"Chill out, Freddie. I'll protect you," I joked.

"Quit joking around, Chloe. This is serious."

The door swung open, and two men built like mountains stood before us, dressed in black suits and wearing ear pieces, indicating that they were some type of security. They nodded to Freddie, and he pushed me through the door first, before following behind. The heavy door slammed shut, and the male mountains shoved past me, each one turning back to look me up and down with lascivious expressions on their faces. They led us to a staircase at the back of what I now assumed was a nightclub, or probably a strip club like the one

I'd just left. Was that what this was all about? Strip club wars?

"Are you stealing me from Jack's to make me strip here instead?" I asked, but Freddie shook his head.

"Always with the questions, Chloe. No, this isn't a strip club. And no, I don't want you dancing, not like that. It isn't you."

"How would you know what's me? You haven't seen me for seven years, Freddie," I snapped.

"You're right. I don't know you as well as I used to. But I know enough to say that's not how you want to make a living. And I know enough about your boss to tell you, things could be a whole lot worse for you right now, if I'd have walked away tonight."

"How, Freddie? How could things possibly be worse for me? I've probably lost my job tonight. Teresa and I have zero rent money. Our rent is due in like three days and we have no idea how we're gonna pay that. Oh, and the landlord is a sleazy asshole, who'll probably try to get me to pay him in kind. That's not even touching on the tuition fees and other stuff I need for university. You've fucked up my night and my life."

I didn't get an answer from him though, because we'd arrived at a dark wooden door, with cameras pointed at it and two new guys standing guard on either side.

"Are we seeing the Godfather?" I smirked across at the men all gathered around the door, like it was the gateway to somewhere other-worldly.

"No, just my big brother." Freddie glared back.

"Oh goody, a reunion. Just what I wanted to do tonight instead of earn my rent money."

My stomach turned at the thought of seeing Luca Marquez again after all these years. If I could've bolted back down the stairs, I would've in a heartbeat, but I was trapped.

One of the gorillas guarding the door mumbled into his ear piece and then opened the door for us to enter. I stood still until Freddie pushed me forward, forcing me to stomp like a sulky teenager into the office in front of us. Freddie closed the door behind him and I huffed in annoyance and plonked myself down into a leather sofa in front of me. Folding my arms over my chest to cover myself, I moaned out loud. "This is ridiculous."

The office was eerily dark. The only light came from a lamp on a huge mahogany desk and a wall of screens showing security footage of the club, the corridors and outside areas. There was a large fireplace with a roaring fire, and a glass drinks cabinet next to it, set into the wall, with every spirit I could think of stacked up there. The whole aura of the office oozed power and intimidation. A dark figure sat in the shadows behind the desk, in some kind of show of supremacy. To try and make me feel nervous no doubt, unsettled. I knew it was Luca, and he didn't scare me. I'd known him as a twelve-year-old boy. I last saw him when he was a nineteen-year-old coward, leaving me behind. He always liked to play the part of the aloof, untouchable mysterious one, but I knew him better than that.

The room was silent for about thirty seconds, before my resolve to stay quiet finally broke.

"Well, this catch up has been great, can I go now?" I said in a sarcastic manner meant to rile them both up.

"Why did you bring a whore to my door, Freddie?" Shadowy Luca growled.

"Yeah, Freddie. Why did you do that? Because all strippers are whores, you should know that, right? Was it to piss your brother off, or do you think I'm a sure thing?" I chipped in, shaking my head in mock disgust.

"Do you need me to spell it out for you?" Freddie wasn't letting this one go. "Do you know what would've happened to you if you'd carried on working there?"

"That's her decision, brother."

Luca sounded as bored as I was with this whole scenario. He wasn't even looking at us. 'Charming,' I thought. He was so important now, he couldn't even give his little brother the courtesy of looking at him when he spoke. I wasn't sure I liked this new Luca one bit.

"Yes it is." I altered my gaze from the shadow behind the desk to where Freddie stood. "So tell me what your problem is, *Freddie,* or take me back. You know, Teresa will call the cops. Do you want them crawling all over this place tomorrow?"

Freddie shook his head at both of us, as if he couldn't believe what he was hearing.

"You want to know why I saved you? Fine. Tonight you were dancing. Taking your clothes off for money. But tomorrow, you could've been shipped off to fuck knows where. Sanchez is a trafficker. A sex trafficker. He specialises in a certain... *type* of sex slave. I'm guessing that's where you were heading before too long."

I gulped quietly in horror, but managed to keep my cool exterior in place.

"You think I can't look after myself? I've been looking after myself just fine for years. I don't need you or anyone else."

"Freddie, you can't save every fucking stripper Sanchez employs. Just send her on her way and I'll smooth things over for you. I'll sort it... as usual."

Luca started to tap away at his computer, obviously indicating that he was finished with this farce, and had already moved onto the next pressing piece of business.

"No!" Freddie shouted.

Luca stopped, his fingers in mid-air, and his head instantly snapped up to where his brother stood. He rolled his chair forward to illuminate his face in the lamp light, and when I saw him, I had to hold in my gasp.

In the seven years since I last saw Luca, he'd grown even more beautiful, something which I would've thought was impossible. His jet-black hair was still long on top, but he'd slicked it back now, giving him a dominant and commanding look. His lightly-tanned skin was flawless, but he had more dark stubble than he used to covering his square jaw, with a sexy roughness that screamed stroke me, hold me, grab me. His green eyes sparkled with wicked intent, and his lips looked full, plump. I found myself imaging what it'd be like to kiss those lips, bite them. Feel them biting, nipping, caressing places I shouldn't be thinking about right now in this office. I felt familiar flutters and moisture pool between my legs. He was a distraction I didn't need. Lord, this boy, well man now, always did this to me. He had the ability to put me under a spell every single time I was in his presence. That was one thing that time hadn't changed. I was always gaga over Luca bloody Marquez, and there was nothing I could do about it. He rendered me powerless.

"Who the fuck do you think you're talking to?" He gritted his teeth and his eyes burned into Freddie. I'd never seen him so angry, and certainly not at his beloved brother.

"Luca, do you even know who she is? Have you taken the time to look at her? She's not some two-bit whore."

Luca didn't even glance in my direction, he was so done with this it was kind of humiliating. I felt embarrassed for Freddie.

"I couldn't give a fuck if she's the Queen of England. Get her off my sofa and out of my club, understood?"

I held my breath and waited to hear what Freddie would say next.

"No!"

Oh, he was really trying to make up for abandoning me

seven years ago. Too little too late, dude, but nice try all the same.

Luca shot up out of his chair, almost knocking it over. Pure, unbridled fury boiled over, as he stalked around the desk to face his brother.

"Are you challenging me, *little* brother?" He sneered, and I could sense the destructive power play bouncing off the walls.

"I'm challenging you to look at her. I mean really look at her, and then tell me you wouldn't have done exactly the same thing tonight, if you'd been at the club," Freddie said, holding his chin a little higher and standing his ground against this new, mighty Luca.

I glanced cautiously up at Luca, as he leered over his brother, breathing deeply down at him in annoyance. He was still a foot taller than his little brother, and he oozed power, he commanded it. He wore a dark suit, but not like the security guys. No, his was 100% designer, fit to perfection to showcase his muscly frame. The top two buttons of his dark grey shirt were undone, and he'd loosened his black tie. He was dressed for business and ready for sin, all at the same time. I couldn't breathe, the air was stifling. Would he recognise me? Would it upset me if he didn't?

The last time he saw me, my curly hair was frizzy and wild. My body was certainly a hell of a lot different to the one I was hiding under Freddie's jacket, about three or four cup sizes different. My attitude hadn't changed, though. I was still the ultimate boss of my world.

Luca put his hands on his hips and shook his head, then turned to face me. I froze. I couldn't second guess how this was going to play out. Seconds passed as he gazed at me, starting at my high heels and stocking clad legs. Then up my body, that was carefully hidden under the oversized men's jacket, and finally to my face and my eyes. I saw it, the instant he recognised me, the flicker of recognition for just a second, then it disappeared. What it meant, I had no idea? But something had been there, something passed between us. He knew exactly who I was, and I still affected him in some way, no matter how small or how he tried to hide it. It made my tummy flip in triumph, but I still bit down on my bottom lip, nervous to hear what he would say or do next.

"I know who she is," he said, quietly turning to Freddie. The brothers stared silently at each other before Luca finally broke. "Fine. What do you want me to do?"

"I want you to look after her. She's vulnerable," Freddie replied.

"Ha! I am not vulnerable," I snapped back. "I can deal with any assholes that come my way, don't you worry about me."

"Still as stubborn as ever," Luca said without looking at me.

"It's a case of having to be, when you've lived alone on the streets for years like I have."

Luca seemed to wince slightly at this little revelation,

but Freddie, as always was the one to pipe up.

"Hey, you two. Enough with the arguments. We aren't kids anymore. And Chloe, if we'd known you were on the streets, we'd have helped you. We had no idea, honestly."

I wanted to argue that they'd left me. That they didn't care. But what was the point? I had zero energy and I was rapidly losing patience.

"Whatever, Fred. Look, I need to go. I have an important assessment to take tomorrow, and I have to be up early for class."

"You're going nowhere, not for a long time." Luca turned to look me dead in the eyes, pointing at me to emphasise his seriousness. His jaw clenched shut and the pulse in his neck throbbed on double time. "You've got a target painted on your back, you both do. The sooner you go into hiding, the better. I can protect you both, but only if you do what I say."

"I'm not going into hiding. It's an important year for me. I've already paid to get myself through the first three years of med school. I'll be damned if I let your crazy lifestyles stop me now. Forget it, I'll take my chances."

I stood up to leave, but Luca took a step forward and glared at me. The sinister way he snarled down at me with those delicious plump lips made me tremble.

"Sit." He commanded, and just like that, I did.

"Chloe, we'll help you with anything you miss whilst all this is going on. But please, just this once, let us protect you. We owe you that much at least." Freddie looked so contrite, so honest, I just nodded back.

"What the hell. It's only my life and career. Not like it's anything important, right? I suppose you'll 'take care' of Teresa for me too?" I said, sounding ungrateful, but honestly, I didn't know how I felt about any of this. Was I really earmarked for some kind of sex trafficking gig? My skin prickled, and I shivered involuntarily.

Ignoring my question, Luca strode over to the door. Even the way he walked made me go giddy, with what I thought was long since buried desire. I wished he'd taken his jacket off so I could check out how good his ass looked in his tight trousers. I bet it looked damn fine. The corner of my mouth curled up into a cheeky smirk as I thought about it, and gazed longingly at the back of his jacket. Reluctantly, I shifted my gaze away from his ass, to then catch Freddie frowning at me. I shrugged my shoulders, and he chuckled to himself and shook his head in mock despair. He could always read me like a book, and pick up on my unspoken thoughts. I'd missed him and the crazy connection we both had.

"Leo, Dan. Can you take Freddie to the safe house? Fred, you need to lay low. I'll call you on this mobile," Luca said, going over to his desk and pulling a mobile phone out of his drawer and handing it to Freddie. "Don't call anyone else. Don't go out, and don't do anything unless I've okayed it. Are we clear? If you need anything you go through me first, yes?" Freddie nodded, then motioned over to me with his head and said, "And Chloe?"

"You let me worry about her," Luca said half-heartedly. It was clear he wanted Freddie out of the room before he sent me packing, or palmed me off onto someone else, ridding him of the guilt or responsibility.

"Oh no, I want to know where she's going. I want your assurance she'll be safe and nowhere near that club or that monster ever again. I'd die to protect her from him and you know that, brother. What would you do, huh? What would you do to protect Chloe, Luca?" Freddie was playing with fire, even I could see that.

"Don't push me, Fred. She can stay with Gina, or one of the other girls until it's sorted." Luca maintained his dismissive attitude, but Freddie didn't look happy.

"How is that safe?"

"It's all you're getting from me. Take it or leave it," Luca spat out, standing and glaring eye to eye with Freddie, his muscly arms folded over his broad chest. They didn't budge for what felt like ages, then Freddie sighed.

"Okay. Whatever. I trust you, brother."

Freddie turned, then sat down next to me on the sofa, and grabbed me unexpectedly into a massive bear hug.

"I hope we can catch up when all this is over. I've missed you, little sis. I really have."

I was taken aback by his change in attitude, but the friendliness he was showing me now wasn't unwelcome. I needed a hug.

"I missed you too, Freddie. Can I keep the jacket for a

bit? It's not really g-string weather tonight," I said, pulling it closer around me and breathing in his smell from the fabric.

He laughed a proper belly laugh, then said in a hushed voice, "Yes, Chloe. Keep the jacket on. You'll give my brother an even bigger headache if he sees what's underneath it." He grinned. "You can give it to me when we meet up again, or just keep it forever. I don't mind, sis."

He seemed reluctant to let go of me and took a deep breath in, as if he was breathing in my scent and saving it to his memory. I looked over Freddie's shoulder to see Luca watching our display of affection, and grinding his jaw in agitation. He wasn't pleased, I knew the signs all too well. It made me feel smug and satisfied that he was the one on the outside. I'd spent years on the outside looking in where Luca was concerned. So a touch of redemption, no matter how small, felt damn good.

"Okay, Freddie. You gotta put me down, we can't stay here forever." I smiled, pushing him away lightly.

He cupped my face and planted a big, sloppy kiss on my lips, making me scrunch my nose up and laugh.

"I still don't like your sloppy kisses, Freddie."

He stood and walked towards the door without looking back.

"Stay safe, Chloe. I love you, little sis." And then he was gone, leaving me alone with Luca.

Luca wasted no time calling the last two gorillas into the office. He obviously didn't want to be alone with me any longer than he had to. I glared daggers into his back. He was such a bloody coward.

"Can you take Miss Ellis to Gina's? I'll call ahead and inform her of her new...guest."

I huffed and stood from the sofa to make my escape, keeping the jacket closed tightly around me, so as not to flash anyone with my lacy secrets underneath. Luca was escaping back behind his desk without looking me in the face, when something caught his eye and he stopped. He put his hand out to stop me, and then my stomach sank to the floor. I'd totally forgotten I'd worn it tonight, and I knew straight away he'd seen it. He reached forward and touched the St. Christopher necklace that hung around my neck. The same one that'd hung there for seven years. The feel of his hot, rough fingers brushing feather like against my delicate skin, sent thunder bolts of electricity through my body and straight between my legs, making me quiver and hold in my moan. I heard him take an unsteady breath in, but he wouldn't raise his eyes to look into mine. If he had, he'd have seen the years of angst and longing for him, that'd built up within me and then been buried deep. They were still there, they always would be. Lying dormant, ready to be ignited on his say so. He spun round to address the gorillas at the door.

"On second thoughts, take her to mine. Sanchez will be vying for blood and that's the safest place for her. It wouldn't be fair on Gina, or any of the other girls to deal with the shit Sanchez brings with him."

LUCA

My eyes bugged out of my head, but before I could even formulate a reply, the two goons had come either side of me, and were ushering me out of the office and back down the stairs to deliver me to their assigned destination.

Chapter Four
CHLOE

Seven years ago...

"Chloe, time to get up or you'll be late for school." My Dad hollered at me from the kitchen downstairs.

I groaned, wishing it was Saturday and I could fester in my bed all day. Why were school days always the days you needed more sleep? I sneaked an eye open to look at the clock, and noticed a scrap of paper on my bed side table, that hadn't been there when I went to sleep the night before. I sat up in bed, and when I saw what lay on top of the paper, I cried out in pain. Something truly awful had happened, I just knew it.

I lifted the silver chain up, and the St. Christopher pendant that hung from it twirled around in front of my eyes. He'd had that pendant hanging around his neck ever since he'd moved in next door. He never took it off. Once, I'd asked him where he'd got it from and why he always wore it.

"It's the only thing I have left of my Mum's." His stunning, perfect face shadowed in mourning for the Mother he'd loved and lost.

So, why was it here now on my bedside table? I lifted the paper it'd lay upon, and saw scrawled in his messy handwriting six words. Six simple words that I'd find myself clinging onto for the next few years. Six words that I thought held so much truth, but ultimately set me up for the biggest heartbreak of my young life, and caught me, trapped me in its lie.

'I will come back for you.'

Chapter Five
CHLOE

Present day

The two beefy hunks bundled me into the back of a black SUV, and one of them barked over at me to buckle up. I was never one to follow orders, so I ignored him and leaned forward, sticking my head in-between the two front seats to start my interrogation.

"So, who are you guys?" I asked, looking from one to the other.

"That's none of your business," the blond one replied stiffly.

"Well, you'll probably be stuck watching my ass until I can get away, so we might as well know each other's names, right? I'm Chloe, by the way."

I stuck my hand out in-between the seats. I figured if I could get these two on my side, I'd have a better chance at running away and getting back home sooner. Either that, or I could gather some useful information.

"I'm Vince, but everyone calls me Vinnie," the dark-haired one said, shaking my hand. "He's Marco." He pointed at the grumpy blond guy, who looked over at Vinnie accusingly, and huffed in annoyance.

"So, I can call you Marc?" I said, poking his arm.

"No, my name's Marco. You can call me Marco, or sir, and please don't touch me."

"Whatever, Marc. You need to chill out and learn not to take your job so seriously." I sneered, slumping back into the back seat. "Sir...seriously. As if I'd call anyone that!" I tittered quietly.

Vinnie laughed, and Marc scowled at the road ahead as he drove. I had a feeling I was gonna like winding these two up, especially Marc, with the enormous stick he had up his ass.

"How long have you been working for Luca?" I thought I'd start off with the easy questions. Gain some trust and build a rapport with them.

"Me, about three years. Marco here, since forever," Vinnie replied.

"Well, I don't remember you, Marc, from when I was fifteen and hanging out with Luca and Freddie every day." Marco was a tough nut to crack, but I guessed he was the one with the most info.

"So, you two just drive women around all night and guard Luca's office. Your parents must be so proud."

I hoped to get a reaction from one of them, I got my

wish.

"You don't know fuck about what we do and you don't want to know, little girl. Just know this, you're in dangerous territory right now. You'd do well to remember that and keep your pretty little mouth shut," Marco snapped, pulling his jacket back to reveal his handgun.

"Dude, you don't have to scare the girl," Vinnie said.

I chuckled. "You think I'm scared of a handgun? Let me tell you something, I've been dealing with shit from the Marquez family since I was eight-years-old. So let me tell you something, I don't scare easily and I'm used to danger. You think you know me, think again." I guessed right, Luca was into something illegal.

Vinnie chuckled, but Marco just looked straight ahead, his expression gave nothing away.

-

We pulled up outside large, black metal gates, and Marco pushed a button located on the dashboard that activated the opening mechanism. The gates slowly eased open to reveal a short driveway up to a large, white two-storey house surrounded by high walls, with cameras in every corner.

"Nice place." I nodded. "Is this your club house?"

"This is the boss's home," Marco stated proudly, pulling up next to a black sports car. "He lives here alone. Well, he did until tonight." Marco turned to me and raised his eyebrows. "Tell us, what makes you so special, little girl?"

"Wouldn't you like to know?" I replied, opening my door and grinning back at him. "Maybe if you'd been friendlier on the drive over, I might've told you."

"We aren't supposed to be 'friendly' with girls we deal with in our line of work." Vinnie smiled, as if to apologise for their lack of communication.

"Good job I'm not in your line of work then, isn't it." I grinned back.

Marco led us to the highly polished, black double doors at the front of the property, and keyed in a code. The doors opened, as the code was accepted, and we strode inside.

"Wow, this place is so cool."

I walked across the small entry hall into the open-plan living area, and went down a couple of steps towards the windows which ran the full length of the room, from floor to ceiling. It was pitch black outside, but I could still tell it had a spectacular view of the beach, with its snowy white sand and crashing waves. The décor was simple blacks and whites, and there were no photographs or personal artefacts on display. Luca's home showed nothing of his personality, or perhaps it did. It was a front. Perfect on the outside, flawless even, but hiding dark secrets underneath.

I spotted a pack of cards on a console table nearby, and my rebellious side kicked into gear.

"Do either of you guys play cards?"

"Not when we're on duty," Marco said folding his arms.

"You're off duty now." I held my hands up in the air.

"Look, I'm where you needed to take me." I huffed out in boredom. "Oh come on guys, humour me a little. I've had a pretty shitty night, so a couple of hands of poker might cheer me up."

Vinnie shrugged at Marco. "Sounds better than sitting around making small talk. Are we playing for money?"

Seeing as I had no money to start with, I kicked off my Louboutin's and gave a cheeky smile.

"How about strip poker?" They both raised their eyebrows at me.

"Oh, come on! I have three items of clothing on." I opened my jacket to reveal what was underneath and Vinnie laughed.

"You're one crazy girl, you know that?"

"So I've been told!" I danced over to a white lacquered dining table, and sat down at the head of the table.

"How many cards do I need to deal out for poker?"

Marco raised his eyebrows in exasperation. "Do you even know how to play poker?"

I shrugged nonchalantly. "I played a few years ago with my Dad. I've forgotten some of the rules, but I'm sure you guys can help me." I gave Marco my best puppy dog eyes and he growled.

"The boss will kill us if he finds out we're playing cards, never mind strip poker."

"Good job neither one of us will tell him then." I smiled. "Marc, you really need to live a little. Let your hair down. If you take that stick out of your ass once in a while, you might even have some fun."

Vinnie roared with laughter.

"Come on, girlie. I'll deal. You just pray the cards are lucky for you tonight, sweetheart." He winked at me as he dealt the cards. Marco sat in the chair opposite him, and to my right, glaring at Vinnie as if he'd agreed to a game of Russian roulette.

We each looked at our cards. We ummed and ahhed, and eventually we were all ready to show our hands.

"I don't think my hand is any good is it?" I pretended to look hopeful as I put down my cards with zero value.

"Better luck next time, Chloe."

Vinnie laughed, and I slipped Freddie's jacket off my shoulders and onto the floor, then sat back in my bra and panties. I noticed both guys trying but failing miserably not to check me out. Vinnie adjusted himself where he was sitting and I stifled a giggle.

I played a good game at pretended to be disappointed, but I was in my element. As my Father always taught me, lull them into a false sense of security, and then hit them where it hurts.

"What've you got this time, Chloe?" Vinnie wiggled his eyebrows at me.

"I have these three tens, are they any good?" I sighed and batted my eye lids like a stupid, naive woman.

"Shit, that's three of a kind," Vinnie said. "Are you sure

you're new to this game and not hustling us?"

Of course I was hustling them. I spent most days honing my craft, when Teresa and I were stuck indoors with no money and nowhere to go.

"No. I haven't played for years. Guess it was a lucky hand guys, so get em off."

Marco huffed, and threw his cards down, with only a measly pair of fours to show. Then both men shrugged their jackets off their shoulders and threw them to the floor.

Their night got progressively worse from there on in. They didn't spot my sleight of hand, or even question why I was winning all the time. And I was doing a pretty awesome job of acting like a clueless sap.

"I think I have something here." I grinned sheepishly, as I placed down a straight flush; four, five, six, seven, eight, all spades.

"Aww man, she's killing us!" Vinnie threw his head back, then looked over to Marco and his face froze.

I'd already got them both stripped down to their underwear, and I was chuckling evilly in my corner of the table, when I heard the front door bang closed.

"What the fuck is going on here?"

I looked across to where Luca stood, his handsome face twisted and contorted into fury. His fists balled at the side of him, and his jaw clenched so tightly shut, I bet we could've heard his teeth grinding if we'd listened hard enough. My skin burned under his gaze, and I felt exposed for the first time tonight. It must've looked a sight to walk in on, me and the two guards, stripped down to our underwear at the dining table.

"Sorry, boss. She wanted to play cards, so we thought it was best to keep her happy," Vinnie said

"You thought it was a good idea to play cards with a card sharp, whilst you waited for me to get home? And Strip poker at that? Seriously, it took you guys to get down to your underwear to figure out she's a cheat?"

"I'm not a cheat... I'm an artist!" I cried, infuriated at his use of the word cheat. I wasn't a cheater. I was a winner by any means necessary, that's what Dad always told me.

"A con artist," Marco replied bitterly, glaring over at me.

"You're just pissed cuz you lost." I smiled. "Anyway, I didn't con you out of your money, just your clothes. You wouldn't be complaining if it'd been the other way around and I was sat here naked, would you?"

"You might as well be from where I'm standing. It's not like your underwear leaves a lot to the imagination." Luca was seriously pissed off and not trying to hide it one little bit.

Vinnie thought my predicament was amusing, but Marco didn't, and neither did Luca.

"You won't find it funny when I kick your ass out and fire you." Luca threatened Vinnie, and both men stood up and started to gather their clothes together.

"Upstairs now, Chloe." Luca ordered. I just sat back and folded my arms, daring him to look my way, but fearful of what his gaze would do to me.

"What part of that don't you understand?" He moved closer to where we sat, his eyes full of anger, but never reaching mine.

"Where upstairs?" I asked.

"First door on the left, that'll be your room while you're here. Go." He snapped, throwing his arm in the general direction of the staircase, his eyes fixed on Vinnie across the table.

I stood and started to walk away, giving my hips a sneaky, sexy sway as I walked off, hoping in some sadistic way that they'd all be checking me out.

"Oh, and Chloe? Stay away from my men in future."

I turned around, but Luca eyes were fixed, staring at the floor. So much for *him* checking me out.

As I reached the top of the stairs, I heard him say to his men, "Cards, darts, pool, whatever it is, you don't play it with her. She's a hustler. Her Dad taught her everything he knew, and she'll beat both your asses before you even know what's happened. She's the best."

I smiled proudly. Yes, I was the best, Luca. And don't you ever forget it.

"Cool," Vinnie replied. "She's awesome."

"She's off limits is what she is. Stay away from her, I mean it."

I had no idea if he was warning them off me because he feared for their ego if they lost a game, or because he was jealous of another guy giving me attention. I found myself hoping it was the latter.

Chapter Six

The room Luca had put me in was beautiful, all silver and white luxury. It felt like a plush, mega expensive hotel room. The bed was the comfiest I'd ever laid on, and the sheets were soft, thick Egyptian cotton, the best money could buy. It looked like Luca had done well for himself, or rather the illegal shit he was into these days paid well.

I had my own private bathroom, with chrome fixtures and a massive walk-in shower with jets coming from the walls as well as the ceiling. If I'd had a shower like this at home, I would've spent the majority of my time in there. The bedroom windows faced the beach, so I'd wake up to that spectacular view every morning. Was Luca planning on keeping me here? Because after a day or two of this, I wouldn't want to leave.

I paced around the room, looking for a telephone or computers with internet connection, but found nothing. Then I listened out for a knock at the door, or some indication that he might come to talk to me, but again nothing. I sank down exhausted onto the bed and stared at the ceiling. What the hell had happened to me tonight? Yesterday, life was pretty simple. Tough, but simple nonetheless. Now, here I was lying in a bedroom in the home of my first love, hell my only love, and laying low to save myself from some crazy, trafficking dude, who may or may not sell me into slavery. Life was never dull when the Marquez brothers were around.

Tiredness caught up with me and I found myself drifting off. But just before sleep took me, I heard his heavy footsteps on the stairs. I held my breath and watched as a shadow appeared under the gap of my bedroom door. Was he going to come in? Or knock on the door and check up on me? What would I do if he did? Pictures of what could happen between us played over in my mind like a racy porno. Then I chastised myself and shut them down. What the hell was I thinking? He was an asshole. A heartbeat later, the shadow walked away, and the lights from outside went off.

-

The next morning, I was woken by the glorious sunshine streaming down onto the bed and warming my bare skin. I leant up on my elbows and looked around. Everything felt strange in the light of day. What on earth was I doing here, sleeping in Luca Marquez's spare room? I had to leave today, and I definitely needed to ring Teresa, and fill her in on everything. Our rent was due in two days, and even though I was banned from the casinos in the local area, I figured a trip across state, to try out some new places, might help build up some much-needed funds for us.

The aroma of bacon and eggs started to filter its way into my senses, and I sat up looking around for something to cover myself with. I only had my bra and knickers from the night before. I'd left Freddie's jacket on the living room floor last night, so I couldn't use that. There was a built-in wardrobe along one of the walls, so I pushed the door aside to see if there was anything I could borrow. Row upon row of shirts, jackets, T-shirts and jumpers lined the wardrobe. I found myself stroking my hands across them, and then taking a deep breath in to see if they smelt of him. They did and it made me feel horny again. Jeez, what was wrong with me? I'd gone from sophisticated woman to needy horn bag in one night. I had to get out of this place, it was messing with my head.

I grabbed a plain, white dress shirt and threw it on, sniffing the manly scent once more, before shaking my head clear of all my naughty thoughts. It felt big on my tiny frame, it smothered me, much like its owner used to. But at least it covered my tits and ass and would keep me warm.

I headed downstairs in the direction of the food smells, and when I opened the door to the kitchen, I was surprised to see Vinnie at the oven, frying up a feast of a breakfast.

"Morning, Chloe. Did you sleep okay?" He asked, looking me up and down, and spending a bit too long ogling my bare legs.

"Yeah, fine. Do you always cook breakfast here?" I stood next to him, leaning against the counter, and picked a crispy slice of bacon up to nibble on.

"I like cooking," he replied, then tutted at my rudeness for stealing the bacon, and tried to grab it out of my hands. But I scooted away too quickly. "Coffee? Or are you a tea drinker?"

"Coffee is fine. Black, no sugar."

"Same as Luca." He looked at me as if he was telling me something I didn't know. I already knew how Luca took his coffee. It'd been the reason I took mine the same way when we were younger. I'd only had milk and sugar if I was at home and he didn't know about it, but eventually his taste for black, no sugar, became mine too. I guessed we shared the same bitterness for life.

"I need to call my friend, Teresa. Tell her where I am. She'll freak out otherwise. I can't find any phones or computers, though. Can I borrow your mobile?"

"Already taken care of." A deep voice behind me stated clearly.

I turned around to see Luca, stood at the door in dark jeans and a black v-neck sweater. Tattoos were visible on his chest where the v rested. He was glaring at my body now, not my face, and he seemed...bothered.

"Is she okay?" I asked. He didn't reply with the answer I was looking for.

"Put some clothes on. My men don't need to see you walking around half naked." He turned to walk away from me, but my laugh had him spinning back around.

"Well, I would if I had any, but your brother stole me in my underwear and I've been stuck here all night. You're lucky I put this shirt on. It was this or nothing."

Vinnie gave a wolf-whistle which made me smirk.

"Stay in your room then," Luca growled, stalking off.

"Yeah, great idea. How about you get the handcuffs out and chain me up whilst you're at it." I shouted out to him.

"Kinky," Vinnie chuckled.

"Don't fucking tempt me," Luca spat back.

He was acting like a grade-A asshole right now. I remembered he was always a moody guy, but he was taking that assholery to a whole new level. I felt like taking the shirt off and walking back to my room stark naked, just to piss him off.

"Asshole," I whispered under my breath and sat down at the kitchen table. No way was I going to miss out on a full breakfast and first-class coffee because of his grouchy mood.

"So, what's the story between you two?" Vinnie asked as he flipped his pancakes and turned the bacon over.

"Our story?" I bit my bottom lip. "It's...complicated."

"I can see that. I've never seen the boss show so much emotion in...well, ever."

I knew what he meant. Luca was closed off, emotionally detached. But I knew how to get under his skin, I always had.

"We go way back. I lived next door to him and Freddie for years. We have a lot of...history."

I found it difficult to put into words what Freddie and

Luca meant to me, Luca especially. I'd spent half of my life loving him unconditionally, and the other half despising him for being such a coward and leaving me. I'd never found out what happened that night, seven years ago. All I knew was they all disappeared; Luca, Freddie and their father. The police found traces of blood and a bullet lodged into the wall, but nothing else, or so they told us.

"So you think you'll stay around for a while?" Vinnie put a plate of bacon, eggs, pancakes and waffles in front of me and then sat down next to me.

"I doubt it. I think all the bridges are burned as far as me and the Marquez brothers are concerned." I sighed and bit into another strip of bacon.

"I don't believe that for a second." Vinnie stood up to leave, but his raised eyebrows didn't go unnoticed by me. Did he know something I didn't?

-

I spent the rest of the day in my room. As much as I loved sparring with Luca or Marco, I felt tired and wanted to be alone. I sat watching the beach outside, where surfers waited to catch the perfect wave. The odd dog walker went past, as their dog pranced along the seashore, jumping over the trickle of the waves meeting the shore and barking in delight.

I was just about to start climbing the walls, when a knock sounded on my door.

"Come in," I called from the windowsill where I sat.

The door swung open, and Marco came strolling in

loaded down with shopping bags. Vinnie and a few other men followed behind, and started depositing boxes and bags onto the bedroom floor.

"What's going on?" I asked confused.

"New clothes." Marco gestured to the bags around him. "New shoes, new erm...under things." He blushed saying this, and I couldn't help thinking that he was kinda cute really.

"Did you get these?" I stood up and glanced into one of the bags, noticing the name of a popular designer I could never have afford in a million years.

"No. Bosses orders. Gina bought them and we collected them from her just now. They should be the right size. Let us know if not."

Marco nodded at me and ushered the other guys out of the room, locking the door behind him.

Jeez, there must've been hundreds if not thousands worth of stuff here. Everything from dresses, jumpers, jeans, boots, shoes, underwear and nightwear. There were even toiletries, perfume, make-up and some hair products especially for curly hair. I'd no idea who this Gina was, but at the very least, Luca must've told her I had curly hair. It left me confused as hell. One minute he's barking orders at me as if I'm the biggest pain in his ass, then he's buying up a whole store of clothes for me and paying special attention to my hair and make-up needs. What was up with that?

Another knock came at the door and I opened it to find Vinnie standing there looking awkward.

"There's gonna be a party here later tonight. I just thought I'd tell you so you were prepared, you know, in case you wanted to get dressed up or whatever."

"Thanks, Vinnie. Should I be dressed up?"

"I don't know. The boss will probably kick my ass for even telling you about it, but it's not like you won't hear the noise or the music."

Vinnie stood at the door looking at his feet like a gawky teenage boy, then sighed to himself and looked up at me.

"Maybe it's better if you stay in your room. Wouldn't want to upset the boss any more than you already have, right?"

"Are you kidding me? And miss out on a party? No way!" I replied, and gave a sexy grin as I went to push the door closed. Then I figured, with Vinnie being in such an accommodating mood, I might try for one more favour.

"Hey, Vinnie. Can I borrow your mobile? I really need to talk to my roommate, Teresa. I just need to know she's okay. I won't tell anyone you lent it to me." I pursed my lips and gave him a sexy, smouldering look. As if his relenting to this favour would bring further 'favours' his way.

"Sorry, Chloe. No can do. Boss would cut my balls off." With that he sighed and walked away.

I slammed the door shut with a frustrated groan, and made my way over to the treasure trove of goodies awaiting me on the floor, to help distract me. My bad mood was tempting me to rip every damn thing up into pieces to spite

Luca for being such an ass, but my head said, 'girl, don't take it out on the shopping, for the love of God." My head won out.

Maybe, I could put off leaving Luca's for a little bit longer, have a bit of fun teasing him instead. The idea of toying with him was just too damn tempting.

Chapter Seven

Later that afternoon, I heard another knock on my door, and was shocked when I opened it and found Luca standing on the threshold. He looked like a gorgeously sinful devil, full of lustful promises, with his jet-black hair and hypnotic green eyes. Those eyes didn't meet mine, but he glanced in a disinterested manner past me into the bedroom, and held a mobile phone out to me.

"Freddie wants to speak to you," he snapped and crossed his muscly arms over his well-defined chest. Making the old me yearn for the chance to feel those arms around me, just once.

I lifted the phone to my ear, expecting Luca to walk away, but he stood his ground.

"Hey, Freddie. I'm fine. No need to check up on me." *Unless you're gonna break me out of here and stop all this bullshit, or at least come and visit and make me laugh.* I thought restlessly.

"Is Luca being okay with you?" Freddie asked in a

hushed tone. He knew his brother well enough to know he was standing near to listen in on this conversation.

"Oh, you know, being a closed off prick as usual. But he can't help being an asshole, can he." I grinned over at Luca as I said that, and his eyes met mine, boring into me as if to try and scold me like a child. *Tough luck, Luca. That glare doesn't work on me anymore. Well, not as much as it used to. Oh hell, who was I kidding? He totally had my knees knocking and my pulse racing.*

Freddie laughed. "Chloe, you still know how to push his buttons, don't you? I bet his teeth are almost ground down to his gums by now, aren't they?"

"I think he's got a few millimetres left, but I'll work on it." I smirked, and turned my back on the open door and the six-foot-tall package of seduction staring my way.

"Listen, I know the situation last night was shitty, but I really was doing what's best for you, Chloe." Freddie sighed. "I wouldn't forgive myself if I'd walked away and Sanchez had sold you."

"It's okay, Fred. I think I understand, but I'm not the same little girl you left behind seven years ago. I've been through a lot since then. I can take care of myself better than you realise." *It was a case of having to, after you both deserted me and left me to the wolves.*

"I know. We owe you this much, though. For once, let us do the dirty work. You've helped us enough over the years." I could hear the warmth coming from him over the phone.

I gave a heavy sigh. "Okay, Freddie. Anything for you." *And you're right, you do both owe me. But don't ever fool yourselves into thinking I'm some weak-ass female. I know my strengths, and I can play to them pretty well.*

"I'm looking forward to seeing you, when all this is over," Freddie sang down the line.

"Me too. See you soon, Freddie." I handed the phone back to Luca, hoping to touch his hand as he took it away, so I could see if there were any more sparks when he touched me, but he didn't make contact. Disappointed, I went to close the door, but when I noticed the shopping bags around me, I felt compelled to say something.

"Thanks, by the way."

"For what?" He asked, staring me dead in the face like I was so inconsequential he couldn't believe he was stopping to listen to me.

"For the clothes and other stuff. It was...thoughtful."

He grunted. "It was necessary. I can't afford for my men to become distracted by you."

He went to walk away, then stopped and turned to face me again.

"Don't kid yourself into thinking I'm some kind of hero in this drama of yours. You need to realise that there's a reason men like Sanchez do as I say. He might think he's a big man, but I'm the fucking king around here, and whatever you think of Sanchez and what he can do, know this, I can do a million times worse."

I slammed the door shut and huffed out my annoyance at his ridiculous threats. He didn't scare me. He'd never scared me. God forbid, the mighty Luca Marquez should ever notice me and be distracted himself. Did I want to distract him? I'd made it my life's goal to distract and win Luca Marquez's attention when I was fifteen, but now? I doubted he noticed anyone these days, unless they worked for him or made him money. I laid back on the bed and let my mind drift back to that last day, seven years ago.

Seven years ago, on a hazy summer's afternoon, I was heading back home after spending the day with my friend, Hannah. We'd been trying out different hair styles and make-up techniques, and I'd kept mine on, in the hope that I'd bump into Luca in the street, and finally wow him. I had my favourite red halter-neck top on, the one that made my boobs look bigger than they were, and my little denim shorts, cut just above my ass.

When I walked past the row of shops around the corner from our house, I peered down the alleyway in-between, and that's when I saw him. Pressed up against Kate Silvers, the sluttiest girl in our school. They were about to kiss, I just knew it. She had her hands around his neck and he had his arms around her waist. I felt so mad I had to stop myself from stalking down the alley and breaking them apart. How dare she look at him, let alone touch him. But more importantly, he knew he was mine. Why would he cheapen himself and chase her? She'd made out with most of the guys in our school. I hated her with a vengeance.

When I got home, I waited at the side of my house, and when I saw him walking past, I jumped out in front of him and slapped him hard across the face.

"What was that for?" He cried, rubbing his cheek as if he was really hurt by little old me and my girlie slap.

"For taking that hoe-bag, Kate Silvers, out on a date. Did you kiss her?" He stayed quiet, shuffling his feet. He couldn't even look me in the eye. And I couldn't stop myself from slapping him again.

"Jesus Christ, Chloe. Quit with the slaps. What the hell has gotten into you?" He shouted. I had to work really hard to keep my tears at bay.

"She isn't good enough for you, Luca."

"No one ever is, as far as you're concerned," he sighed.

"I'm good enough. You're mine, Luca. You have been ever since you came here seven years ago." I knew I looked and sounded desperate now, but I was so fed up of waiting for him to notice me.

"I'm nineteen-years-old, Chloe. I'm too old for you. What do you think it'd look like, a nineteen-year-old being with a fifteen-year-old? I could end up in prison, Chloe. Your family would kill me." He always found reasons to keep me at arm's length, he was the king of excuses.

"It's only four years. When I'm twenty, you'll be twenty-four. That's not so bad." I tried to reason.

"It looks bad now, though. Please, Chloe. Don't keep pushing me on this," he begged, glancing around cautiously to see who was watching us. No one was.

"Who cares what anyone else thinks? I know I don't." I kept pushing him. I always did where Luca was concerned.

"No, Chloe. It's not gonna happen. You're special to me, you know that. But right now, we can't be together. Not how you want, anyway."

I stared up at him, and all thoughts of reason flew out of my mind. I stood on my tiptoes and kissed him, a delicate, soft kiss on the lips. He didn't move away, and I was sure he kissed me back; I definitely felt some movement from his lips. When I stood back on my feet and peered up into his eyes, I felt something pass between us. I couldn't say what it was. Maybe love? Lust? Or hope? But it was something. He let out a deep sigh, but never broke eye contact with me. Feeling like I'd gained the upper hand somehow, I spun on my heels and stomped away, hoping he got an eye-full of my ass in my tight denim shorts as I did.

That was the last time I saw Luca Marquez, well until last night that is.

Chapter Eight

Hours later, I could hear the prep going on downstairs for the party. I had no idea why there was a party going on in the first place. Luca was the last person to want to party, but I wasn't going to complain. I felt excited about having the opportunity to meet more people, who knew Freddie and Luca. Plus, the chance to dress up and wind up Marco, and more importantly, Luca, was way too tempting.

I found the perfect party dress, amongst the bags and boxes the guys had delivered to my room. A little red Versace number. It was tight, short, and had a fitted bustier to keep the girls in check. There were two criss-cross black straps, studded with gold buttons, which ran along the length of each strap. A nod to the original bondage and safety pin styles of Versace's yesteryears. It felt edgy, sassy and would make me stand out in a crowd. Something I definitely wanted to do tonight. Gina had good taste. I just hoped we didn't share the same taste in men, as we did in clothes. I'd hate to have to kick her ass.

The music started pumping through the house, and the laughter from the patio outside drifted up into my room, but I wasn't ready to go down yet. I wanted to make a show-stopping entrance when the place was full, to ensure maximum impact. I would get a reaction tonight from Luca, even if it killed me.

Eventually, the lure of alcohol, dancing and chatting up hot muscly men became way too tempting, and I made my way out of the bedroom and down the stairs into the open-plan living area. I worked extra hard at keeping my head high and my confidence in check, as I walked into the crowd of beautiful people. The women were simply stunning, all skinny, polished to perfection and dressed to the nines. The men, a lot of them I recognised from the club, were ripped, horny and prowling around the women like they were in a candy store, ready to take their pick. Was it that kind of party? I certainly hoped not. I found myself backing up to where the bar was situated against the back wall. I poured myself a whiskey and stood quietly, taking in the scenes around me whilst sipping my liquid courage.

One blonde, skinny model type was rubbing herself up against Leo, the security guy I met the night before. I saw him bend down so she could whisper in his ear, and as she did, she nipped the bottom of his earlobe. *'Well, that's a subtle come fuck me, if ever I saw one,'* I thought sarcastically. She may as well have come naked, carrying a sandwich board saying I'm here for cock. I didn't like her, but judging from

Leo's reaction, he was already smitten. I watched them disappear hand in hand upstairs, and I was suddenly thankful I'd locked up my room.

I glanced over at the sofa area and saw Dan, sitting back with his legs open and looking extremely self-satisfied. A tiny red-head in a green dress that'd ridden up to her ass, was straddling him and grinding all over his crotch. I wasn't judging her. I'd done much the same dancing at the club. But when I saw her slip her hand into his trousers in front of everyone, I wanted to go over and tell them to take a note out of Leo's book and get a room. Oh hell, was this some type of orgy?

"Chloe. You came down."

I turned to see Vinnie staring straight at me, a look of apprehension on his friendly face.

"Does Luca know you're here?"

"No." I grimaced. I was pretty sure that if Luca saw me, I'd be ordered back up to the bedroom. And with what I'd seen so far, I wasn't entirely sure that'd be a bad thing. Then the thought hit me like a truck, was Luca somewhere with a girl grinding on him, or worse? It made me feel sick to think about it, so I decided I needed a distraction and fast.

"Come outside with me to the terrace?" Vinnie asked. "It's quieter out there, and you can meet Gina."

I was intrigued to meet this Gina woman. So I followed Vinnie outside, keeping one eye on the crowd to see if I could spot Luca. I couldn't.

The outdoor area looked breath-taking, with fairy lights strung up in the trees. The outdoor pool was lit up in shades of blues and purples, and there were torches along the path heading down towards the beach. It was definitely a more romantic setting than the hot bed of sin I'd seen so far.

Vinnie led me to a tall table at the end of the terrace, where a tall, blonde woman in a black lace off the shoulder dress stood sipping some type of yellow cocktail.

"Chloe, this is Gina DiMarco. Gina, this is Chloe," Vinnie said, doing the introductions.

Gina put her cocktail on the table and stood back, looking me up and down.

"Wow, Chloe. You certainly know how to wear that dress. You look stunning."

Hmm, I might like her just a little bit, seeing as she'd paid me a compliment.

"You have great taste, Gina. I love it. I love all the stuff you got for me. Thanks for doing that, by the way," I replied, giving her a polite but guarded smile.

"It was my pleasure. I live to shop and I got to shop on someone else's credit this time, which is always a bonus." She grinned. "Your Luca wanted you to have everything a girl needs and let's face it, if we left it to the men, you'd be wearing crotchless panties and little else."

My Luca? Okay, I was starting to really like this woman. She was making me feel a lot more at ease, more than I'd felt since I'd arrived.

"He isn't my Luca. But I think you know that already." I gave her a marked stare and she nodded.

"Vinnie, I need a top up. Would you mind?" She said, handing Vinnie her glass and turning her back to him to speak to me more privately.

"Chloe, I hope you don't think I'm speaking out of line, but Luca is a very dear friend, and I've got a feeling you may become a great friend too. So, I'm going to be completely honest with you."

I nodded, readying myself for the bitch fest she was about to unleash on me.

"I've known Luca for about four years, and in all that time he's never even invited a woman back to his home for coffee, let alone to stay over. Don't get me wrong, he's been with women. That's what he uses me for."

I gasped out loud, probably louder than I intended, as she instantly corrected herself.

"Oh no, not like that. I've never, we've never...been together. No, I run a high-class escort service. I provide Luca with...girls."

I took another gulp of my whiskey, and wished I could jump into the pool and swim away from this conversation. Awkward and hurt was an understatement for how I felt.

"My girls call him the Ice King. He never instigates a conversation with them. He'll answers their questions as succinctly as he can, but he prefers to...you know...do the deed and split. He's never been with the same girl more than once, which has always seemed...weird. But now that I see you, Chloe, I'm kinda getting it now."

I wasn't sure I wanted to ask the next question. "Why do you say that? What is it you're getting?"

"Why he always asks for a certain type. He likes brunettes, only brunettes, just like you. If they have curly hair, even better. He likes big tits and he loves curvy girls with skinny waists, which in that dress, I can clearly see you have it all. You, Chloe, are a walking wet dream for Luca. You're exactly what he asks me to find. I know you and he go way back, so now I get it. He's been trying to find someone like you, but now he's finally got you back. It's really sweet actually, like a modern-day fairy tale. The Ice King has found his hot, smouldering queen to thaw his frozen heart."

I couldn't stop myself from laughing at her idealistic imagery.

"I think the last thing we are is a fairy tale, Gina. I feel like I'm in a flipping nightmare."

Gina shook her head and looked at the floor.

"Vinnie told me about Sanchez. A few of my girls have come from his club to me. He's an evil fucker, but Luca will look after you, Chloe. You don't have to feel scared."

"It's not Sanchez I'm scared of. I can look after myself." I stood a bit taller, as if to reinforce my strength and self-belief. "No, I mean, Luca. He's always been hard work, but he's changed. He's even more closed off and arrogant than he used to be. And believe me when I say, I'm the last girl he'd want here."

"We'll see." Gina looked over my shoulder, and seeing Vinnie coming towards us with a tray full of drinks, she whispered, "I think Luca likes you a little more than you realise. And as for Vinnie? He likes you a hell of a lot. Be very careful, Chloe, okay? Look after yourself."

Gina hugged me and the scent of her heavy, expensive perfume swirled around us, then she let go and made her excuses to leave Vinnie and I alone. I liked Gina, but as I'd learnt on the streets, I should always keep my guard up. I couldn't afford to let anyone in, especially with so many enemies out there. How did I know she wouldn't scuttle off to Sanchez, and tell him where I was? Or tell Luca something I'd said to get me into trouble? Time would tell, and time was something I seemed to have a lot of, now I was cooped up in this place under house arrest.

"Gina seems nice," I said to Vinnie, to scope out his reaction.

"Gina is a diamond. You can trust her, Chloe. She's one of the good guys."

-

The drinks were really flowing and I was in a serious partying mood. I felt the music flowing through my veins, and I couldn't stop myself from getting into the party vibe. I was a dancer after all, and the beat of the music always brought out the sexy moves. Add in the alcohol, and those moves came thick, fast and extra sexy. Most people had moved into the main living area from outside, and with the low lighting and flashing colours, you could imagine yourself in an exclusive intimate nightclub.

I started swaying to the music, dancing next to Vinnie. Next thing I know, he's wrapping his arms around my waist and grabbing my hand to spin me around. I laughed, throwing my head back and feeling like the young carefree twenty-two-year-old I should be. I held my arms above my head, as I slipped into stripper dance mode. Then I closed my eyes, letting the beat take me away from everything, except the feeling of being here now with Vinnie. The alcohol in my system gave me the freedom to really let loose.

I swayed, grinding against anyone who was around me, but mostly Vinnie. He didn't seem to mind, and I was too lost in my head to think about the way his hands stroked my arms, or the way he brushed my curls off my shoulders, to whisper low into my ear over the music.

"I've never met anyone like you before, Chloe. You're so...wild, but delicate at the same time. You really know how to fuck with a guy's head, don't you?"

I was just about to tell Vinnie that I had no idea why he thought I was a head fuck, when I spotted him. Pulling away from Vinnie, I glanced over at Luca, dressed head to toe in black and standing at the door to the pool and terrace area outside. I guessed he must've been on the beach this whole time. Maybe the party hadn't been his idea after all, and he'd escaped down there to get away from the hordes of people.

Luca didn't do big crowds, and I knew for a fact he didn't like socialising like this.

The way he stood still, staring over at me, made goose bumps erupt all over my body. The alcohol that'd fed my carefree nature only minutes ago ran dry, and left behind a flurry of butterflies flowing through my body. Butterflies laced with fear. It felt as though there was no one else in the room, only Luca and I, trapped in this vortex, tethered to each other by an invisible thread. His beauty took my breath away, but his aura made me his slave. I didn't even hear Vinnie, as he chattered away next to me. All of my attention was focused on him.

Noticing my distraction, Vinnie turned to follow my line of sight, and when he saw Luca he muttered, "Shit," under his breath. Luca chose that moment to stalk towards us, and I braced myself for storm force ten.

"Party's over, Chloe. Go to bed."

Typical. He was treating me like the fifteen-year-old girl he'd left behind.

"No, I'm staying here," I stated, like the petulant fifteen-year-old he saw.

"PARTY'S OVER! GET OUT!" Luca shouted to the whole room now, and the music was cut dead, instantly. He certainly knew how to kill a good vibe, and the rest of the room obviously agreed with me, as they groaned in protest.

"FUCK OFF. ALL OF YOU!" He roared and pushed his way in-between Vinnie and me.

I'm not sure whether he knew that I heard what he said next, or if he really cared.

"You don't ever get to touch her again. Do you understand?" He snarled aggressively at Vinnie. "She's not like the rest of the whores here, she's different."

"I know that, boss, and I like her. I really like her."

Oh no. That wasn't the response I'd expected, and I wished I'd listened to Gina's advice from earlier in the night. Vinnie was a good guy. The last thing I wanted to do was to string him along. I'd fucked up big time tonight, but I'd deal with the fall out tomorrow with a clear head. No good could come from trying to instigate a 'we can only ever be friends' chat with Vinnie at the moment. I was too emotional to have any sort of chat with either one of them.

So I chose to ignore them both, and slopped off towards the staircase to escape to my room. My mind was a jumble of emotions and desires for a tall, dark, brooding asshole that I knew would chew me up and spit me out. Once inside, I threw myself onto the bed and buried my head into the pillow. I felt as if I was on an emotional rollercoaster. Luca was the head-fuck here, not me. One minute he pushes me away, then he warns his men to stay away from me, as if he wants me for himself. He tells me off for how I act, then he buys me clothes and things to make me more comfortable. I'd got no clue what he thought about me, or where I stood.

Don't get me wrong, I loved winding him up, getting under his skin, but it seemed his game was a hell of a lot more devious and calculated than mine, and it twisted me up in ways I'd never experienced before. I wasn't sure how much longer I could take the mind games, before I finally cracked. I wasn't even sure I wanted to play these games any more. I think he'd become a better player than me over the years, but I'd never admit that out loud to anyone.

I rolled onto my back to stare absentmindedly at the window and hopefully drift off to sleep, when the bedroom door slammed open hitting the wall. I rolled back around to face the music. I already knew who was standing there.

"What do you want, Luca? I'm trying to get to sleep."

"What the fuck was all that about, Chloe?"

I sat up glaring daggers at him, ready to unleash my full arsenal.

"You're not my fucking father, Luca. You can't throw your weight around and warn guys off. I mean, who the hell do you think you are? You haven't bothered to contact me in seven years, not a letter, a phone call, nothing. I've been here for one day and you're already dictating what I wear, who I talk to, what I do."

He stalked towards me, his whole body going rigid with fury and he pointed his finger at me, drilling holes into my soul with his devil eyes.

"It's for your own good. You need to be kept in check, Chloe. You're a fucking liability half the time. I never know what you're gonna do next. You're too unpredictable, you're dangerous."

There it was in a nut shell. I was too unpredictable. I'd waltzed into his perfectly ordered world and fucked it up for him. I lifted myself up onto my knees, so I could try to meet him at eye level.

"I didn't even want to be here in the first place!" I jabbed my finger at his chest and he took a step back, as if my making contact with him would scorch his skin. The evil glare in his eyes dulled slightly and was replaced by...I'm not even sure...was that confusion? Regret? Trepidation?

"Tomorrow morning, I'm gone. I'm taking my unpredictable ass back to my apartment, and I hope I never see your scowling face ever again. Then you can fuck as many women as you want here, without me cramping your style and making things awkward for you. Happy now?"

Those tricky to read eyes bugged out of his head in shock.

"You're going nowhere," he snarled. The vein pulsing in his neck gave him away, he was close to exploding. His teeth were clenched so tightly, he was liable to crack them at any minute.

"You'll stay here until I tell you it's safe to leave. Trust me, when it's time to go, I'll happily drive you home myself."

I huffed my annoyance and folded my arms across my chest. My eyes were reduced to slits of fury and contempt for his bossy, stick up his ass way of dealing with me. However, even I couldn't deny that his domineering, bossy stance, also made me feel lust and fire in my veins, it always had. My nerves spiked and my breathing deepened to a pant. I sneakily squeezed my legs together to intensify the growing pulse and flutter that his power trip was creating down there. If he carried on, he could probably make me come without even leaving the doorway.

He crossed his arms to mirror my stance and steadied his breathing.

"You're one spoilt brat, Chloe Ellis. Do you know that?"

I rolled my eyes.

"I'm trying to protect you here and all you do is act up, cause me grief, upset my men and then throw a tantrum. What the hell was that about tonight? What? You're gonna whore yourself out to the first guy that shows you some attention?"

Oh, hell no! He did not just go there.

"Fuck you!" My lust rolled into anger, then boiled over into vengeance. "You know what? I haven't dated anyone for over four years. Not even kissed a guy, and you have the nerve to call me a whore. I'm not the one with the Madame on speed dial, providing round the clock fucks tailored to their every need."

His face fell and I could've sworn he gasped, but it was so soft I couldn't tell. He dropped his gaze to the floor, then spoke with a slight crack to his voice.

"You have no idea what you're fucking talking about, Chloe. You know fuck all about me or my life."

"You don't know me either, Luca," I said, sitting back

onto my ass and channelling a new kind of power. "But you should know I'm no whore, you know that much about me at least."

"Then stop acting like one around my men."

Damn him, he couldn't even look me in the eyes when he said that.

I shook my head a sly smile on my face.

"I was dancing. I wasn't taking my clothes off, or dragging men upstairs like half the women here tonight. For Christ's sake, Luca, give me some credit."

Suddenly and uncharacteristically he nodded.

"I know. I'm sorry," He whispered so quietly I found it difficult to hear. Then he turned to leave, closing my door behind him.

I lay back down and let out a confused, frustrated sigh. What the fuck was all that about? In all the years I'd known Luca Marquez, and in all the times he'd broken my heart; that was the first time I'd ever heard him say the word 'sorry'.

Chapter Nine

The next morning, I put on some black, ripped skinny jeans and a tight beige sweater. Then I tied my hair up into a high ponytail and headed downstairs, to face up to my shitty situation, and deal with the events of last night. The living area was empty and surprisingly tidy, considering it'd been trashed hours before. I went through into the kitchen to find Leo, Vinnie and Marco, sitting at the table drinking coffee, looking hung over and feeling decidedly sorry for themselves.

"Morning guys! Enjoy your night?" I said rather too loudly, and chuckled when Leo held his hands over his ears in disgust at my volume.

"You don't look like you're suffering like us," Vinnie replied, his eyes looked like piss holes in the snow.

"Ha! I could drink any one of you under the table and then some. I know how to hold my drink, you know. I'm well trained."

Vinnie nodded as if he was impressed. "Was that another trick your Daddy taught you?"

"Too right." I smiled slyly. "If you're gonna hustle a guy,

you gotta be able to keep a clear head whilst drinking with him."

I poured myself a coffee and sat down next to Vinnie.

"Where's your boss this morning? Is he hiding in his room, hanging like a pussy like the rest of you?" I asked, trying to hide my anticipation that Luca could walk in at any moment.

"He left for work hours ago. Boss rarely drinks. I think he was stone cold sober last night. He told us to get clear heads and then join him later. He doesn't want the stench of stale alcohol all over his office."

"At a nightclub?" I laughed. "Is her serious? The whole place must wreak of stale alcohol every morning."

"Not if the boss is around. He has very high standards," Marco said with an air of admiration, sticking his nose in the air as he sipped his coffee and gazed out the window. "Shame some of us here don't have the same standards in our own lives."

I didn't know if that was aimed at me or the other two. I'd hoped it was to Leo and his fuck fest with the blonde, but knowing Marco it could mean either one of us.

"I feel just fine about my life and what I do," I snapped back. "I pay my way *legitimately* and I'm training to be a doctor, you know…helping out others in their time of need and becoming a useful member of society. My standards are the right side of the law. Can you say the same, *Marc*?" I hit that ball right back into his side of the court. I'd be damned if

I was gonna let anyone stand in judgement of my life choices.

"Good for you, Chloe. Make sure you keep it that way," he replied, glancing over at Vinnie with a sour face as he said that last part.

"I will."

I stood from the table and made my way out to the pool. I wasn't in the mood for Marco's sanctimonious bullshit.

Minutes later, I heard someone approaching my sun lounger.

"Chloe, I'm sorry about last night. I hope I didn't get you into trouble." Vinnie sat down on the lounger next to mine, his feet planted on the floor and his hands laced together in-between his knees.

"Don't worry about it Vinnie, it's all good." I sighed. I was about to tell him that Luca apologised, but thought better of it. That was something I wanted to keep to myself, to keep private. I also knew Luca wouldn't appreciate anyone else knowing what we said to each other when no one else was around, especially an apology like that.

Vinnie started fidgeting next to me and I sensed he wasn't finished with our conversation.

"What's up?" I asked, feeling slightly irritated that he wouldn't just come out with it. I hated indecisive men...well anyone indecisive really. I wanted to tell Vinnie to grab any opportunity by the balls and just go for it, but then I suppose that would've given him the wrong impression about my possible reaction to his 'cease the day' moment.

"I just...I was wondering...it's silly really and you can say no-"

"Just spit it out for Christ sakes." I snapped a bit too rudely.

"Do you want to go out some time? With me, I mean?"

I had to tread carefully here, I didn't want to cause any drama. Well, anymore drama than I already had.

"Vinnie, I don't think that'd be a good idea, do you?"

He hung his head but didn't reply.

"You're a good guy, but I'm not in the market for one of those right now. I'm sorry."

He looked up at me, his eyes were bloodshot from the night before. I had no idea he'd drunk quite so much. If I had, I would've reigned in my sexy, sassy dancing.

"You're right, Chloe. I get it...I do. If anything changes though-"

I gave a short laugh. "You'll be the first to know." I finished for him.

"So, friends?" Vinnie asked, raising his eyebrow at me.

"Always," I replied, standing up and patting him on the shoulder as I walked away. Then I twirled around and gave it one last try.

"Any chance I could borrow your phone to call my friend? I wouldn't tell anyone, it'd only be to check in with her."

Vinnie shook his head and grinned up at me.

"You never give up, do you?"

"No, not me. Never." I wiggled my eyebrows, knowing my eyes were sparkling at him right now, and doing their best 'please give in to me' look.

"Sorry, Chloe. That's never gonna happen."

I shrugged. "Oh well. It was worth a try."

He laughed as I sauntered away from him.

Vinnie was a good guy, I had meant that, but he wouldn't have the first clue how to deal with someone like me. I had a stronger character than him. I'd have killed his male ego and pussy whipped him within days if we were together. I needed someone who could stand up to me and all the bullshit that seemed to follow me around. Someone with bags more testosterone than Vinnie was packing. I liked a challenge, and I needed someone who could challenge me mentally and emotionally. Keep me on my toes and make me feel alive. I'd already found that guy, but he still couldn't see me. I doubted he ever would. I guess that ship had already sailed.

-

Later that afternoon, when Luca finally showed up, he walked straight past me sitting in the living room and went straight upstairs. Even just entering a room, he sucked all the air out of it for me, making it impossible to breathe, and turning my fragile equilibrium into a hormonal frenzy. He didn't even glance my way or acknowledge my presence, that's how much I figured on his radar. But he held the bloody remote control to mine. A fact he was oblivious to, or possibly just didn't care about. Two minutes after that, Marco followed behind him, and put a bag of Chinese food in front of me. The delicious aromas wafting out of the bag sent my taste buds crazy.

"Boss got you this. Said it's your favourite. And no, you can't borrow my phone," he stated and then walked straight back out of the house and drove away. I rolled my eyes at his assumption that I'd ever ask *him* for a 'secret' favour.

Inside was my favourite, Kung Pao chicken with spring rolls and fried rice. What the hell was all that about? He couldn't even say 'Hi' to me, but he thought about me on the way home and stopped to pick up my favourite takeaway? Head-fuck central right there, radars and control all over the fucking place.

I drifted in a daze into the kitchen to plate up the food, and sat in front of the TV watching Netflix and consuming every last mouthful of deliciousness.

Then I headed back up to my room and fell asleep, feeling dazed and confused about what was going on here. I felt like I was drowning and he kept pulling me back out, only to push my head back under again. Some might call it sweet torture. I just called it downright cruel. It was time to up my game and reinforce my armour. I was no one's object to toy around with, least of all his. As much as Luca Marquez sent my desires spiralling out of control, and my body into meltdown, my head was blaring the warning sirens. Protect your heart, Chloe. Protect you.

–

A few days later, whilst I was sunning myself by the pool in a gold string bikini that Gina had expertly chosen for me, I noticed Luca, standing at the door watching me. Was he checking me out? From the way he seemed to 'arrange' himself in his trousers before he walked out, I would've said so. I'd noticed a few sly glances my way just lately. Looks that sent prickles over my skin and tremors through my body. I'd put it down to him thinking, plotting ways to wrap up this whole Sanchez saga and get me out from under his feet. His facial expressions never gave any hint to how he was feeling, apart from perpetually pissed off with the world. When he came over and spoke, my suspicions were confirmed.

"I've put something in place today. Something to keep Sanchez sweet and off your back. I just thought I'd let you know."

He didn't look at me as he spoke, instead he stared at the pool. I couldn't take my eyes off him, though. How did he always manage to look so deliciously sinful and fuckable, despite being in a constantly shitty mood? He really had the whole bad-boy package down. The swagger, the intensity. That whole aggressive and unattainable allure, which women loved to hate, but always fell for every single time. He'd had it when he was nineteen, and I'd followed him around like a love sick puppy. But he literally oozed it now, and I had to look away. He was the fire and I was the proverbial moth to the flame.

"Thanks. Does that mean I'll be free to go about my life

again?" He didn't turn to face me.

"It might take a little longer than a few days, but it's being dealt with."

Then he stalked away into the house, as I stared at his tight ass, looking yummy and biteable in his jeans. He'd left me with a million and one questions that I wanted to ask, but felt I couldn't. Not to him anyway, he was seriously distracting me from my shit just lately. He was unsettling my yen or chakra or whatever the fuck people called it these days.

I stood up and sauntered into the house, my head full of whys and what ifs. I found a few of Luca's men waiting on him in the living area, and when I noticed Vinnie loitering around, I beckoned him over to me to talk quietly away from the others.

"What's going on, Vinnie?"

"To be honest with you, Chloe, I've no idea. Boss never shares private business with us, but something big is going down. I know that much. Security at the club and here is being stepped up, especially around you."

I had no idea what that meant. Hadn't Luca said it was close to being sorted? Why would I need extra protection? Maybe I didn't want to know. Sometimes, ignorance was bliss. It had been in my Dad's case. If he'd have known what a cheating whore my Mum was, it would've broken his heart. I was thankful she waited until he died, before parading her stable of boyfriends through the town.

"You know, I still don't know what business it is you guys

are into. I know Luca has the club, but I'm not stupid enough to think he makes all his money through that." I was going for the bullseye here.

"And you know I can't tell you, Chloe. That's Luca's call, but you're right, the club is...useful," he replied cryptically, looking upwards in thought and rubbing his prickly chin.

I left it at that and headed back to the pool to do a few laps before lunch. I was going stir crazy cooped up in the house, so any exercise I got helped to stem the boredom and quash my ever-growing tension.

I'd just finished my twenty-third lap when I noticed Gina, sitting by the pool, dressed in a red strappy sun dress and looking quite demure for a high-class Madame. She waved over at me, so I pulled myself up out of the pool to join her.

"You didn't need to stop on my account." She smiled up at me as I towelled myself off.

"I was almost finished anyway. It's nice to see you again, but I think you've come at the wrong time, there's only me here."

She cocked her head to one side and studied me for a while before answering.

"I didn't come to see Luca. I came to see you, Chloe. Actually, that's not exactly true. Luca asked me to drop in and check if you were okay."

I let out a loud laugh. "Check up on me more like. What does he think I'll do, steal his silver?"

"No, I think he's genuinely concerned that maybe you're lonely, or need someone to talk to."

"Shame he can't ask me himself. He can't even bring himself to look at me these days. No, he has to send you to ask me if I'm okay. What a joke! I mean what is up with that?" I felt seriously pissed off with his aloof, condescending ways. He seemed to forget his past, our shared past so easily.

"If he's been ignoring you, Chloe, I don't think it's for the reasons you say." Gina looked across at me and put her hand on my knee, then smiled and sat back.

"Chloe, I'll let you into a little secret. Since you came to this house, Luca hasn't used my services, not once."

"Why would I want to know that? So, he's pissed he can't get his rocks off because I'm here. Big deal, I'll be gone soon."

She shook her head at me. "That's not what I'm saying, Chloe. He came by my place at least three to four times a week. And now? Nothing. Do you think you might be the reason he's avoiding using my girls?"

I knew where she was going with this, but I still didn't trust her one hundred percent.

"I'm sorry my being here affects your business. I'm sure he'll make up for it when I'm gone."

"Jesus, Chloe. Do I need to spell it out for you? He doesn't want my girls because he wants you. You two sound as bad as each other. Hell will probably freeze over before either one of you admits to the other how you're feeling."

I was gobsmacked, and couldn't help but laugh at the

irony of it all.

"Gina, I spent every day for seven years telling Luca I loved him, and he pushed me away every day. I'm done. I don't need his crap in my life. I'm going to become a doctor in a few years anyway, and I plan to work really hard in my specialised area. I'll forever be independent; answerable to no one but me. That's what I want and that's how I like it."

Gina stood to leave. "Okay, Miss Independent. But we all need a little love and affection in our lives sometimes, so don't forget to keep that part of your life fed and watered."

"Maybe you'll have to expand your business to cater for me, get in some hot males."

"And let me guess, your preference would be tall, dark and handsome with sparkling green eyes and a moody disposition."

I rolled my eyes as she laughed hysterically at her own joke.

"Maybe short, fat and bald would be better. Less hassle in the long run," I bit back.

"Chloe, I don't think there's a man alive, other than Luca, who could hold your interest for longer than a night or two. I think it's the same for him too."

"What, he struggles to find guys that can hold his attention?"

"You're not funny you know, and I know you're using humour to hide what you really feel. Now finish your swim and burn off some of that sexual frustration that's seeping out of your pores, sweetie. I'll see you soon, okay?" Gina gave me two air kisses and breezed back towards the house.

"Wait, Gina! Can I ask a favour?"

Gina stopped and turned around, her interest obviously spiked at what I could possibly want from her.

"Do you have a mobile phone I could borrow? Just to make one quick call?"

Her jovial smile turned down straight away, and I knew she'd be warned not to help me out like this.

"Please, Gina. I only want to ring my roommate and check she's okay. You can stay and listen the whole time."

She bit her lip. I could tell she was wavering.

"I won't tell a soul about it, I promise." I gave her my best puppy dog eyes, and slouched my shoulders to make myself look even more trustworthy.

"Fine!" She huffed, reaching into her tiny shoulder bag and pulling out her jewel encrusted iPhone. "But if anyone ever finds out I did this, I will kill you myself, Chloe. Understand?"

"Yes. Thank you, thank you, thank you," I replied, hugging her as she handed the phone to me.

Luckily, Teresa's number was ingrained into my brain after my own mobile had been stolen a few months back. I usually rang her when I needed help, or a ride, or anything really.

The phone rang out a few times and my tummy flipped over as I worried that maybe she'd been hurt, or her phone had gotten into the wrong hands.

"Hey, who's this?" Teresa's guarded voice whispered down the line.

"T, it's me, Chloe. Are you okay?"

"Oh my God, Chloe. What the fuck is going on with you? I've got guys ringing and coming to the apartment every day looking for you. Where are you?"

"I'm okay, T, honestly. Did you manage to get the rent money sorted? Are you okay?"

She sighed heavily down the phone at me. "Yes, I'm fine. And yes, I got the money to Mr Grabby hands. Some guy came round, said he was a friend of yours, he had the full rent money and then some. Where are you, Chloe?"

"Cool," I replied, avoiding her last question. "Listen, I'm gonna be home soon. I just need you to sit tight for a little while longer. Don't tell anyone I called and don't answer the door anymore, okay? I quit my job, at the club. That place was dodgy to say the least. So whatever you do, stay away from there."

"I don't think I'll be hanging out in a strip club any time soon, Chloe, but seriously, I need to know where you are dude. I can't sleep at night for worrying about you, girl."

I'm not sure why I gave up so easily. Teresa was always pulling my private shit out of me without me even realising most of the time. It was her gift.

"I'm stopping with Luca, that guy I told you about from my past, until this-"

I didn't get to finish. The phone was snatched from my hand, and Gina shut the call down.

"That was a dick move, Chloe. You know you're not supposed to tell anyone where you are."

Her eyes turned cold towards me, and I felt shame under her frozen glare.

"I'm sorry, Gina. I do trust Teresa, though." I shrugged, hoping I hadn't just given our fledgling friendship the kiss of death. I really was growing to like Gina DiMarco.

"Well, for both our sakes I hope she lives up to that trust, because if Luca finds out I lent you my phone, I'm in serious trouble."

"I'm sorry, Gina. If it comes to it, I'll say I stole it from your bag when you were in the bathroom or something."

She nodded, then her smile towards me warmed up again.

"Fine. It's done now. No need to worry over something that might never happen. Anyway, I'm off. Get back into that water you little minx and work off that sexual frustration that's clouding your judgements lately." She giggled to herself as she turned around and click-clacked her way out.

Sexual frustration? Was I sexually frustrated? How would Gina know that just by looking at me? Could other people tell? Oh hell, I might be a stripper with a smart mouth and a penchant for bringing the sass, but when it came to sex or rather the opposite sex, I was pretty clueless. I dived into the pool and swam forty more lengths, just to make sure any frustrations were well and truly burnt off.

Chapter Ten

Seven years ago…
One week before they left me…

"They're called constellations, Chloe. A group of stars that form a pattern up in the sky. Look, over there is Ursa Major. Some people call it the big dipper, but that's only part of it. It's more like a big bear. Can you see it?"

Freddie and I were lying in his back yard, our bodies flat out on the rough patchy grass and our eyes searching up in the night sky, stars twinkling innocently above us.

"I don't even know what I'm looking for, it all just looks like stars to me, Fred." I squinted, as if that'd help some amazing star pattern suddenly come to life in front of me.

"There see, those seven stars." He pointed at the sky, his head touching mine as he leaned across. I still didn't see anything, but I liked being close to my surrogate brother. It made me feel all warm and fuzzy inside.

"Oh yeah." I lied, because I guessed I could lie here all

night and still not see what Freddie saw, but I hated to upset him.

He loved the stars and space, anything that wasn't of this world. I think it gave him a release from his rotten life back here on earth. It helped him to remember that even when things got too much or too unbearable, we were all just smaller parts of a bigger realm called life.

"The stars in the night sky are like a map, Chloe. If you can find Ursa Major, you can find the North Star. Centuries ago, before people knew their way around like we do, they used the stars to guide them."

"Like in the bible, yeah? I've heard those stories. I'm glad I wasn't alive then. I'd have been lost forever. I'm rubbish at reading maps. But a star map? Forget it. I've no idea what goes where and you tell me most nights, Freddie."

"You don't give yourself enough credit, Chloe. I bet you can still find Orion. Remember Orion's belt? Those three stars are the easiest ones to find. If you can see those, you've found Orion."

"Yeah, I see them." No I didn't, but I'd never burst his bubble and admit that.

I heard the crunch of his boots, and felt the familiar shiver trickling down my spine, before I heard his voice break through the silence of our stargazing.

"What the hell are you two up to?"

Luca stood towering over us, his hands stuffed into the pockets of his jeans and his eyes looking accusingly from me to Freddie, as if he'd caught us doing something we shouldn't. Was that jealousy I detected behind his glare? Probably not, but I could always hope.

"I'm teaching our sis about the night sky."

Freddie rolled his head towards Luca, then he looked at me and gave me a cheesy, smug grin.

"Yeah, I'll be able to navigate my way through the desert soon. Go me!" I rolled my eyes back at Freddie and he chuckled.

"We'll always be with you, Chloe. There's no need to navigate yourself anywhere."

I liked hearing that, it made me feel safe and...loved.

"Dad wants you inside, Fred. He's had a letter from your school and he wants you to explain. Sorry bro, I tried to sort it for you, but he wants you."

Freddie winced and lay still for a minute before huffing into a sitting position and then standing. Luca sat down next to me as he did, and I stayed lying down, attempting to keep my breathing steady whilst Luca was so close to me.

"If I don't come back out again in ten minutes, come looking for me." He gave his big brother a stare that said, 'I mean it, come save me,' and Luca nodded back at him.

Once Freddie had disappeared inside, Luca lay down next to me. I was hyper aware of the heat from his body so close to mine, making my skin tingle and my body clench in ways I didn't understand. I just wanted to turn my head and kiss him, roll onto my side and pull him closer to me. I was always doing the chasing as far as Luca was concerned, but I wanted him, and if you wanted something or someone so badly you had to fight for it, right?

"So, what are we looking at?" His deep voice sent my heart into a flutter. I found it so hard not to touch him.

"You know what? I have no idea. Stars, just night sky and stars, but don't tell Freddie I said that. I'd hate to break his heart."

Luca chuckled softly beside me, then turned his head to face mine. I did the same. Our lips were literally inches apart. We were so close it was insane. This felt like a 'moment' for us. Finally.

"What are you thinking about?" He asked, furrowing his brow.

"Do you really want to know?" I bit my bottom lip, not meaning to look seductive, but I guess that's how it came across to Luca.

"Always. I always want the truth from you, Chloe."

"I like being here, lying here, feeling close to Freddie...and you. It feels safe. You make me feel safe."

He smiled, a rare smile that pulled at my heart strings and touched me to the very core. Luca Marquez didn't smile for anyone, but he did for me.

"I like making you feel safe."

I held his gaze with mine for what felt like an eternity, before I jumped in at the deep end and said what I was really thinking.

"Will you wait for me?"

His head whipped back slightly, as if he was puzzled and not quite getting what I was asking him.

"What do you mean?"

"I mean, will you wait for me to catch up with you? To be the right age for you to give me a chance? I don't want you to fall in love with anyone else whilst I'm catching up to where you need me to be."

The expression on his face softened and he rolled onto his side to speak to me. He didn't laugh at me, like some older guys might've, Luca never teased me. He always wanted the truth because he always gave the truth back.

"Chloe, it's not about me choosing the right age for you to be or putting a date on things. It's got to be natural. You can't force these things."

I felt the tears well up in my eyes. He was giving me the brush off, yet again. Lying so close, so temptingly close, then pushing me away.

"Don't do that, Chloe, please." He leant up on his elbow and wiped a tear from my eye. "I didn't say no, I said don't keep forcing it. If it's meant to be, it'll happen."

"It is meant to be. I love you, Luca. You're mine and I don't want to share you with anyone."

His smile was sincere and melted me all over again. How could he be so cruel, keeping me at arm's length, and then be so adorable and protective at the same time?

"You know what, Chloe? I promise I'll always be here

for you. Will that do for now?"

I shrugged, it sounded like I was being friend-zoned.

"I suppose, if that's all you can give. I won't ever give up though."

I whispered the last part to myself as I stared back up at the sky, and when Luca responded, my heart almost burst free from my chest.

"I'm counting on it."

He moved his left hand to lie next to my right on the grass, our skin touching ever so slightly, sending shocks of electricity to course through my body. The stars seemed trivial and unimpressive next to this beautiful boy, who held my heart in the palm of his hands. My life felt interconnected, entwined forever with his in that moment. He curled his little finger around mine and it meant the whole world, more than any words he could say. He would wait for me. He loved me. He just couldn't tell me.

We stayed like that for ages, lying side by side, silent but saying so much with our fingers laced together. It was the sweetest, most romantic thing that'd ever happened to me in my whole fifteen years. It might've looked trivial to anyone on the outside, but it was huge for us. Luca was reaching out to me, to my soul. He would wait for me and I would love him forever.

Chapter Eleven
CHLOE

Present Day

I stood under those same stars next to Luca's pool, gazing up in awe of the beauty and grinning to myself. I still couldn't find Orion or his belt or Ursula Major, whatever Freddie had called it. My star map just showed twinkling gems of wonder, and reminded me that whatever happened in the darkness of the night, the sun always rose to herald a new day with new hope.

It had been a few days since Luca's revelation that I may have my life back soon, but I'd heard nothing else from him since then. He was like a ghost in his own home, heard but never seen. I was going stir crazy and suffering severely from lack of human contact.

Suddenly, I heard the patio doors sweeping open and I spun round, expecting to see the ghost himself. Vinnie was dressed in black jeans and a smart black button down shirt, the buttons around his neck were open, showing off his chest hair.

"Where's your medallion, hot stuff?" I laughed, making it obvious I was sweeping my eyes up and down his body.

"Fuck off," he snapped, then he went quiet before stating. "I left it at home. The chain catches on my chest hair."

I threw back my head and laughed.

"Oh my God. How did I guess you were one of those posers?"

His cheeks reddened, so I walked over to him and rubbed his chest with my hand.

"Don't panic, big boy. I'm sure wherever you're going tonight you'll have all the girls falling for you, even without your lucky medallion."

He shuffled his feet nervously. Oh hell, was he building up to asking me out again? I hoped not, maybe the chest rub had been a step too far.

"It's my night off, but I'm heading to the club still to...you know...kick back."

"Yeah, kick back...is that what they call it these days?" I chuckled.

"Wanna come with me? Not as a date, just to... I don't know, get out the house?"

I was going to knock him back straight away, but the thought of escaping the four walls that were keeping me prisoner right now sounded way too appealing.

"Won't Luca cut your balls off for defying an order?" I asked, raising my eyebrows and expecting him to say yes and change his mind.

"He'll be there too, working. I don't see why it'd be a problem? It's not like I'm taking you somewhere that isn't safe. The clubs full of our security."

I was shuffling past him and heading through the door to my room to change, before I'd even given him my answer.

"I'm in! Give me twenty minutes to change and freshen up, then I'm all yours." I hollered over my shoulder, then I flew up the stairs and burst into my room, flinging open the wardrobe doors.

I knew just the outfit to wear. It was a silver, crystal encrusted mini dress. It was off the shoulder and would cling to every curve I had. Gina had also bought a pair of silver Jimmy Choo's and a silver clutch bag that was too cute to be kept hidden away in this room. These items needed to be worn in a public place, it'd be a crime not to show them off.

Twenty minutes later, my big, bouncing, chocolate curls hung around my bare shoulders and down my back. The dress sparkled like the stars I'd just been gazing at, and my smoky eye shadow complimented the silver outfit and made me feel daring and risqué. I was ready to hit the dancefloor and cause some serious mayhem.

"Woah! You look hot, Chloe."

Vinnie stared at me with his mouth hung open, looking like a fool as I walked down the stairs. I had to take each step slowly, in case I fell ass over tit in these skyscraper heels. To him, it probably looked like I was making some grand sexy entrance.

"We do make a good pair, don't we?" I made it to the bottom step without incident, then snaked my arm through Vinnie's, as we headed to the door.

I was playing with fire being flirty with him like this, but knowing Luca would see us at the club, I couldn't stop myself. I was a sucker for punishment, always had been. And Luca deserved to have my sassiness rubbed in his nonchalant, dismissive, gorgeous face.

In Vinnie's car I played around with the music, skipping over hard rock, heavy metal and rap, until I found the perfect song to complement my mood.

"Great! Chick music." Vinnie complained, as Demi Lovato sung about being confident.

It was how I felt right now though, and I sang along at the top of my lungs. Vinnie shook his head but smiled, letting me have control of his radio and his ear drums for the entire ride to the club.

Minutes later, we waltzed through the entrance, past the line of clubbers waiting to get in, and headed in the direction of the bar and the pumping base. This was my first time seeing the club itself. My last visit here had been through the back door and into Luca's lair.

The club was awesome. All gold and black, with a DJ booth raised up high in the middle of the dancefloor. The bar we were stood at was mirrored with glitter and silvery gold accents. It all screamed sumptuous luxury and excess, and I loved it.

Vinnie and I threw back a few shots of tequila, before settling on our main drinks for the night, beer and cocktails. A few of Luca's security guys shot disapproving glances our way, but no one dared to come up and talk to us. That was until Marco spotted us, and proceeded to fight his way through the crowds to give us his opinion on our night.

"What the fuck are you doing, Vinnie? Do you want to get fired? Have you got a death wish or something?" Marco stood with his back to me as if I wasn't even there.

"If Luca sees you here with her, he'll skin you alive."

"That's a bit dramatic, don't you think, Marc?" I was goading him now, pissing him off on purpose. I knew he hated me calling him Marc, but I didn't care.

"Anyway, we're only here dancing. It's not like we're making out or anything." I sipped my cocktail suggestively through the straw and gave him a cheeky wink.

Vinnie visibly swallowed and Marco growled, before stalking off and throwing his parting words over his shoulder to us.

"It's your funeral. Don't say I didn't warn you."

I swung round to address Vinnie, my balance going slightly squiffy with the tequila that was settling into my system.

"Is he going to run off and tell on us like a grass?"

Vinnie took a big gulp of his beer before answering.

"No, you can trust Marco. He wouldn't want to get

involved."

I didn't really care what Marco or any of the other's thought about me being here to be honest. I was a grown woman for Christ's sake. I could come and go as I pleased, and right now, I'd had about enough of all the cloak and dagger shit that'd been going on. I was done with being hidden away. If Sanchez wanted to take me, he could try, but I was no push over. He'd have the fight of his life on his hands. Anyway, I reasoned with my drunken self, he probably doesn't even care about little old me anymore. I made up my mind that after this night out, I was going back to my own apartment and getting on with my life, living it the way I wanted to. Completely Luca free.

Chapter Twelve
LUCA

Time was running out. I didn't know how much longer I could pretend I had a plan. I had no fucking plan. No idea what to do to keep Sanchez away from Chloe, other than warning him off. But that was a big no-no, he'd only become more fixated on her if he knew she meant something to me, which she did. I could claim her as mine, but then again, that'd make the target on her back even bigger, and I doubted she'd go for that one. She seemed to hate my guts these days. We were both screwed. Short of bumping him off myself, or locking her up forever, I didn't know what else to do. That's why I'd increased security, because word from Sanchez's camp was, he was pissed and out for revenge. Wiping him out completely was becoming my best option.

It was also getting harder and harder to avoid her back at the house. Not to mention *it* was getting harder and harder, every time I looked at her flouncing around in those skimpy bikinis and outfits that Gina had bought her. She had this way of swinging her hips that made all her curves bounce in such a 'come fuck me' way. I swear my balls were getting bluer by the second. I didn't know if I could hold myself back any longer. All I could think about was bending her over, seeing that ass up in the air in front of me, and fucking her tight little pussy so hard she'd feel me for days after.

Chloe fucking Ellis. That woman would be the death of me. She wasn't content with giving me a constant hard-on when I was a teenager. Watching her around the neighbourhood with all that soft, creamy skin, and those perfect perky tits, stalking around the place in those ass hugging denim shorts. No, she had to find me now and tease my cock even more with how she'd grown. Boy, had she grown. She was like a Victoria's Secret angel and the star of the porno in my mind all rolled into one. My sanity was hanging on by a thread and I was sure my men had noticed. I couldn't afford for them to see any weakness in me. Especially now, when we were so close to all-out war with Sanchez.

Hell, my mind was at war with itself. The half that was a red-blooded male said, *'fuck it. Just fuck her in every possible way you've dreamt of over the years, until she's screaming your name, and coming all over your cock.'* I wanted to find out if she tasted as good as she looked. Have her fuck my face, as she sucked my cock. Hell, I wanted her to come on my cock, my face, my tongue, my hands and fingers; I wanted it all with her. But the other half, the half with some morals, reminded me of her father and the promises I'd made. He was a good man, her Dad. He taught me more in the years that I'd known him, than my own poor excuse for a father ever did. His advice rang in my ears today, as clearly as it did seven years ago...

I was leaving the house and I casually glanced over to next door, in the hope of catching a glimpse of Chloe. Her father, Stan, was in the driveway working on his old Ford. His head was buried under the bonnet as he clanked away, using some tool he'd brought up from his tool shed. He stood back from the car scratching his head, then noticed me as I walked past.

"Hey, Luca. How's things?"

Stan always took the time out to talk to me and Freddie, none of the other neighbours did. We were the odd family on the street, you see. The ones who didn't belong there.

"I'm working at Al's now, thanks to you that is."

Al's was a mechanics in the town and Al the owner had agreed to give me a month's trial working there, based solely on Stan's recommendation. People respected Stan, they took his word as gospel. So I wasn't going to let him down, knowing he'd placed his valuable trust in me. Plus, Stan had taught me everything he knew about cars. I'd spent hours with him, stripping engines apart and putting them back together, just for the hell of it.

I loved being around Stan and the positive vibes he gave off. It didn't hurt that I'd get the chance to watch Chloe too, whenever she came out of the house to bring us cold drinks or cookies, dressed in her little outfits. It felt cruel that she was so much younger than me, and yet she was all I could think about. None of the other girls in the neighbourhood held a torch to Chloe Ellis. She was my perfect girl. Looked like an angel, but with a body most definitely made for sin. Only problem was, she was just too young.

"Think you could take a look at this? If you're not too busy that is?"

Stan gestured to the open bonnet of his car and I nodded, sprinting up the driveway and bending down to have a look at the engine. Stan's knowledge far outweighed mine, so I wasn't sure why he was even asking me for advice, but it felt good to feel useful. That was something my own father never made me feel.

"So, you got a girlfriend yet, Luca?" He asked, leaning against the side of his car.

I shook my head. "I don't have time for that, too busy looking after Freddie and...stuff."

I looked back at the house that'd never felt like a home, not once in the seven years we'd been forced to live there. The minute Freddie was old enough, and I'd managed to save enough money, we were both out of there. I was determined to get us both away from my father and his right hook.

"That wouldn't have something to do with my daughter would it?"

My head shot up to look at Stan and gauge his reaction.

He was looking back at me with kind, friendly eyes. Not what I expected at all. I couldn't answer though. I didn't tell lies. So I decided to keep the truth quiet inside.

"She's a lot like me you know, our Chloe. She might come across all cocky and confident, but she's delicate. She has a pure forgiving heart, but it's easily broken."

He was nodding purposefully at me as he spoke. I knew it was his subtle way of warning me off.

"Don't get me wrong, Luca, you're a good kid. I just need to make you aware of a few things, okay?"

I nodded back at him.

"Okay."

"I know my Chloe likes you, she likes you an awful lot. A blind man could see that. All I ask is that you let her down gently. I don't want to see my baby have her heart irreparably broken."

I had no intention of breaking her heart. It was my heart that was breaking most days, holding everything in, suppressing how I felt.

"I won't ever hurt her, Sir," I said, looking him dead in the eyes so he would know I spoke the truth. "She's too special to me, I could never hurt her. You have my word on that."

And there it was, I'd said it. She was special to me. The most special thing I had going on in my shitty life right now. Every night I went to sleep going over everything we'd said to each other that day in fine detail. Recalling what she'd worn, how she'd smelt, what she'd feel like to touch, to hold in my arms, to have underneath me. Then I'd wake up with her on my mind, hopeful that I'd bump into her that day. She was all I thought about. In fact, it was getting kinda creepy how often I was thinking about a fifteen-year-old girl, and not in the most innocent of ways either. Maybe I needed to take a few other girls out on dates, just to try and slow down this growing obsession I seemed to have with my underage neighbour.

"You see son, people think we're invincible, strong. But people like me and Chloe, we hurt easily and deeply, but we do it privately."

He dropped his gaze to the floor and spoke in a hushed tone.

"Do you think I don't know my wife is cheating on me with any guy who gives her the time of day?"

To be honest, I had no idea Chloe's Mum had been cheating, but I didn't reply. I just carried on listening.

"I found out years ago, but I won't leave her. I'll never leave her. Do you know why?"

I shook my head.

"Because she's an evil, vindictive cow, my wife. And I know she'd use Chloe to get at me. She'd hurt her and screw her up even more than she has done over the years. I can't leave my daughter to live alone with that cruelty, and I can't take my daughter away with me because...well legally, I can't. So I stay here. I put up with her cheating ways so I can be here for my girl, and save her from anymore heartache. Give her the love and guidance my wife can't. I live for Chloe, so you see, her happiness means the world to me. If she's heading for heartbreak from you, I'd appreciate a heads-up, so I can prepare and do my best to help her heal."

I was knocked for six. Stan had just surpassed the already high position he'd held in my mind, and shot right up to Saint or even God like status. That he'd sacrificed his own happiness to save his daughter from heartache did something to me. It made me realise I felt the same way too. Yes, I was hanging around in a home full of violence and abuse, waiting for the day when I could escape with my brother, because I couldn't leave him all alone. But at the same time, the thought of leaving Chloe made me feel physically sick. When the time came and I was in a position to escape with Freddie, I wasn't convinced I'd be able to do it. A life without Chloe, felt like no life at all.

"There won't be any heartbreak for Chloe from me. I can assure you of that, Sir," I replied confidently.

He walked over to me and patted me on my shoulder.

"We get one life, son. Don't let what other people think hold you back."

I knew what he was saying. He was referring to the age gap, but it was too big a deal for me. I had to wait. I'd promised myself that I'd wait. I thought of what my Mum would think if other people were shaking their heads in disgust at her eldest son. I'd never want to bring shame to *her, Freddie or Chloe for that matter. It was too much for me to bear. I wanted to lead a good life, the opposite life to my father.*

"I know," I replied. "I just have a few...things to sort out before I start thinking about the future."

He smiled and then looked down at the engine.

"I think I'll pop her into Al's, give you a chance to work on her when you're getting paid for it. You're a good man, Luca. Remember that."

He closed the bonnet and wandered off into his house, leaving me staring after him, feeling like I'd been given a warning and a green light. If I wasn't confused before, I most certainly was now. Why couldn't I have been born second instead of Freddie? Life sucked sometimes.

I heard a loud knock at my door, pulling me out of my daydream. Moments later, Leo strode in, carrying the paperwork I'd asked him for on a shipment we'd recently dealt with. He came to the side of my desk to drop them down and I turned to grab them. That's when something caught my eye on the security monitors that filled the left wall of my office. A sight that made every nerve in my body twitch, and the veins in my neck almost pop in fury. Vinnie. Bloody Vinnie, on the dancefloor with his grubby hands all over her. All over my Chloe. She didn't look too disappointed about it either, as she ground her ass into his crotch and rubbed herself up and down him. I wanted to rip his fucking head off and tear down the whole fucking club. I was so angry. He'd been told already and he'd ignored my direct orders. He couldn't touch her, not now... not ever... She was mine and he needed telling.

I shot out of my chair and flung my office door open. I didn't even flinch when I heard the almighty bang it made against the plaster in the wall. Fuck it. I'd get it re-plastered in the morning. Hell, I'd redecorate the whole club if it took away the images of him pawing at her like that in front of everyone. Bastard.

I took the stairs two at a time, and flew through the doors into the main club like a bat out of hell. I could see my security guys nervously glancing at each other. They knew why I was here. I stomped over to the edge of the dance floor area and held my hands on my hips, scanning the area to find them. Then silver sparkles caught my eye, and the vision of her ass, her curves poured into that dress, made me go full on caveman. I had to fight down the urge to stalk over to her, and throw her over my shoulder. Carry her off to my cave and spank her for what she'd done. Shit, the image of Chloe bent over my knee, ready for a good hard spanking, her curvy ass naked and ready for me, made me rock hard. I had to adjust myself before I could even think about moving. Tonight, this shit ended.

Chapter Thirteen
CHLOE

Being in a club again and letting the music take me away, take over my body, was the best feeling I'd had in ages. I felt a little guilty about the saucy, seductive way I was grinding up against Vinnie. But hell, we were in a club, that's what people did right? It didn't mean anything.

The dancefloor was packed solid as everyone got lost in their moves, and the DJ switched the track over to Tyga telling us to have a Taste. I was busy gyrating and singing along, when a bolt of nervous electricity went through my body. I automatically glanced up at Vinnie, who was in a trance, totally oblivious to his surroundings. I didn't need to turn around to know he was there. My Luca radar was on full alert and blaring loud and clear into my ear lobes. A second later it wasn't just the radar blaring, it was Luca himself.

"Get your dirty fucking hands off her," he shouted across at Vinnie.

Luca was stood behind me, and as he spoke his hands found their way to my hips and he pulled me back into him. I could feel his hardness pushing into my back. Was it the confrontation that was turning him on or me?

Vinnie chose that moment to look up, his consciousness returning with a bang, as his eyes grew wide and he started to shake his head and plead his case.

"It's not what it looks like, boss, I swear. I just brought her along because she was bored and I didn't think it'd matter. She's safe here. What's the big deal?"

I heard Luca take a deep breath in, he was glaring over my shoulder at Vinnie. His face was inches away from mine and I could feel the tension in his taut muscles as he fought himself. Held himself back from launching into Vinnie and pummelling him into the ground.

"You don't bring her anywhere. She isn't yours. You don't get to talk to her, touch her or dance with her. Nothing. Do you hear me? This place is crawling with people. It's not safe and neither are you if I ever see you again, got it? Now get out. You're fired."

Vinnie just stayed put, gawping at Luca as if he'd just spoken to him in Japanese.

I couldn't let Vinnie take the wrap for this though, it wasn't fair.

"Don't take it out on him!" I screamed, whirling round to face Luca head on and jabbing my finger into his solid chest as I spoke. "I wanted to come because I'm fed up with being locked away, and you know what? I'm not doing it anymore. I'm done! I'm going back to my own apartment and there's nothing you can do to stop me."

I folded my arms over my chest, making the girls almost pop up out of my dress. Luca's eyes almost popped out of his head as he noticed them and my tummy flipped. He *was* checking me out!

"Like hell you will!" He snapped, gritting his teeth and panting.

Next thing I knew I was hanging upside down, having been thrown over Luca's shoulder, and carried out of the club via the side doors towards his office.

"What is it with you Marquez brothers and carrying me out of clubs like this?" I shouted and he laughed. He fucking laughed at me.

"Put me down you asshole. Let me go!"

"No," he snapped back, and pushed his way through another set of doors and out into an underground car park.

He stalked over to his black sports car, and dropped me on my feet. I instantly went to walk away from him, back to the doors we'd come through, but he grabbed my arm and forcefully pulled me back against him. He pushed me up against the car, my back against his front and I could feel that hardness again. Damn it felt like he was packing something impressive back there, but I shook my head. I couldn't let his voodoo magic cock distract me from my goal. He was obviously turned on by arguments and confrontation. I doubted that his arousal had anything to do with little old me.

He put both of his arms either side of me, to trap me in

his grasp, and he whispered low and menacing in my ear.

"I swear to God, Chloe, if you don't get that tight little ass of yours into this car without making a scene, I'll be putting you over my knee and spanking the hell out of it. You'll be covered in my red hand marks for days. Trust me."

I turned my head to the side, feeling his hot breath panting close to my cheek and neck. I gave a sly grin as I sighed. "Is that a promise?"

A slight groan or growl sounded at the back of his throat, and he yanked me off the car back into him. The lights of the car flashed and he snaked one steel arm around my waist, as he opened the passenger door with the other.

"In!"

He pushed me down into the seat and then reached across me to click my seat belt into place. The nearness of him made me grow wet with want. I wanted him so badly. I tried to imagine what he'd do if I pulled him down onto me, crashed my lips against his and slipped my tongue into his mouth to taste him. Would he push me away if I ground my hips onto his long hard cock through his trousers, and tried to release some of this pent-up frustration, by getting the friction I needed from him? My heart was beating fast and my nerves sparking in all the right places. But I knew he'd push me away. He always did. I was just Chloe, the little sis. The last person he'd see in that way. He never had, no matter how sexily I'd dressed, how hard I'd flirted or how many times I'd told him I wanted him.

"There. This time you'll wear your fucking seatbelt when you're in one of my cars."

He moved back out of the car, running his hand over the belt that was over my stomach as he did. The feel of his fingers drifting softly across my dress, so close to where I wanted him, made me gasp sharply. I looked at him, to see if he was as affected as I was, but he wasn't looking at me. He hardly ever did.

He slammed the door closed and stalked to the other side of the car, sliding into his seat and securing his own seatbelt as he started the engine.

I think most women would agree, that being in a car with a hotter than hell guy driving, is such a fucking turn on. Luca was no exception. The way his muscly forearms flexed as he gripped and turned the wheel, controlling the car with such power and precision, and driving at speed made me fantasise about him controlling me in the same way, driving into me with that level of power and precision. I'd purr even better than this supercar if he treated me like this. I had to stop myself from unbuckling my seatbelt and straddling him as he drove. Images of us pulling over and him bending me over the hood to thrust into me made me close my eyes and lean my head against the window, playing it out in my mind. I'd have to add that to my bank of fantasies I used most nights about Luca to get myself off. Since moving into his house, I'd been pleasuring myself a hell of a lot more than I usually did. His presence brought that slutty side out in me.

Just as fantasy Luca was flipping me over and coming all over my tits, I realised we were slowing down and I forced my eyes open to see we'd arrived back at his house. Luca spun the wheel to screech the car to a halt outside the house, and without a word, he left the car and stormed off into the house, leaving me sat there like a fool, watching his back disappear inside.

"Welcome home," I sang to myself as I unbuckled the seat belt and opened my door.

Chapter Fourteen

When I got to the front door, I could see Luca pacing up and down the living room like a caged lion, with a tumbler of whiskey in his hands. I slammed the door shut behind me and he stopped dead in his tracks and faced me, looking like he was ready to shoot me dead where I stood.

"I've had enough of your shit, Chloe. It ends tonight. Do you hear me?"

"You don't tell me what to do, Luca. No one does." And I meant it. He'd done nothing to warrant being so controlling over me. I wasn't his. He'd made it very clear that he didn't want me. He'd never wanted me.

"Under my roof, you'll do as I say."

"I don't want to be under your roof. I want to go home."

"Fine!" He shouted so loudly I jumped at his voice. I'd never heard him like this before, not even when he'd screamed at Vinnie. "I'll take you home tomorrow and you can get on with your life. But tonight, you stay here."

I pushed off from my position at the front door and

stalked over to the stairs, then ran up them as fast as my ridiculous sky-high Jimmy Choo's would let me.

"Fuck you!" I called over my back.

At that moment, I truly hated, no... despised Luca Marquez. I hated him for thinking he could speak to me anyway he liked. That he could treat me like an object, a piece of shit, and think it was okay. I hated that he thought he was so much better that me. I was no weak ass female. I could look after myself. And I hated him because I'd given him my heart and soul, gift-wrapped and guaranteed forever, and all he'd done is turn me down. Throw me away like a cheap toy that was never wanted.

I put so much effort into slamming my bedroom door shut I was surprised it didn't shatter. But no sooner had I slammed it closed, it flew back open, and a furious Luca stood in the door way. He was panting like a wild animal, his eyes boring into mine with a heated glare that burnt through me, making me falter slightly. His hands were balled into fists at his side and he looked ready to pounce.

We stood staring at each other, as if this was some weird, angry stand-off. Luca broke first.

"What the fuck is it you want from me, Chloe?" He panted "Just fucking tell me?"

"You know what I want," I whispered back, but to be honest I had no idea what I wanted. Another total head-fuck was clouding my judgement. I was swinging between lust and fury like a crazy woman.

"No, I don't." His voice was a little less coarse, and he took a few tentative steps into my room, but his body remained taut and tense.

"I'm not saying it anymore. I'm done, Luca. You never listen to me anyway."

"I'm listening now, Chloe. Talk to me."

I was toying with the idea of telling him how I felt, how he drove me crazy. How I couldn't function, because I was going insane with all of the different ways I wanted to make him mine. I spent most nights fantasising about the ways he'd fuck me. How his cock would feel. What it'd be like to come with him inside me. But I was older now, more guarded. I'd put myself on the line too many times for this man. I didn't have the energy for yet more disappointment and rejection.

"I can't."

I turned to walk into my bathroom, and he darted across those last few steps, and spun me back round to face him. He didn't let go of my arm as he stood over me still panting, his eyes burning like wild fire.

"Do you want to leave? Leave here and never see me again? Is that really what you want, Chloe?"

I couldn't speak.

Looking up into his eyes, I couldn't speak. Because if I said yes, I would've been lying. I could never lie to him.

"I don't want you to leave," he whispered. "I don't want you to walk away from me. I can't let you do that."

All I could do was stand still and listen to him. I thought

maybe he was telling me he wanted me, but I couldn't be sure. Years of mixed signals had fucked up my ability to understand anything where Luca was concerned.

"Do you hear what I'm saying, Chloe?"

He levelled his eyes at me, and in all truth, I didn't know what he was saying, so I shook my head.

He leant forward to speak into my ear, and his arms that were holding me in place drifted down to hold my hips.

"I...fuck it...I want you, Chloe. I've always wanted you. You're mine, no one else's. I want *everyone* to know you're mine."

He kept his head in the crook of my neck and planted soft little kisses along my ear, then down towards my shoulder, making me lean my head to the side to give him better access.

"Okay," I sighed. Just one little word that'd change my whole life. One little word that'd bring me everything I always wanted. Him.

That one word gave him the green light, and the animal that had stalked hungrily into my room only minutes earlier took possession of him, claiming me as his. His soft kisses down my neck and around my jaw turned hard and needy. Then he pressed his lips hard against mine, and his tongue slipped seductively inside to taste me. His hands held my head in place as he began fucking my mouth, giving me a preview of how he wanted to fuck my body, brutally, relentlessly and with total domination.

He slipped his hands down to my ass and squeezed hard, making me gasp as he growled low in his throat.

"The things I'm gonna do to your ass, Chloe. You have no idea how many times I've jerked off thinking about fucking your tight little ass. Fingering it as I suck your pussy and make you scream for me. I'm gonna do dirty, dirty things to you, Chloe."

I couldn't speak. Images of Luca taking control and taking me anyway he wanted made my panties soaked. I hated being out of control, but for him I'd do anything. I'd be his dirty little whore if that's what he wanted. I'd enjoy it too.

He bent down and yanked my legs up around his waist, picking me up, before turning me towards the bed and throwing me down on it. I lay on the bed panting, desperate for him to take my clothes off. For me to strip him down and feel his skin against mine. He stood at the side of the bed, his chest heaving in and out at a rapid speed and his eyes fucking me as he dragged them up and down my body.

"I've waited a long time for this," he groaned, as he crawled onto the bed and held himself over me like a wild animal. "I'm so wound up, Chloe. You've worked me up so much I can't think of anything else but being inside you, making you come."

He pulled my dress down to expose my tits, then he palmed them hard, rubbing and pinching my nipples, making me writhe and squirm under him.

"I'm gonna fuck you so hard, I'll ruin you for any other

guy who even dares to try and fuck you after me."

"I don't want anyone else," I replied in a breathy desperate tone.

I pushed my tits forward, arching my back as he leant down and sucked one nipple into his mouth. One of his arms wrapped around my back, pulling me further into him, whilst he held himself above me with the other. Then he swirled his tongue around gently, before sucking and nipping on me. Giving me pleasure and pain, sweet torturous pain. He was rigorous in his appreciation of each nipple, building me up into a frenzy of desperation to feel more. If he didn't move to my pussy soon, I was going to explode.

I gasped as he licked down from my tits to my belly button. Dragging my dress down over my waist and then pushing it over my hips.

I grabbed at his shirt trying to unbutton it, but going agonisingly slowly. Luca sat up and ripped the rest of his shirt open, the last few buttons popping off in all directions, then he threw it across the room. His chest was an artwork of sculpted, muscular perfection and stunning tattoos that told the story of his life. I sat up, stroking over his pecs and down along his abs. Hard, delectable muscles that rippled under my fingertips. I reached down to unbuckle his belt and get rid of his trousers, my eyes never leaving his. Heat and desire was spiralling out of control.

My fingers were clumsy and he took over, dragging his trousers down. He was going commando and oh lord, my eyes almost fell out of my head when I saw his thick, hard cock jutting out from his body, pointing at me, begging to be sucked. I pressed my lips against the head and tasted the salty little drip that was glistening on the top. Luca took a deep sexy breath in and held his head back as I licked, sucked and swirled my tongue around him.

Then he took control again, wrapping his fist around the base of his cock and pumping it slowly, as he used his other hand to push my head down further, directing where and how he wanted me. I sucked him and glanced up to find him looking down at me with pure lust in his eyes as he fucked my mouth.

"You're gonna take me down your throat, Chloe. Every fucking inch...but not now."

His voice broke slightly as I felt his cock start to grow and throb under my tongue. Then he pushed me away and his glistening, wet cock popped out of my mouth.

"I'm not coming in your mouth yet. I want your pussy first," he moaned. Then he yanked my dress down over my hips and along my legs. I had a black lacy thong on, which he obviously approved of.

He ran his fingers slowly across the seam of my panties, barely touching where I needed him to be. Then he pulled them aside, and his fingers circled my clit and teased my folds as he inserted two long fingers into my pussy. He stroked me from inside, curling forward to rub and massage that sweet spot. It was as if he held the secret map to my body. One touch and he had me pulsing. One stroke and I was itching, burning for release. A thrust and slow rub and I was moaning for him to take me, let me feel him.

I reached down to hold his cock and give back some of what he was giving me, but after a few pumps of my fist I lost control of myself, and couldn't focus on anything other than the growing sparks that were building in my pussy. I was heading to a spectacular climax, bigger than anything I'd ever felt before.

"You're gonna come on my face, Chloe. I want to taste you and feel your tight little pussy quivering on my tongue."

He lent back and yanked my panties down my legs. Then he picked my legs up under the knee and pushed them aside. I lifted them higher, baring myself to him.

"Perfect." He sighed. "You're beautiful like this. All laid out, wet and begging for me to make you come. Fucking perfect."

Then he settled in-between my legs, his tongue licking toe curling circles around my clit before it darted into my pussy, making me cry out. It felt so fucking good. He lapped at me and moaned, then he kissed my pussy like he would've kissed my mouth. I grabbed his hair in an effort to push his face further into me, to show him how crazy he was making me. His mouth moved back to my clit and he sucked and nibbled, as I ground my hips into him and groaned.

"Oh, God...Yes...Just like that...please, God...yes...I'm so close."

I felt him smile as he carried on his assault of my senses, "Not God, Chloe. Just me."

Then he pushed my knees right up to my side as he licked down my slit again before reaching my asshole. I groaned and threw my head back as he circled my ass with his tongue. No one had ever done that to me before, and although it should've felt dirty and wrong, with Luca it felt sensual, erotic, taboo and so fucking sexy. I'd never felt so completely wanton and desperate for him as I was right now.

"I'm coming...Oh God...Oh...Oh..."

I bucked my hips into him, as he licked back up to my pussy and speared his tongue inside me again, then sucked hard on my clit, alternating his pressure and sending me spiralling over the edge. My pussy clenched hard on his mouth, nerve endings exploding like fireworks and my body trembled with the intensity of it all. The throbbing and pulsing went on and on as I cried out, unable to deal with the level of pleasure he was giving me.

"So sweet," he said, milking every last drop of my orgasm from me, as he lapped at my pussy and licked over my sensitive spot. Seconds later, my clit went into spasm, throbbed hard and out of control and I threw my arm over my face. I couldn't take anymore.

I felt Luca lift himself up over me and then his massive cock was there at my entrance, pushing hard to get inside. When he pushed forward with that first thrust, I bit into my arm to stop the scream that threatened to break free and shatter this precious moment. It felt like a hot poker, a thick hot poker had ripped me apart. It took a few more thrusts before I started to feel like I could accommodate him slightly easier. He was stretching me so painfully I started to sweat. Would he be able to tell that this was my first time?

Hearing Luca pant into my ears, his control shredded as he rutted into me, made the soreness subside and I felt the familiar burning again inside my pussy and around my clit.

"So fucking tight," he gasped between grunts. "You feel so fucking good, Chloe."

His thrusts were moving me up the bed, making the headboard bang against the wall, and the bed squeak where it stood. I grabbed onto his ass as he pounded into me, feeling the muscles in his ass clench tight on every forceful push.

"Always...knew...you would..." He emphasised every word on each thrust as he worked us both up to an earth-shattering orgasm.

"I'm coming," I cried, as he lifted his head up to look down at me. His eyes were clouded over and his mouth hung open. I locked my legs tightly around his waist and wrapped my arms around his neck, hanging on for dear life, before I fell off the proverbial cliff yet again.

"Wait." He increased his pace slightly to meet me on the edge and then he cried, "Now!" And we both came hard together.

Tears fell down my cheeks as my pussy squeezed his cock and Luca hung his head gasping.

"Fuck, Chloe...so tight...feels...too good."

His cock throbbed as he released every last drop of his cum into me. His thrusts became slower and erratic as he came down from the high we'd both been catapulted to.

I'd spent years fantasising about this moment, and in all those years, I'd never dreamt it'd feel like this. All I wanted to do was hold him close and smell him, feel his skin next to mine. I felt so close to this man I could've cried. I didn't think it was possible to love Luca any more than I did, but right now, in this post orgasmic state, I'd have done anything for him.

He kissed me gently on the lips and pulled himself up off me to sit back between my legs, and that's when the bottom of my world fell out.

"There's blood." His face drained of colour and my orgasmic bliss began to wane, replaced by embarrassment, shame and fear.

"Did I hurt you? Why is there blood? Chloe...oh fuck."

The look of confusion and then absolute shock that appeared on his face as the truth dawned on him, made me wish the ground would open up and swallow me whole. I shot up off the bed and ran for the bathroom, locking the door behind me so I could die of shame right there, in private, on the bathroom floor.

Luca banged on the door, he sounded seriously pissed.

"Open this god damn door, Chloe! Now!"

Was he mad with me? Had I made a fool out of him or

something? I didn't understand his reaction.

"For fucks sake, don't shut me out!"

He was pounding so hard on the door I half expected the panels to crack and for him to be there 'Here's Johnny' style.

"Just fuck off," I shouted back. If he was going to be mad at me for not being the experienced dirty girl he wanted, then I could be mad that he'd been such a man-whore over the years.

"Jesus, Chloe. Why didn't you tell me? You're twenty-two-years old... you've been a stripper...how was I to know you were..."

I couldn't stop myself. I flung the door open, pure venom dripping from every pore.

"I'm sorry I disappointed you. Sorry I wasn't the slutty whore you'd signed up for tonight. You know, not all strippers are doing it for sexual kicks. I wasn't. I needed the money. So if it's experienced pussy you're looking for, Luca, better head back to Gina and her girls. You'll get what you paid for there."

His nostrils flared at the mention of Gina's girls. That really was a sore point for him. Was he ashamed of that? Embarrassed?

"At least I've taught you one thing tonight." I glared at him now with a sly smile. "When I make a promise, I keep my word. I told you I'd wait for you, and I did. You couldn't wait two minutes could you?"

I slammed the door shut in his face, but he didn't pound on it this time. I heard one bump, maybe a hand, maybe his head, and then heavy footsteps retreating. He was leaving. He'd got what he came for and now he was done.

I slumped down to the floor, fighting off the tears that wanted to flow. I wasn't going to let him break me. I was stronger than that. I played the events of the night over and over in my mind, and reassured myself that I wasn't in the wrong here. I'd done nothing wrong.

Chapter Fifteen

I sat on that bathroom floor for what felt like hours, feeling sorry for myself, then talking myself around again. Eventually I got a cold butt, so I decided to run a warm bubble bath and soothe my now aching, overworked body. As I sank down into the hot water and let a long slow breath out, it began to feel like a cleansing of my body and my soul. Lying in the steaming tub I made up my mind, I had to look on tonight's catastrophe as a form of closure, a final, blissful goodbye.

I'd brooded for so long over Luca Marquez. I had to face the fact that we were never meant to be. We were just too different. Those stars that Freddie loved so much just weren't lining up right or writing any kind of future for Luca and me. There would be no happy every after, no twist of fate bringing us together. Just a whole heap of heartbreak and the dreaded walk of shame for me tomorrow.

I let out some cold water and added more hot, but eventually my skin became so wrinkled I had to get out and dry myself off, before I turned into a total prune. I wrapped a huge fluffy towel around myself and pressed my ear to the door to listen out for anyone on the other side. There was nothing, just silence. I clicked the lock open and peered cautiously around the door. The bedroom was dark, cold and empty.

I left the bathroom and stepped quietly over to the object of my downfall, the bed, which had now been stripped bare. How ironic. I glanced around me to see if he was hiding anywhere, perhaps standing in a dark corner watching me, but he wasn't. All that was in this room was me, standing by the bed, with a note placed in the middle of the mattress. I was expecting a 'Dear John' letter or a brush off, ridding Luca of any blame for what'd transpired this evening. It wasn't what I got.

I did wait for you.
I've never loved anyone else.
Only you, Chloe.

Oh my God, was he telling me he loved me? I slumped down onto the mattress and then lay on my side, with my hands covering my face. Why did my life have to be such a fucking mess? I had it all figured out two minutes ago. I'd made my decision and I was leaving. Now, I just wanted to curse him for being so god damn stubborn and not telling me this years ago. Why had he left me seven years ago? And why had he never come back?

History had told me that the promises written and left behind by Luca weren't always kept, so I guessed this one could be a lie too. I folded the note back up and placed it on the bedside table. I closed my eyes and tried really hard to block out the memories of our evening in this bed, willing them away so they wouldn't plague my dreams. Then minutes later exhaustion took over and I drifted off to sleep.

-

The next day I woke to a quiet, empty house. After freshening up for the day and dressing in a cute baby pink sundress that finished just above my knees, I wondered out of my room to see if anyone was around. There were no signs of life. No used crockery in the kitchen, no cooking smells. Only the hum of electrical items and the whoosh of the breeze blowing outside.

Typical Luca, he was doing his usual cowardly act. He never had been able to face up to reality. He always chose to run and hide. Nothing had changed over the years. That's why I'd always been the one running towards him, I was stronger. Go me! I thought, as I wondered around opening drawers and cupboards to try to find any clues to hint at what Luca's life was like now. I didn't even know what he did for a living, apart from his 'useful' club, as Vinnie had put it. I found nothing.

Walking over to the front door, I wondered what'd happen if I just opened it and left. Went back to my apartment to carry on with my life, hustling for money and living one pay check to the next. I missed going to school, and I kind of missed Teresa's bossy, couldn't give a fuck attitude. That was all I missed, though. For some twisted reason I wanted, no needed to see this thing through with Luca. Stay and find out what he meant in his note last night. I was done with living on what ifs and if onlys. I was older, and even though I felt out of control right now, I had to take control of my future. That included drawing a line under the feelings I had for Luca Marquez.

-

He never came back that day. I shuffled around the house, did a few laps in the pool, and watched a whole box set on Netflix before I decided I was done waiting for him. I took a soak in a steaming hot bath and then took myself off to bed, wondering if he'd still be a coward tomorrow.

I was woken by the sound of laughter and voices downstairs. I checked the clock, 2.36am. I rubbed my eyes, fluffed my hair and threw the covers off. Slowly, I crept to the door, creaking it open slightly to listen to the chatter downstairs. Two voices, that's all I could make out. One was clearly Luca's, his deep velvet tones were unmistakeable. The other voice had a flirty, high pitch. He'd brought a woman home.

I felt sick, then angry. How dare he do this to me! After last night he'd left me a measly note, then avoided me all day. Now he had the bare-faced cheek to invite a woman home. For what? A revenge fuck? To throw my inexperience in my face? Or show me how much he actually didn't care? I wouldn't take it, though. He should know me well enough to know I wouldn't hide in my room crying.

I stalked over to my drawers and yanked them open, pulling out the black lacy nightie Gina had bought for me. It barely covered my ass and the girls were showcased fabulously in the built in cups. He said he loved me in black lace. Better prepare yourself, Luca. I'm about to blow your fucking mind!

With one last glance in the mirror to check my curls were sexily mussed and not sticking up all over the place, I darted confidently towards the stairs, and headed down to the living area.

As I hit the bottom step I felt both of them watching me, but I didn't turn to face Luca and his fuck for the night. I kept my head forward and fixed on the kitchen door, and put on a dreamy, sexy voice as I said, "Evening." Then pushed my way through the door. I needed to grip the edge of the sink for support as I settled my nerves. The laughter from outside had stopped dead, so I moved back over to the door to listen.

"Sister?"

"No."

"Cousin?"

"No."

"Please don't tell me she's your wife, and you have some fucked-up marriage involving kinky threesomes every night?"

"Definitely not."

"Well, this is awkward."

"Why?"

The living area went silent, and I held my breath as I waited for one of them to speak. The woman broke the silence.

"Listen, you brought me here tonight. But since she walked across there you haven't taken your eyes off that door, and you're so tense you look like you're about to explode. So I'm guessing she's more than just a random houseguest."

Luca didn't say anything, all I could hear was the chink of a glass as one of them sipped their drink.

"You know, I've heard the rumours about you."

"Yeah? Enlighten me." Luca sounded bored now.

"You're cold, emotionally detached and you never ever invite a woman back to your home. I thought maybe you'd seen something different in me tonight, when you asked me here. But now I've seen her and the way you're reacting? I get it."

This I had to hear.

"You didn't bring a woman home tonight, did you? You brought me here as an object, a thing, to toy with her. Am I here to make her jealous? Or upset her in some way?" She sighed. "I don't know what your game is with her, but I don't want to be used as your pawn, Luca. I'll see myself out."

The slam of the front door sounded her exit and I went towards the kettle to make a hot drink. She was right, Luca was playing a game, and I wanted no part of it either. I was done with his mind games.

I made myself a hot chocolate and then tentatively I sauntered back into the living area, but it was in darkness, utterly deserted.

Chapter Sixteen

Tap, tap, tap.

I woke to a gentle knocking on my door, but feeling totally unsociable I ignored it and turned over in bed, determined to ignore the world for as long as I could.

"Hello? Little sis, you awake?"

My eyes flew open at the sound of the familiar voice, and I sprang up into a sitting position in bed.

"Freddie! Oh my God, what're you doing here? It's so good to see you." I genuinely meant it too.

He came walking into the bedroom grinning like the Cheshire cat, and sat down on the edge of my bed. I didn't care that I was in a black, lacy nightie that showed a little too much cleavage, and my hair probably resembled a bird's nest at that moment. It didn't matter, because Freddie was like my big brother, and I didn't care what he saw me looking like. I launched myself across the bed giving him a massive hug.

"I missed you, you big oaf!" It was nice to wake up to something positive for a change.

"Not that I'm complaining, but why are you here?" I asked, wondering if Freddie's return would mean I was free to leave. I honestly didn't know how I felt about that.

"Luca called me yesterday. He said he thought it'd be better for both of us if I came here." He glanced around my room nodding in approval.

"Nice prison cell you've got."

I chuckled, he was kind of close with that assumption.

"Try dungeon of hell," I replied coldly, staring down at my lap and twisting my hands together.

"Is everything okay, Chloe?"

"Yeah, well apart from being locked up here. Why do you ask?"

He shrugged, then looked back up at me.

"Luca seemed...different... on the phone. I don't know, he was more human, I guess? Chattier and less snappy." He gave a small chuckle. "He asked me how I was and he never asks me that."

"Maybe he's trying to be a better brother?" I reasoned back.

"Or more likely you've had an effect on him. Some kind of weird, Chloe voodoo that you're so good at conjuring up, like when we were kids."

I rolled my eyes and pushed off the bed to head into the bathroom.

"I doubt anyone could change your brother, least of all me."

I started to brush my teeth as Freddie came to the doorway and lent up against it to watch me.

"You underestimate yourself these days, you never used to. I hope he hasn't been knocking that confidence of yours."

I spat the toothpaste into the sink. "Why? Would you kick his ass for me?"

"Damn right I would."

From the look on his face he was serious, but I knew Freddie couldn't kick a cat's ass, let alone Luca's.

"You being here, does that mean I'm free to go?"

"Not exactly. It's more a case of keeping our valuables stashed close together. All eggs in one basket so to speak."

"Great, so more days spent killing time here, when I could be working or getting my life back on track."

"It could be worse, Chloe."

"How?" I started to wash and moisturise my face before I started on my hair routine.

"You could still be without me! At least now you get to enjoy my sparkling wit every day!"

"Oh, how I've missed your witty charms," I sang back to him. I made out I was teasing, but it was true, I had missed him. At least Freddie didn't avoid me or treat me like a leper. Things would certainly get interesting now Freddie was back. I wondered how Luca would change. Would he even acknowledge what'd happened between us? Or would he use Freddie as a distraction?

-

Freddie and I spent the day catching up, being childish and watching T.V. It was whilst I was sitting on Freddie's lap, watching The Simpsons and laughing at Homer, that Luca showed his face for the first time that day. If I wasn't so pissed off with him, I'd have been drooling even more than I was. He was practically oozing sex in his dark blue suit and white shirt. The way it fitted over his shoulders and hugged his muscular frame made me want to run my hands over his body, then rip it all off. Damn my stupid, female hormones and crazy insatiable lust. He scowled over in our direction, as he asked Freddie what his plans were for the evening.

"What? He gets to go out, but I've gotta stay here?" I snapped back, daring him to look me in the eyes, but he never did.

"Chill, Chloe. I wouldn't leave you here on your own," Freddie replied, stroking up and down my arm.

Luca gave a low growl and stormed out of the house, slamming the door.

"The doors in this house must have the best hinges ever. They only ever get slammed," I moaned.

"Damn girl, you sure have riled him up this time. What's been going down between you two?"

I had to hold myself back from saying it was Luca who'd been going down on me. I wasn't ready to impart that secret to anyone yet though, but when I did, Freddie would be the first I'd tell.

Chapter Seventeen

Day five, post Luca and that fateful night, and things were still pretty tense and miserable in the house. Freddie provided a welcome distraction, but I was growing impatient with the lack of attention coming from the man himself.

That morning, I'd sneaked down to the end of Luca's garden to take a walk along the beach. The fresh sea air and sounds of nature helped to ground me, and bring a certain sense of calm that'd been sadly lacking in my life lately. I sat on the sand watching the waves and let myself just be, no dramas, no moody men and no restrictions, just me and the beach. Perfect.

"Hey you." A gentle, friendly voice called out behind me.

Gina had her shoes dangling from her left hand as she came over to sit next to me.

"Hi, Gina. Are you okay?"

"Yeah, I'm good. Looks like you aren't doing so good though."

"I'm better today than I have been for a while, don't

worry about me." I bent my knees to tuck them under my chin and sighed.

"Listen, I'm gonna just come out with it. I came over because I'm guessing you could use a friend right now."

"It's nice of you to come over, Gina, and I could use all the friends I can get, but what makes you say that?"

She looked straight ahead biting her lip, then glanced back at me.

"Don't take this the wrong way okay, but Luca likes sex."

"Don't all guys?" I smirked, but my stomach dropped. What the hell was she going to tell me?

"Yeah I know, but Luca...he's kind of...I don't know...highly active? Anyway, he rang me a few days ago saying he needed my services."

Oh God, here it comes. I was going to have to endure another delightful episode of Luca, flaunting his manliness and his women in front of me.

"He asked me to hook him up, but then he never turned up. Chloe, he never showed up that night and now he's ignoring my calls. So I'm putting two and two together and guessing somethings happened between you two. Am I right?"

"You could say that." I stared straight ahead at the waves, not wanting to see the look in her eyes.

"That's what I thought, and I'm guessing things aren't all smooth sailing. He can't bring himself to cheat on you, but he needs you at the same time."

"We'd need to be in a relationship for him to cheat on me."

"Seems like it's a relationship in his mind. Remember, men don't think the same way as us, Chloe. We're the smarter sex after all," she said gaily.

"Aint that the truth." I looked across at her to see humour and kindness in her eyes.

I took a deep breath and dived in at the deep end. "We slept together, a few days ago, but things ended, well...badly."

"Badly how? Did you push him away?"

"No."

"Was he rough with you?"

"No, it's...complicated and I can't talk about it, but he's avoiding me and I feel so mad. I just want to punch his cocky, moody...bloody sexy face in."

She laughed out loud.

"I think most women feel like that about him. Okay, so he's avoiding you. Do you think that's because he's embarrassed about whatever it is that did or didn't happen between the two of you?"

"Maybe. You know he brought a woman back to the house the night after?"

"No!"

"Yeah, classy move, huh?"

"What happened? Did he...?"

"No." I smirked. "I walked past them in that black lacy nightie you got for me and she walked out. Accused him of playing games and using her to get at me."

"I think she's right. Nice move by the way. Showing him you won't take his shit and rubbing his nose in it with your sexy night wear." She winked at me and I couldn't help but smile.

"He deserved it. He's an asshole."

"Do you want my advice?" Gina asked.

"It can't hurt, but I can't guarantee I'll use it. I kinda live by my own rules."

"I can see that." Gina smirked. "Well, Chloe, men never grow up. They just get bigger muscles and become more stubborn. Luca does anyway. If you wanna know what he's thinking, you've gotta ask him. If I know Luca, and I think I do, hell will freeze over before he admits he's done anything wrong or makes the first move."

"He made the first move that night," I bit back.

"Maybe I'm wrong. I mean, you've known him a lot longer than me, so you know best. Couldn't you just corner him and talk to him? It might surprise you what's actually going on in that weird, pretty head of his."

"I'll think about it," I sighed. "Thanks for coming over, Gina. You're a good friend." I smiled over at her, and she put her hand on my shoulder and squeezed, before giving me a hug.

"Anytime, Chloe. I'd love to see Luca smile occasionally and I think you're the girl to be able to do that to him. Whenever you need to chat just call me, or get one of the guys to...I know you don't have access to a phone, but I'll come over anytime."

"Thanks, Gina."

She lifted herself off the sand and made her way back to the house. I watched her leave, then settled myself back onto the sand to watch the clouds drift by. The calm before the storm, I mused.

Chapter Eighteen

My day of reckoning came two days later, as Freddie and I lay together under a blanket on the corner sofa, watching a horror movie in the dark. We had a huge bowl of salted popcorn balanced between us, and were scoffing our faces between hide-behind-the-pillow moments. The front door opened and we both looked over to see Luca stroll in, wearing his trademark designer suit. Black this time, with a grey shirt open at the neck, no tie. He took one look at us and slammed the door behind him, before stalking off to his office at the front of the house.

"What crawled up his ass?" Freddie whispered.

"I don't know, but I'm going to find out," I said, throwing the blanket off me and striding purposefully to the corridor leading to Luca's office.

"I think I'll make myself scarce. I'll be in my room," Freddie said, jogging up the stairs to escape being caught in the crossfire.

I came to the dark, wooden door and didn't stop to

knock, I just threw the damn door open and went inside. Shutting the door behind me, I stood and crossed my arms over my chest and stared at him. He was sitting at his desk, a glass of whisky in front of him. He was leaning forward with his hands braced either side of his head as he stared down at the drink, then over to where I stood.

"Not now, Chloe. I'm not in the mood," he growled, rubbing his temples in frustration.

"Fuck you. You don't get to dictate what I do, and I'm doing this...we're doing this, now. What the fuck is wrong with you?"

He shot up out of his chair, pointing his finger at me.

"No! We're not going there. Just get out. Go back to Freddie. You both look pretty cosy lately. I'm sure he can pick up from where I left off."

My blood, which was boiling and simmering nicely, exploded like a volcano.

"You absolute, fucking asshole! How dare you bring Freddie into this. He's my oldest friend, your brother, and he's shown more compassion to me in the few days he's been here than you ever have."

"Funny that. Do you think that's because he wants to be a good friend, or is it because he wants to get into your panties? Don't be so naïve, Chloe."

"Coming from you, who thinks it's perfectly fine to invite random women back to the house the day after you've fucked me, that's rich. Tell me, if I hadn't come down that night and ruined your little intimate party for two, would you have gone through with it? Would you have fucked her here, with me sleeping under the same roof?"

He sat back down in his chair and knocked back the whisky in one gulp, then poured himself some more.

"No, I wouldn't. I might be an asshole, but I'm not that vindictive." He glared at me.

"You're so clueless, do you know that?" I walked over to the other side of the desk and placed my palms flat on the surface, then bent down to meet his eyes.

"You think I'm spending time with Freddie because I'm attracted to him? Are you for real?"

"You've always had a connection, I've always seen it. I used to watch the two of you most nights when we were kids, lying on the grass looking at the damn stars. Tell me, why didn't you ever kiss him, back then? I know he wanted you, he still does." The scowl never left his face as he threw out his accusations.

"Oh my God, can you hear yourself? You have absolutely no clue what you're saying. You're deluded! You don't know the first thing about Freddie and me."

"I know you have private jokes, you were always thick as thieves back then, and it's getting like that now. Every time I walk into the house, you're draped all over him or he's pawing all over you."

"You're jealous. You're jealous of your own brother and you're so blinded by that, you can't even see the truth can you?"

His eyes bored into mine now. "So enlighten me then, tell me what's going on."

"He's *gay*, Luca. Your brother is gay. Do you not know that?" The anger on his face fell away as his mouth dropped open in complete and utter shock.

I kept going. "He told me he was gay when he was thirteen. He confided in me all those years ago, because he felt like he couldn't tell you. I know why now, you never listen, you just see what you want to see."

Luca sat painfully still, total disbelief playing over his face. He couldn't take his eyes off mine.

"I...I don't know what to say...Why wouldn't he tell me? That's so...huge. I..." I started to feel sorry for him, so I tried to help ease his guilt, not that he deserved it.

"He always looked up to you. He wanted to be just like you. But he thought you'd see it as a weakness. He didn't want to be weak in your eyes." I sighed and stood up, moving away from the desk I'd been looming over. "He'll probably kick my ass for telling you, but to be honest, he thinks you've already guessed and just won't talk about it."

"I had no idea." He shook his head and downed another mouthful of whisky.

"He's been seeing a guy he met at a club for a few months now. It sounds like it's getting serious, so I hope you're not gonna be a complete dick and start treating him differently. He's a good guy, the best. Don't shut him out."

"I'd never do that. He's my brother. I couldn't give a fuck who he's...fucking...as long as it's not you."

I ploughed on head first, determined to get my answers.

"I can't read you, Luca. I've no idea what you want. One minute you're being cold and pushing me away. Acting like the biggest dick on the planet. The next you're leaving me notes and telling me things that leave me with a total head-fuck. You need to stop the games and just be honest with me."

He took a deep breath in and looked at me over his eye lashes.

"I make men fear me, in my job. I have to make grown men fear me, and yet you're the one thing that scares the hell out of me, Chloe."

"Why? What have I done?"

"I can't read you either. I don't know how to act around you. I feel like...if I say the wrong thing you'll leave, so I don't say anything."

Finally, we were getting somewhere.

"All you have to do is talk to me, Luca. I'll always give you the truth, you know that."

"Maybe that's the problem. The truth scares me, because I don't know what the truth is anymore."

I'd never seen this Luca before, the vulnerable one behind the whole alpha asshole facade. It was a new experience for me to deal with.

"Sometimes you have to just put yourself out there, take a jump into the unknown to get what you want," I sighed.

"You know I can't do that."

There he was again, the guarded Luca was back, walls erecting as we spoke and gates about to shut for the night. I stuck a metaphorical leg forward to stop it closing.

"Well, I can. I've spent my whole life doing it with you, so here I go again. I love you, Luca. I always have and I always will. Don't get me wrong, I'm fucking pissed off right now. You've been a grade-A douche bag these past few days, but I'll never stop loving you."

"Why didn't you tell me?"

"I've told you every day since I was eight-years-old!"

"I don't mean that. I mean, why didn't you tell me about your...situation? Why couldn't you trust me?"

I shook my head and bit my lip.

"The subject of my virginity isn't the kind of thing I'd bring up in general conversation. I know you had a shit upbringing, and you're kind of socially inept, but even you must know that's not the kind of thing a girl would talk about with a guy like you."

"But it made me feel-"

"What? What did it make you feel, Luca?"

"Guilty."

I walked around the desk and leant down to roll his chair back and put myself directly in front of him.

"I didn't want you to know. I felt embarrassed."

"You shouldn't have. You have nothing to be embarrassed about, Chloe. I do, though. I treated you like a...fuck toy."

"No, you didn't. You did what you wanted at the time. I wanted that too."

He ran his hands over his face, so I reached forward and pulled them down to look at him.

"I don't want to carry on playing games. I..." I was going to carry on telling him how much I'd missed him. How badly I wanted him, but I didn't need to.

He stood up and wrapped both hands around my face. His fingers laced into my hair at the nap of my neck, and he pressed his lips softly against mine. He kissed me gently, then licked across my lips making me open up to him. As always my tongue and lips responding to his, twisting and stroking in sensual licks. The taste of whisky and Luca sent my head into freefall. I snaked my hands around his neck and pulled him into me. I wanted to melt into him, be consumed by him.

"I wasn't lying when I said I wanted to do dirty, dirty things to you, Chloe," he sighed into my ears in-between kisses on my neck. Then he pulled away to look deep into my hazy, lust-filled eyes. "You've no idea what a fucking turn-on it is, knowing you're all mine, only mine. Only touched by me."

I had no words, all I could do was feel. His kisses were like a drug to me, sending me sky high and spiralling into a bottomless pit of ecstasy. I didn't know which way was up and which was down, and I didn't care. How had I gone so long without feeling like this? It was like an awakening for me. I wanted everything with him. I'd have happily locked myself in this house forever if he'd asked me to, because nothing in this world had even felt as good as Luca's mouth on mine, Luca's body close and under my fingertips. I needed more.

I undid the buttons of his shirt and pushed it off his shoulders, then ran my fingers slowly up his back, across his taut, hard shoulders and down his chest to his stomach. Every part of him felt solid, powerful, and I wanted to lick and taste every tantalising inch. I kissed his shoulder and then down towards his bicep, as I brushed my fingers lightly across his abdomen, along the dusting of hair that disappeared into his trousers. He looked down at me and circled his fingers around my own shoulders, then hooked the thin straps of my flirty sundress down, until it rested around my waist.

I glanced back up at him through my own hungry eyes and silently willed him on.

"Pink satin this time? This could be my new favourite."

He ran a finger from my shoulder down to my breasts and circled his thumb where my nipple was straining under my bra, making it bud even harder. Then with his other hand, he pulled down the cup covering my other breast, and leant down to stuck it hard into his mouth.

"You have the softest, most fuckable tits I've ever seen, Chloe. I love how they respond to my touch."

He carried on licking and stroking, sucking and rubbing, making my head fall back and my eyes roll into the back of my head.

"For a guy who...barely talks..." I managed to groan out between my little appreciative moans. "You certainly like to talk when you're ...doing this."

He smiled a wide smile and peered up at me, blowing on my wet nipple, before swapping to the other one. "I like talking like this, it turns me on."

Well that was the exact opposite of what Gina had told me, but I figured maybe, hopefully, I was different to those girls. I ran my fingers through his hair and guided his mouth where I wanted him, putting all thoughts of other girls out of my mind. I didn't need the green-eyed monster rearing its ugly head now, we'd already dealt with enough tonight.

"I love how sweet you taste. How soft your skin feels when I lick it. How hard your nipples become when I suck on them."

I just gave a sigh in response and he chuckled. "I can't wait to taste every delicious inch of your body, Chloe. When I'm done with you, there won't be a part of you that I haven't had my mouth on."

He kissed a trail back up to my neck, and my skin prickled and tingled under his attention. I felt light-headed with the sensations he was creating.

"When I'm done with you, there won't be an inch of your body that I haven't come in, or on. I'm going to ruin you, Chloe."

I gasped. "I hope so."

He yanked hard at my dress, indicating that he wanted

it gone. So I pushed myself up to let him pull it over my hips and down my legs, to pool on the floor. His hands grabbed my ass, squeezing and massaging hard.

"The way your ass feels with this silk covering it up makes me so hard. I need to buy you more silk. I want to fuck you while you're wearing a pink silky nightie, and stroke your ass while I ram my cock into your tight little asshole."

His dirty talk was certainly doing the trick. I wished I had a silk nightie for him to do just that. The image of him losing control like that, and the words and thoughts he used, made me quiver for him.

He reached down to where my panties covered my pussy, and traced one finger down the middle, before moving the fabric aside.

"Jesus, you're so wet. You want me badly, don't you?"

He growled and I nodded, struck dumb with the overload of erotic sensations coming in waves through my body. Making my nipples hard, my tits feel heavy and my pussy start to pulse lightly wanting to be filled.

I loved how Luca took charge, opening his belt forcefully and with a determined look on his face, then ridding himself of his trousers with such ease. He was going commando again and the sight of his cock, swelling and jutting out, made me desperate to touch him. That little bead of moisture, glistening on the tip so temptingly. I wrapped my hand around him and ran my thumb over that wet little drop, then put my thumb to my mouth and sucked. His pupils dilated and he moaned, as he fisted himself and watched me close my eyes tasting the saltiness that was Luca.

"I would get you on your knees to finish the job, but I want your pussy too badly. I want to feel those velvet walls of yours squeezing my cock tightly when I make you come."

He pulled my panties off and threw them onto the floor. Then he grabbed underneath each of my knees and pulled them up, until my legs were open, my feet resting on the surface of the desk.

He fisted his cock again and ran it around my clit and along my pussy, sighing heavily as he did.

"Look at us, Chloe," he said, as his own greedy, hungry eyes gazed down at where he was rubbing.

"Look at us. This feels right, doesn't it?"

"Yes," I managed to say, as I watched the large, rounded head of his cock circle my folds, rub my clit and smear my wetness around. He was so agonisingly close to my entrance, that I wanted to grab his ass and push him in myself, but he wanted this. He wanted to watch us together and take this part slow.

He made one last delicious circle of my clit before he stroked his cock down towards my opening and pushed in so, so slowly I gave a cry at the stretch I felt.

"Don't close your eyes, Chloe please. I want you to watch us. See how fucking beautiful it is when I push my cock inside of you. Tell me how it feels, baby."

He pulled out, then pushed just the tip of his cock into

me.

I sighed. "It feels...like you were made for me," I replied, not able to put into words what the stretch actually felt like, it was too good.

We had our foreheads touching as we both breathed deeply, and gazed down to watch how perfectly we fit together. He was right, watching his cock sliding in slightly then back out, circling my clit and sliding back in again, was the single most erotic thing I'd ever experienced. It made the outside of my pussy burn and pulse. The inside throb and ache for him. And my clit was developing its own beat with the blood pulsing around it, making it hard, sensitive and so receptive to him.

"You were made for me," Luca gasped, as he grabbed my ass with both hands and with one big thrust, he pushed his cock right into me, making me cry his name out loud. My pussy was stretched to agonising proportions before slowly adapting to accommodate the size of him.

We were so close now with his cock buried deep inside me, but I craved even closer contact. So I grabbed his head and pushed my tongue into his mouth, kissing him hard. I fucked him with my mouth whilst he fucked me with his cock. Crying and moaning into each other as he massaged and circled, thrust and pounded his hardness into my soft.

"So tight," he growled out. "I love how tight you are." His thrusts came faster and more urgent. "So fucking good, Chloe."

All I could do was grab onto him for dear life, and rest my head on his shoulder as he pounded into me. The build up to my orgasm was painfully close, it was all I could focus on. My walls burned and my pussy began to tighten, as nerves sparked. My clit was so sensitive I ground myself into him, his coarse hair giving me some friction. I needed more though, and as an expert at reading my body he knew straight away, as he reached down and began to rub my clit.

The combination of his cock hitting me in places I never knew existed, creating waves of pure heaven, coupled with his expert fingers teasing out my orgasm, made me throw my head back crying and then he lay me back on his desk. All laid out ready for the grand finale.

"Come for me, Chloe. Come hard for me, baby," he grunted.

He held both hands on my hips as he powered into me, thrusting so hard I could hear the banging of the drawers in his desk, as they jiggled around with the force and intensity of our movements. That banging was the final turn on for me, it was so base, so primal. We were fucking like animals and I loved it.

"I'm coming," I screamed, as my orgasm took control of my whole body, making my legs shake, my back arch, my body convulse, and my pussy clench and throb so hard my brain turned to complete mush.

"Fuck yeah," he shouted, as he rammed harder, making the waves within me roll on and on. When I thought my orgasm was waning, he jutted his hips and ground into me more forcefully, making my orgasm respark and become more intense than the last. So this was what multiple orgasms felt like? Jesus, no wonder it was the stuff of legends, the sexual pinnacle. I felt like I was going to die the most exquisite, torturously incredible death. Just when I thought I couldn't take anymore, my body defied me, and kept firing off more explosions. My pussy had turned into the fourth of July. Luca was a fucking master.

"Fuck, you're so tight. I can't control it anymore," he growled out and I felt him thicken and then grunt out his own release. His thrusts turned erratic and desperate, then slowed to a beautiful, sensitive end. My pussy had well and truly milked him dry and he fell onto me completely sated. The sweat of his body coated mine, as we both gasped in air to try and steady our breathing.

"Oh. My. God." I just about managed to breathe out.

"Amazing right?" He smiled as he spoke, his cock was still buried inside me and his arms circled around my hips as he held me tightly to him.

"Beyond amazing," I replied, running my hands through his hair and panting.

"That was only round one, Chloe. I plan on having a lot more fun with you tonight."

He held himself up over me and peered into my eyes as our breathing began to slow. The look of love I saw in him made my heart prickle in my chest. He used one hand to stroke my cheek and I felt like crying.

"I love you," I said, stifling a sob but failing to stop a tear from escaping my eye and rolling down my cheek.

He wiped it away and placed a soft kiss where my tear had been.

"Come on. Let's go upstairs to bed. I need to cuddle you," he replied.

I couldn't help but feel a twinge of sadness that he hadn't said it back. I knew from his eyes that he loved me too, but sometimes, and especially in times like these after such an intense encounter, a girl needed to hear the words. A cuddle sounded good too though, and all I wanted was to feel him close to me. I wanted nothing more than to fall asleep in his arms.

I nodded and he pushed himself up off me and reached into his desk to pull out tissues. He cleaned me up and then lifted me into his arms and carried me over to the door. My legs were wrapped around his waist and my arms around his shoulders. I nestled my face into his neck and breathed him in.

We hadn't bothered getting dressed when we made our way out of his study, along the corridor and into the living area. Neither of us had thought about covering up, as he climbed the stairs with me wrapped around him like a baby monkey. But when we got to the top few steps, he tensed up his muscles.

"Freddie had better not choose this moment to come out

of his room," he growled. "I'll have to kick *his* ass if he sees your naked ass." He smacked my ass as he said that and I laughed.

"I don't think my ass holds much interest for Freddie."

He wasn't convinced though. "I don't care. I don't want anyone else seeing this ass. This ass is mine," He said, squeezing it with both of his hands. "For my eyes and my hands only."

I sniggered as a familiar, male voice sounded from behind a locked door.

"You do know I can hear you both from in here."

I hid my face in Luca's neck.

"Good. Stay where you are, little brother. Unless you want an ass kicking."

"I'm going nowhere," Freddie shouted. "Oh, and for the record, I'm putting my headphones in now and listening to very loud rock music for the rest of the night to help me sleep and block out any...night time noises. So you kids go ahead and do what you gotta do."

"Oh my God!" I groaned in embarrassment and Luca laughed. It was nice to hear him laugh, it made me feel all warm and fuzzy. He was always so serious. I planned to make it my life's mission to have him smiling and laughing more, just for me.

Chapter Nineteen

We never did get to round two. As soon as my head hit the pillow, I was out for the count. I didn't mind though, because waking up the next morning, with Luca curled around me, more than made up for anything I'd missed out on the night before. His arms held me close to his chest, my back to his front, and his legs were tangled with mine. From the soft, steady breathing I could hear and feel on the back of my neck, he was still asleep. So I lay there quietly, enjoying the peace of the morning and the warmth of his body. I couldn't remember the last time I'd felt this safe and contented. I suppose that's what good sex does to you. That, and a hot guy to do it with.

About ten minutes later I felt some movement behind me as he stirred and then the delicate kisses on the back of my neck. He mustn't have known I was already awake and he was giving me the gentlest wake-up call ever. I moved my hand down to where his rested over my tummy and laced my fingers with his.

"Morning," I whispered and lifted his hand to kiss it.

He tried to roll me over, but I protested at the lack of tooth brushing that'd occurred so far that morning. To which he replied that he didn't care, he needed to see me and kiss me properly.

"I like seeing you naked in my bed," he said in a sexy low voice. "I think you need to be here every morning."

I smiled and lay my head on his chest. I could hear the strong, steady beating of his heart. It had a calming effect on my soul, and I decided if we never left this bed today, I'd be the happiest girl in the neighbourhood. I was right where I'd always wanted to be.

I ran my fingers gently up and down his chest and took the opportunity to admire his stunning body, and the tattoos that adorned it.

"Do any of your tattoos have a special meaning?" I asked, drawing my fingers around an angel on his arm.

"They all have special meanings." He kissed the top of my head and then pulled his arm over to show me the angel I was tracing.

"You see this one here? If you look closely, and I mean really closely, you'll find a very special something hidden in this tattoo."

I leant up on my elbow to take a closer look, still running my fingers over his arm. I don't know why I'd been drawn to that particular image so much. The angel was kneeling down and what looked like a rosary was in-between her praying hands. Her wings were a myriad of swirls and patterns. I'd always hated those optical illusion pictures, the ones where people claimed to see lions and tigers, or some other weird and wonderful image hidden within the patterns. I could never see them, much like Freddie's constellations in the night sky.

"All I see is an angel with a rosary," I huffed.

Luca picked up my finger and began to trace something. The curve of her knee.

"C," he whispered.

Down her arm and a bump across where it was bent at the elbow.

"H."

Where her wings were attached to her back.

"L."

Then into the wings themselves, where the curls twisted into joined letters that were making my lower lip tremble and my eyes water.

"O and E."

"You have my name tattooed on your arm?"

"I have *you* tattooed on my arm. You're my angel."

I gasped, for once totally lost for words.

"And it isn't a rosary, it's a St. Christopher on that chain she's holding."

I couldn't stop myself. I launched on top of him, hugging him so tight I could've hurt him if he wasn't so tough.

"You like it then?" He chuckled, softly running his hands

down my back and planting kisses along my shoulders.

"I love it. I love you," I cried.

We held each other close for what felt like ages before I reluctantly pulled away and asked the question that'd forever burned onto my lips.

"What happened that night? The night you left?"

He closed his eyes and sighed, then quietly and gently he opened up to me, and recalled the whole sorry saga.

Chapter Twenty
LUCA

Seven years ago…

I still felt totally shitty for taking Kate Silvers out on that God-awful date earlier. I didn't even like the girl. She smelt of stale cigarettes and tasted like cheap liquor when I kissed her. It all felt so wrong. I knew she was low maintenance, though. And I was willing to try anything to get my mind off of Chloe. I figured dating other girls in the area might help. The only problem was none of them held any interest for me. They didn't give me bullshit, drive me crazy, and occupy every spare minute and every spare thought in my day. Chloe, on the other hand, smelt of cotton candy, tasted like cherries and I was pretty sure she felt as soft as velvet. (That one I had yet to test out.) She made my heart race, gave me butterflies, and sent me into a blind panic every time she was near me. So after being on the receiving end of Chloe's wrath this afternoon, followed by that kiss, I was worse off now than I had been before. My head was going the same way as my heart. It was falling under her spell and fast.

Maybe I was thinking too much about other people, I had no idea why. They didn't take my feelings into consideration when they treated me and my brother like trash. Perhaps I should throw caution to the wind and be with her. Be free to love her like I wanted to. What did I have to lose?

It was whilst I was contemplating just that, and while Freddie was busy heating up a frozen pizza for our dinner, that I heard the front door slam shut. My Father stumbled, then fell through the living room door, drunk as fuck and spoiling for a fight.

Freddie walked through with the pizza and put it on the coffee table in the middle of the room. My Father just scowled at it then back up at the both of us.

"You call that a meal? I'm a grown man, how the fuck am I supposed to live on that shit?"

"He didn't bring it in for you," I shot back, wishing he'd just up and leave, pass out somewhere or better yet, never come home.

"Every damn thing in this God damn house is mine. Even both of your sorry asses. Though God knows why I'd want those. You pair of faggots aren't good for nothing."

I felt Freddie shrink beside me, but I wasn't letting him get away with his shit these days. I was learning to fight back. I'd started working out pretty hard and soon I'd have *enough strength to overpower him, give him a taste of what he'd put us through over the years.*

"Look at you," he sneered, as he looked us up and down with disgust; ridicule ready to spurt forth from his vile mouth.

"My sons, my fucking sons. Put you both together and you still wouldn't be half the man I am."

I shook my head, my Father was seriously delusional. If beating on women and children made you a man, I didn't want to be one.

"Take that little girl next door, for example." The hairs on the back of my neck stood on end as he started to talk about Chloe.

"She flounces around here all tits and ass, begging to be fucked, but have either one of you tapped that?" He laughed, giving us a perfect view of his putrid, rotten teeth and a hint of his stale beer breath wafted our way.

"You know boys," he leant forward in his chair, his grubby hands rubbing together whilst his evil eyes shone with wicked thoughts. "I'm gonna do you both a little favour." His grin made me want to puke. He only ever grinned like that before he started on us. That grin meant 'show time' for him.

"That ripe, little teenage ass in those fuck-me denim shorts comes around here every damn day. Her pert little titties pushed into those tight little tops she wears."

His eyes glazed over as he spoke, and I felt my hands

fist beside me. He was pushing all the wrong buttons here, when it came to Chloe, I would go head to head with him. She was off limits.

"Tomorrow," he looked between Freddie and me as he spoke. "I'm gonna invite her in, tell her you're just upstairs and she can wait on the couch. Then I'm gonna fuck her tight little virgin pussy and ass so hard she's gonna feel me for weeks after. I'm gonna rip her apart and enjoy every wriggle, every cry, every kick, scratch and scream she gives me. I like it better when they fight, makes me go harder for longer. You two faggots will thank me in the end for breaking her in. I'll do what neither of you two can manage. I'll give her what she wants."

I couldn't listen to him anymore. I knew exactly what my Father was capable of and I knew he meant every word. He would rape Chloe, and I had to be the one to stop him. I couldn't let him destroy the one good thing Freddie and I had going in our pitiful lives.

I launched myself across the living room at him, my fists flying with as much force as I could muster, but it barely left a mark on him. He even had the audacity to laugh in my face as he pushed me away, and I fell backwards over the coffee table. What happened next, I'll never be ashamed of, and I'll never regret it for as long as I live. I was doing what needed to be done, simply taking out the trash. Protecting what was mine, protecting those that I loved, which is what any real man would do. I wasn't gonna sit back and let him threaten her. Even the thought of his eyes on her made my blood boil. I'd die before I ever let him anywhere near my Chloe.

He sat back, stuffing his grotesque face with pizza and rubbing his rancid cock in his trousers, as if he was warming it up for what he planned to do tomorrow. I made my way to my bedroom and rolled back the threadbare carpet under the window. There was a loose panel of floorboard that was raised up, and I hooked my finger underneath and lifted. There, wrapped in a cloth, was a handgun I'd bought from a guy I'd met through Al's garage. At the time that I'd bought it, I wasn't quite sure why I had. It wasn't like I was a shooting enthusiast or that we lived in a gun-toting, gang filled neighbourhood. But something had told me that day that I'd need it. Today was that day.

I pulled it out of its hiding place and checked the chamber with the bullets to make sure it was loaded. Then, with a sense of serenity and retribution settling over me, calming me for the task ahead, I walked back to the living room.

Freddie was sitting in the armchair looking at his feet and shaking. My Father was oblivious to the effect that he had on my brother and was stuffing the last slice of pizza into his face.

I raised the gun in both hands up in front of me, to point it at my Father. When he looked across and saw me, he started to laugh again, not a hint of fear was in his eyes.

"What have you got there, son? A B-B gun? You should be careful waving that thing around, you could really...bruise me with that thing." He carried on laughing, mocking me.

"Luca don't." Freddie's eyes grew wide.

No one knew I had this gun, not even him. I'd kept it secret because I figured if anyone ever found it, I didn't want to implicate my little brother in any police investigations.

"I wouldn't worry, Fred. Your brother doesn't have the guts. He couldn't shoot a tin can, let alone his own Father."

My Father sat back, rubbing his belly and smirking at me.

"You won't ever touch her," I snarled through gritted teeth. "You won't ever look at her or even think about her again, ever."

"Oh, yes I will." The determination in his voice made it the easiest decision in the world.

"No, you won't." I steadied my arms and pulled the trigger.

My Father shot backwards. A single round hole in the middle of his head dripped a single drop of blood, that dribbled slowly down his face. The back of his head was totally blown off, blood and brains were splattered over the back wall and across the back of the chair.

I'd put him down.

I had no choice.

I had to do it for her.

There'd been two women I'd loved in my life. He'd annihilated one already, I could never bring her back. But I'd die before I ever let him devour and destroy the other. Chloe was mine, and I'd do anything in my power to keep her safe.

It took us hours to clean up the blood and mess, and load my Father's carcass into the trunk of his car. Freddie had gone into shock and was babbling complete shit, making no sense whatsoever. I felt the most relaxed I'd ever been in my life. I wondered why I hadn't got rid of him years ago.

"We can't stay around here anymore, Fred?" I said to my little bro, as he wandered around the house aimlessly, packing up his things and muttering about school, the teachers, the cops and Chloe.

He stood still, staring at me, and shaking his head frantically like a lunatic.

"No...no...we can't leave her. No, we need to take her with us. She's a part of us, Luca. She's our sister."

Part of me wanted to take her. Creep into her home and steal her in her sleep. But when I thought about Stan, and how devoted he was to her, I couldn't do it. She was only fifteen. She had school and friends, a family that loved her. Sure, our world revolved around her, but were we the centre of her world? I didn't think so. She loved us, but she was still too young to come with us. Too young to have a decision like that made for her.

So I did the next best thing. I made a promise to Freddie that when she turned sixteen, we'd come back for her. We'd be on the run from the police, but we'd find a way to get back to her without being detected and let her make the choice herself. To come away with us and live her life alongside ours, or to stay with her family.

"But she's gonna wake up and think we just upped and left her, Luca. I can't do that to her. I can't leave here and not let her know we haven't deserted her."

What he said made sense and I kinda agreed with him. It wouldn't be fair to just leave without trying to tell Chloe we'd be back.

That's why I committed my second crime that night and broke into the Ellis's house. I lurked in the shadows as I made my way up her stairs. Then I inched my way through her bedroom door, my back pressed against the wall. I sighed, as I saw her lying in her bed, fast asleep. An angel, too beautiful for our ugly world. I couldn't wake her. The vision of her flawless skin, plump lips and tumbling curls falling all over her pillow took my breath away. Her eyelashes fanned out over her delicate pink cheeks as she gave an innocent little sigh in her sleep. I felt totally vindicated for what I'd done tonight. She was my angel, my perfect angel, and I'd saved her.

I took a sheet of notepaper from her desk and scribbled down a quick note.

I will come back for you.

Then I folded it in half, and put it on her bedside table, right next to her alarm clock. It didn't feel like enough, though. I had to do more, to show her I meant it. I took my St. Christopher from around my neck and placed it on top of the note. She knew I'd worn that St. Christopher every day of my life. She knew why as well. It was the only thing I had left of my Mum's. But I was leaving it with Chloe, so she'd know I'd be back. I was leaving my Mum's spirit to watch over my angel.

Chapter Twenty One
CHLOE

Present Day

"Oh my God. I...I... don't know what to say. Do you really think he'd have... hurt me?"

I was freaking out, but trying to keep myself cool and calm. I mean damn, he shot his own Father? I knew his Dad was an evil fucker, but still...murder?

"He'd have done it. I know for a fact he would've. It wouldn't have been his first rodeo, trust me." Luca pulled me in closer to him, his head nestled above my own.

I daren't ask him how he knew he'd hurt me, I was terrified what the answer would be. I know he hurt Luca and Freddie frequently, I helped them out most days, but I'd assumed it was just fists and punches.

"And before you ask, no, he never touched us like that."

Thank God. I was starting to seriously question my whole childhood for a minute there.

"So, now I know why you left, but why didn't you come

back? I don't get it."

Luca sighed and stroked softly up and down my arm.

"As time went on it got harder and harder to go back. The day that you turned sixteen, I got in the car to come to you, but I stopped a few streets away from your house, and I just sat and looked around me. It was a good neighbourhood. Decent schools, hardworking people like your Father. I felt like I'd be cheating you out of the best start in life, a chance to make something of yourself, if I took you away from all that. I thought you'd be better off without us. My life was heading down a path that I didn't want you involved in. So I made the decision to leave you be."

I could understand his logic, but he'd made that decision without having all the facts.

"You thought you were doing what was best, but believe me, you leaving and never coming back was hell for me. My Father died three months after you left. Life got pretty shitty after that. I'd have given anything to get out of that house."

He sighed and looked down at me. "If I'd have known about Stan it would've changed things. It couldn't have been that bad though, living with your Mum? I know she was a bitch but you still had the house, school, and your friends."

I sat up and stared back at him lying next to me.

"Are you kidding? The minute my Dad was out the picture she installed a revolving door on the house, for her ever growing line of creepy boyfriends to come over. She even had a guy in her bed the night of Dad's funeral."

"That can't have been much fun, seeing your Mum move on so fast," Luca said, with a sympathetic look in his eyes. He so wasn't getting what I was hinting at. So I spelt it out for him.

"I couldn't give a rat's ass who my Mum was fucking. What I objected to, was them being more interested in getting into my room and my bed, instead of my Mums. Having an overweight forty-year-old, breathing stale beer fumes over you, whilst he wrestles to get your pyjama bottoms off, isn't the best way to be woken up in the middle of the night. And trust me, that wasn't the only time I had to fight them off. My narcissistic Mother, however, didn't believe shit when I told her. No, she just threw my ass out the door before I'd even reached my seventeenth birthday, because she caught the boyfriend of the hour naked in my bed whilst I was taking a shower. I had no idea he was there, but when I argued back she took his word over mine."

Luca hung his head, closed his eyes, and rubbed them with one hand, as if willing away the guilt.

"I'm so sorry, Chloe."

I shrugged and lay back down next to him, my arm snaking around his warm, muscly waist.

"It's in the past. At least I know now what happened, and why you never came back. I guess I kind of understand, even though I wish you'd have checked in with me first. I missed you guys. You...you broke my heart."

Luca rolled over to move his body on top of mine.

"The last thing I'd ever want to do is hurt you, Chloe. Not then, and definitely not now."

I looked deep into those glistening, green eyes and sighed. "Well you have my heart now, so this time...please take better care of it, okay?"

He leant down to place a whisper of a kiss on my lips as he breathed back, "Always."

Then he moved over me to settle himself in-between my legs. I could feel how hard he was, and the yearning I saw in his eyes drove me wild. I pulled him down to me to kiss him again. My tongue slipped past his lips and he met me with his own sensual licks and strokes.

"It's always been you, Chloe," he muttered into my neck, as he trailed soft, gentle kisses up to my ear and then nipped at my ear lobe. His hands skated down my side to my ass, then up along the back of my leg, as he pulled my leg up to bend at the knee. "I want to take my time with you. I want to savour this," he sighed.

I twirled my fingers in his hair and ground my hips into his. "I need to feel you," I begged.

He gave a low chuckle. "All in good time. I need to get you ready. I want you begging for me...desperate."

He was moving down my body now, tweaking my nipples between his fingers and rolling them into hard nubs. His mouth moved tantalisingly slowly over my tummy, my belly button and then he shifted his focus to my legs. He sat up in-between my bent knees and kissed along my calves.

Then he trailed kisses behind my knees, before using drawn out licks and nips along the inside of my thighs.

"I'm begging now," I wined. "Please-"

He speared his tongue and ran a pointed lick from my ass all the way up to my clit. The moan that came out of my mouth was so wanton, but I didn't care. I'd happily ride his face if he made me come like he did last night.

He was seriously good at this shit. He knew when to increase the pressure and the pace. He listened to my moans and groans. He paid attention to my body and how I wriggled and moved underneath him.

"You are so, so good at that. Don't stop, don't ever stop." I willed him to stay there, until he'd drawn every last pulse and spark of my orgasm that was painfully close.

"You're so responsive, Chloe. I know exactly what you need," he said. Then like the master he was, he sucked my clit into his mouth, and pushed two fingers inside me to rub and tease me towards my goal. The feel of his fingers steadily coaxing me into that spiral of ecstasy, along with the erotic way his mouth worked my clit, made me come hard and fast. So fast it gave no warning, just exploded like a surprise party popper, sending my legs to jelly, and my head to mush. I couldn't take my eyes off him. Lying there between my legs, doing things to me that weeks ago would've made me feel embarrassed, but I wanted to bare myself to him, to be his without restriction. I wanted to feel everything with him, in every way possible. I loved that he was loving me like this. I felt worshipped by him. Having him below me like this made me feel powerful, in control. Even though it was clear, he was the one who was in the driver's seat.

He lifted himself up over me. My climax had just started to wane, and he had the biggest grin on his face as he held himself above me.

"Put your left foot on my shoulder," he commanded, so I did. And all I can say is whoa, he blew my mind.

He thrust into me hard with my foot against him. Feeling him this way felt totally different to last night. The way he stretched me was always sublime, but he was deeper and more frantic this morning.

The grunts and panting were so horny, I wanted to make him cry for me like I'd done for him. The sound of the headboard banging against the wall so aggressively spurred me on, made me want to push him further over the edge. I let my foot slide over his shoulder and lifted my other leg. He took my cue and pushed both of my legs over his shoulders, driving into me in hard, deep thrusts.

"I don't think I'll be doing much work today..." he said between grunts. "I'll be too busy...doing you."

I smirked back up at him. His hair was hanging wildly over his forehead as he lost himself in me, in us, with a massive shit-eating grin on his face.

"Sounds good to me," I replied, holding his arms for support as he pounded himself harder and forced me up the bed into that noisy headboard.

Seconds later, I was lost in my second round of orgasms and orbiting somewhere in another galaxy, as he met me with his own moans and throbs. We had a hell of a lot of time to catch up on, and I couldn't wait. How I'd ever get on with the rest of my life, when being with him like this was so...addictive, I had no idea. I was beginning to see why John and Yoko spent all their time in bed. It certainly held a lot more appeal to me now, than it had at any other time in my life. I was one hundred percent, full on, signed sealed and delivered, his. Yep, and I was quoting song lyrics to myself to back it up. It was official. I was a goner.

Chapter Twenty Two

I'd spent the last few days stuck in a loved-up bubble of Luca. Today, he had no choice but to go to work. The underworld wouldn't rule itself I supposed. Still, I missed the cuddles and...other stuff as soon as he left. It had made being on lock down so much more interesting, to say the least.

"Someone sounds cheerful," Freddie said, as he came into the kitchen where I was singing along to Pink at the top of my lungs.

"My incarceration has taken a turn for the better recently." I winked at him and bit my bottom lip, remembering the awesome shower orgasms I'd had an hour earlier.

"Speaking of incarceration, do you have any idea what's going on with that, Fred?" I'd been meaning to bring it up with Luca, but every time I mentioned it, he cut me off and distracted me with...well himself.

"You know about as much as me, little sis. I'm going stir crazy too. If it isn't sorted by the weekend, I'm taking matters into my own hands."

"I know what you mean and I'm with you one hundred percent." As much as I was loving my time with my boys, I needed to get out.

A mobile rang and Freddie pulled out his phone from the back pocket of his jeans.

"What's up?" Freddie nodded along, then after a few 'yeahs' and 'sure', he passed the phone to me.

"Hello?"

"Chloe, I miss your beautiful face. Come over to the club with Freddie this afternoon and surprise me."

"It's not a surprise if you know I'm coming, Luca." I teased.

"I won't know the time you're coming, so that'll be a surprise," he tried to argue.

"Okay, I suppose I can go with that. Plus, the field trip will stem the boredom of my day in lockdown."

I rolled my eyes over at Freddie, as he drank milk straight from the carton, and started stockpiling food under his arms to take back to his room.

"I'm sorry, baby. You know it's all to keep you safe. It won't be for much longer."

"It better not be, or Freddie and I will be starring in our own series of prison break." I hung up the phone and passed it back to Freddie.

"Let me know when you're leaving. I think your brother just gave me a booty call." I laughed and headed out to the pool for some much needed rest and relaxation.

-

Three hours later, I was primped to perfection and dressed in the cutest, short-skirted Dolce and Gabbana summer dress; off the shoulder, ivory and decorated with red peonies. I felt flirty, carefree and ready for a bit of teasing. My chocolate curls were tied up into a high ponytail that reached right down my back, and a pair of red kitten heels finished off the look beautifully.

Freddie used his covert driving expertise to get us from the house to the club, where Leo and Marco met us in the car park. I had no idea what Freddie's urgent task for the day was, but he was insistent that I go to the bar with him for a drink, before he headed off to do what he had to do, and I went on my 'surprise' visit to Luca's office. We both ordered pink gin, and marvelled over how nice it was to see the inside of a different building.

"Getting cabin fever, guys?" Rosa the bar manager said, as she restocked the fridges.

A young, red-headed girl about my age was wiping down the counters, and making a rubbish job of appearing busy and not eavesdropping. She looked like she'd dressed to kill, wearing a tighter than tight red dress and spiked heels. She glared at me, then frowned to herself. Did she think I was a mole that had come to steal the club's secrets? Or some kind of time waster?

"You could say that, Rosa," moaned Freddie, as he

downed his drink. Then he patted me on the back like one of his dudes, and headed back out in the direction of the car park to join Leo and Marco.

Rosa went off into the back of the bar, leaving me with the suspicious red-head scuttling around like a fly. I hopped off my stool and made my way over to the door leading to the stairs up to Luca's office.

"Sorry, you aren't allowed back there. It's management only." She smiled a smug smile that made my back go up instantly.

"I don't think the management will mind *me* going up. Excuse me," I replied sternly, trying to push past her little body that was standing in my way.

"I don't care what you think, you're not getting up there, lady." She folded her arms over her chest and stood her ground. What was up with this girl? She was seriously testing my patience.

"Unless you have an appointment, I suggest you head on back to Gina's knocking shop." She sneered at me, looking me up and down like I was a cheap whore that'd come here to sell herself.

"What the..." I put my hands on my hips, ready to give this minx a piece of my mind, when she made the ultimate save.

"The boss has a girlfriend now. So you'd better spread the word to your little posse. No more sleazy hook ups for you lot."

My shoulders went down and a warm smile replaced the evil scowl that I'd no doubt been giving her. Rosa also chose that exact moment to come back into the bar and raise her eyebrows at us.

"Everything okay, Stacey? Chloe? You're here to see Luca right, Chloe?"

Stacey the red-head's face dropped, and she whipped her head from Rosa's to mine so fast she probably gave herself whiplash.

"Oh my God!" She blurted out, covering her mouth in shame. "I'm so sorry. I thought...well I didn't know... Oh God, please don't have me fired," she begged, and from the look in her eyes, I could tell she was petrified of what I'd do.

"Fired?" I laughed. "You should get a raise for being so vigilant. Good job, Stacey. You're wasted behind the bar. Luca should put you on security." I joked, as she heaved a sigh of relief.

"Not much gets past our Stace!" Rosa quipped, as Stacey stepped aside for me.

"Don't panic," I whispered. "You didn't do anything wrong, not really. And I won't say a word. Trust me."

She grinned up at me and nodded. I had a feeling I'd just made another friend in Stacey, and it felt good to know. As much as I loved Teresa, she wasn't what you'd call a girls' girl. Let's just say, I wouldn't have introduced her to Luca, not in a million years. It wasn't that I didn't trust Luca, no. I didn't trust Teresa not to throw herself at him the first time my back was turned. Teresa was an acquired taste, and although girls had warned me against getting too close to her, I kind of knew how to keep her sweet. Plus, she was a riot on a night out. And after leaving the tyranny that was my Mother's care, I was more than happy to play the good girl to her bad.

I made my way up the stairs to Luca's office, and knocked on the door twice before entering, to find him surrounded by paperwork, money, two laptops and a PC. What the hell was he working on that required so many computers?

"Gentlemen, I have to go. I have an urgent matter that just came up," he said to one of the laptops, as his eyes drank me in and he gave a sneaky grin.

"I want to know the details of that shipment by midnight," a gruff voice echoed back.

"You'll have it when I'm ready." Luca snapped, and shut the laptop down, making my jump slightly.

"Bad meeting?" I said through clenched teeth, hoping that last part hadn't put him in a bad mood.

"Bad day," he growled back, then fixed his eyes on me. "But it just got a whole lot better. Come here." He called me over to where he sat at his desk, then put his arm out to take my hand and pull me down into his lap.

He stroked my cheek then pulled me in for a kiss, putting me into a delicious, Luca-induced trance. Boy, my Luca knew how to kiss. I wrapped my arms around his neck and savoured every minute of him, as he kissed me and held me close. Even in his pissed off state, he still made my knees go weak.

"Thank you for surprising me," he smiled as he pulled his sexy lips away from mine.

"My pleasure," I moaned, leaning down towards him and biting on his bottom lip. "I missed you."

He ran his hand from my knee, up to my thigh, and then lifted my skirt to see what was hidden underneath. The feel of his coarse, rough fingers against my soft skin made me tingle and gasp.

"Ivory lace." He raised both eyebrows. "I like it...but it would look better around your ankles."

"Whatever sex fiend," I said in a low, throaty rasp.

"I'm all wound up. I need your help to find a release," he murmured into my ear.

"I know an excellent way to ease stress and find...relief." I was toying with him now and I loved it.

"Oh yeah?" He smirked, running his fingers up and down my hips, making my skin goosebump.

"Yeah." I ran my nose seductively along the side of his and sighed. "Pool."

"Pool?" He reared his head back and frowned at me.

"Yeah, a decent game of pool always gives my brain a clear out." I smirked back at him.

"I can think of better ways to...clear my brain." He glared at me quizzically.

"But would you be able to say you'd beat the undefeatable, Chloe Ellis, master of the pool halls, hustler extraordinaire?"

He threw his head back and laughed. "Okay my little hustler, you're on."

I hopped back off his lap and he stood, took my hand in his, and led me through to a private room that must've been allocated for the staff. It was decked out like a mini casino, with slot machines along one wall, a self-service drinks area against another, and the all-important pool table in the middle. The rest of the room was taken up with comfy couches and recliner chairs. Just like the club downstairs, it was all decorated in golds and blacks and screamed opulence, even for a staff area.

"Rack em up then, little hustler." Luca reached for the cues, as I placed the balls where they needed to be.

I was looking forward to this. I hadn't played a decent game of pool for a few months. But I knew my Father's lessons and my skills never went rusty. I set the table up ready for a game of 8-ball and sashayed my way over, to take a cue from Luca's hand.

"Be prepared to be shamed, Marquez." I grinned as I bent down to take the first shot.

"Nice view," Luca replied, as he looked straight down my dress to my tits as I was breaking.

"You won't distract me, Marquez. I'm unstoppable."

"It's you who's distracting me, Ellis," he growled back,

then slapped my ass as he walked past me.

I potted a stripe, then set my balls up just where I needed them.

"Your shot, Marquez. Try to hit the ones with the little spot on them," I joked and he shook his head at me.

"I know what to do with my balls, Ellis."

"All guys lose control sometimes." I was so obvious with my distraction techniques, as I bent down on the opposite side of the table from the shot he was taking, pretending to look at the angle of the shot, but really I was giving him another look at my chest.

"Not me." He smashed the balls around the table and expertly potted a spotted ball.

"Nice shot, but don't get too comfortable," I sighed. "I like the challenge."

"Me too," he groaned back, as we exchanged heated glances.

We played on, pretty well-matched in our ability, but I had a few trick shots left up my sleeve. After a few lucky hits and a lot of teasing on his part, I had the upper hand.

"Prepare to be defeated, Marquez." I laughed as I cleared the table and did a little victory dance.

"Fuck this," Luca growled, throwing his cue onto the table and stalking over to me.

"Sore loser?"

"Oh, I won't be the sore one," he said, whipping me around to face the table and bending me forward forcefully. I knew this was his way of claiming back his dominance. He never was a graceful loser.

He lifted my skirt up and ripped my panties down my legs so harshly I gave a squeal at the burn it caused on my thighs.

He kneaded my ass with both his hands, then out of nowhere, *smack*. He hit my ass so hard I cried out, thrown forward by the force of the slap. He kneaded my ass again, massaging and rubbing the sting away, then just when I started moaning, he did it again. *Smack*. Slapping straight across both cheeks this time and making me scream out his name.

"Are you punishing me for being naughty?" I glanced over my shoulder at him, as his hooded eyes stayed fixed on my ass where he was spanking me.

"You needed this, little hustler. You got too cocky. And I like spanking you. I love how pink your ass goes when I do. How hot your skin feels in my hand when I rub it better."

He brought another hard blow down on my ass, then another. Each time rubbing softly over my skin after, and moaning how beautiful my ass looked. I was growing wetter by the second, and the dominant way he was controlling me was a real turn on.

"You love this don't you?" He whispered into my ear. "You love giving me total control over you."

I nodded, my voice lost to the pleasure-pain battle going on in my body and brain.

"I always want to control you, Chloe. I want you to be mine, to do whatever I want, whenever, however I want it...forever baby." He pushed his knee in-between my legs and forced them to open a little wider.

"Always," I managed to say on a breathy sigh.

I heard the jingle of his belt and the rustle of clothes, then the smooth round head of his cock was rubbing up and down my pussy and around my clit.

"Soaked. You're so ready for me, little hustler." He didn't give me a chance to reply. His cock rammed into me hard, sending my hips slamming into the edge of the pool table and making me cry out with the pain of the stretch, the beautiful stretch.

"Fuck," I managed to groan, as he pounded into me like a fucking freight train. Powering into me with an unforgiving pace.

He curled his arm around my hip to give me some cushion against the table and then he took his pace up another notch, thrusting, grinding and driving me to a hard, brutal orgasm.

"Hold on tight, baby," he called out, then rutting into me he shouted. "Now, Chloe."

That was all I needed to explode around him, squeezing his cock so hard in my orgasm that even I screamed out with the force of it.

"Fuck!" Luca threw his head back and pulled himself out of me, then came all over my ass. Hot spurts of cum dripping down, trickling in between the crack of my ass and rolling down my legs.

Once he'd marked me with every last drop, he smoothed two fingers over his cum, and pulled my ponytail back to bring my head up. He forced two fingers, covered in his sticky, saltiness into my mouth. I sucked them just for him, because I loved him and I wanted to taste every part of him. Experience every part of him.

"You are one very...naughty... girl," he groaned, pulling his fingers free, letting them make a popping sound as they left my mouth.

"Only for you," I moaned back, then rested my head on the felt of the pool table, falling into my Luca-induced sex coma.

"It fucking better be," he snarled.

Then he discarded the gnarly, dominant persona and lay over my back, his arms squeezing my waist as he sighed. "I'll never let you go again, Chloe. You know that, don't you?"

"I know. I love you, Luca. So much," I said with as much affection as I could, so he would hear it, feel it, know it without a doubt.

His response?

"Come on baby, let's get you cleaned up."

Chapter Twenty Three

The sun was beginning to set on the private expanse of beach that ran the length of the exclusive neighbourhood where Luca had chosen to live, amongst the rich and elite of the city. The high walls and heavy metal security gates around his property hinted at the deeply rooted suspicion and distrust of others that he had, courtesy of a brutal upbringing. He might live amongst them now, do business with them even, but he didn't trust them. These people were like sharks and if there was one thing Luca knew, it was how to survive in shark infested waters. He'd lived with the deadliest for years. Spending year upon year being conditioned to not trust, stay guarded and defend himself at the expense of others. It was a natural instinct for Luca. Sharks could smell fear, they lived off it. But Luca didn't show fear, he didn't show any emotion. It'd always worked in his favour, to keep himself closed off. It was his best survival technique.

Freddie, for the most part, had been shielded from the worst aspects of his Father. As a result, he lacked the killer instinct that Luca had in spades. He was blessed with a better, more enhanced level of empathy and understanding. He could use emotions to improve his life, bring friendship and love his way. Surround himself with it. He didn't view it as a weakness. Having a strong network of good people around him was Freddie's strength. Fear was Luca's strength. Fear was what he'd always surrounded himself with.

The evening sky was turning a breath-taking shade of burnt orange, red and yellow as the sizzling sun made its way downward, as if swallowed by the sea. The horizon was bathed in warmth. I couldn't help but shudder though, thinking about what might lie ahead in the future, my future. I knew better than anyone how fragile life could be. One minute held in the arms of a loved one, safe and warm. The next they're ripped from you and you're alone, helpless, with no one left to care. When my Father passed away, I lost everything. Since then, I'd lived my life with a 'couldn't care less' attitude. It made me stronger, harder and feistier. I swore I wouldn't depend on anyone. I was my own woman. But now, as things were moving forward, altering my life and changing my path, I realised I was starting to feel helpless again, and I didn't like it. I felt like Luca was taking control of my emotions. Taking from me and not always in a positive way.

After my Father died, I never questioned how someone felt about me, I didn't care. If they couldn't express themselves, or say how they were feeling, I'd have just walked away. When my Mother turned against me, I left her house with nothing but the clothes on my back. It was the best move I'd ever made. But now, with Luca, I was letting him affect me. Letting his lack of emotions get to me. It was making me doubt myself, and I hated that.

"Penny for your thoughts, little sis." Freddie came up behind me as I sat on the sand watching the sunset. The tide was far out, and my knees were tucked up under my chin to keep me warm.

"You don't have enough money to hear all my thoughts, bro."

"Are you bedding down for the night? Camping under the stars with nothing but your thoughts to keep you warm." He sat next to me and bumped his shoulder into mine in an effort to get me to smile.

I took in a deep breath and let out a long sigh.

"Ignore me, Fred. I'm wallowing out here, and even I hate it when I'm wallowing." I turned to look at him. His round friendly face was awash with concern.

"Hey, don't worry. I'm okay. I just came down here to think. I didn't want to bother anyone else with my strange mood." I stretched my legs out in front of me and ran my fingers through the sand at the side, letting the delicate grains trickle through my fingers. It helped to centre me.

"I'll be back at the house in five or ten minutes...maybe fifteen. Then I'll be bouncing around again, singing...you know, my usual annoying self."

"You're not annoying, Chloe." He glared at me for even daring to suggest such a thing. "You, little sis, are a breath of fresh air. Trust me."

It felt good to hear that. Everyone wants to hear positive things about themselves, no matter how old they are.

"Why are you so different?" I knew the answer, but I asked it anyway.

"What do you mean?" Freddie wrinkled his brow.

"You and Luca are like chalk and cheese, black and white, night and day. I always know what you're thinking and yet with Luca, I'm clueless."

"What's prompted all this, Chloe?" He turned his body to face me, a look of concern etched onto his face, replacing the smile.

"I don't know. I think I feel vulnerable. I feel like I'm giving more of myself than he is, and I'm scared I'm heading for a big fall. Does that make any sense?" I looked across at him, but he just shook his head, puzzled by my wittering.

"I've no idea what you mean. How are you vulnerable? You mean with the threats and Sanchez?"

"No. I mean I'm putting myself out there...again...as usual...with Luca, and I don't think he's meeting me half way."

"How do you know he isn't feeling as vulnerable as you are?"

"Because he never tells me how he feels. He's never had to put himself out there. Ever. Freddie, I tell him I love him every day. But he can't even bring himself to say it back."

I hung my head down and concentrated on the grains of sand I was filtering through my hands, afraid to look up and see pity in his eyes.

"Just because he doesn't say it, doesn't mean he isn't feeling it," Freddie replied softly.

"He's never said it though, not once. Why? Am I a plaything? A distraction until he gets bored?"

"Fuck, no! You know he adores you. We can all see it."

"But I can't, not really," I sighed again. "I guess I'm just scared, Fred. I don't want my heart broken. It's been bruised and battered so much, I don't think it'd survive another knock. Oh hell, what am I even saying? Honestly? It doesn't even bother me that much. I mean, I'm not some needy loser that needs to hear 'I love you baby' every day to justify my worth." I held my head high, to signify my nonchalance. I don't think it came off that way though.

"Wanting to hear that you mean something to someone isn't a sign of weakness. Everyone needs to know they're loved. I'd kick Damon's ass if he didn't tell me every day. Luca does love you, Chloe, more than you know. I just think he finds it difficult to put his feelings into words. My brother worships the ground you walk on."

"I highly doubt that, Freddie. He doesn't worship anyone or anything. I'm pretty certain that he means more to me than I'll every mean to him, it's always been that way. I should be used to it by now, but you know... a girl can always hope," I sighed, irritated by my own whining.

"Hell, listen to me moaning. Just ignore me, Fred. Forget I ever said anything. I'm not gonna lose another minute of my life debating how someone else feels or doesn't feel. I have no control over it, it's out of my hands. Wasted energy."

"If you need me to kick his ass, you know I will." Freddie teased back.

"No ass kicking will be necessary. However, I may do a bit of ass whooping if you don't introduce me to your man, Damon, soon. I am your sister after all. I need to vet him, check him out. Make sure he's good enough."

Freddie laughed and stood up. "You'll be the first one I'll be introducing him to when I pluck up the courage to involve him in my crazy life. Right now though, we're enjoying our bubble."

"Aww I love that! Freddie and Damon's bubble of love. I like him already because he makes you happy. If he makes you sad, I'll condemn him to hell."

Freddie took off back to the house, laughing over his shoulder at me.

"I can believe that, little sis. I wouldn't want to get on your bad side, ever."

Chapter Twenty Four

My night was one of broken sleep and various degrees of fucking, courtesy of Luca and his insatiable appetite. He'd come home late from the club, wound up about something, but unwilling to talk about it. He got his frustrations out through sex as usual, and although I wasn't complaining about the multiple orgasms, I would've liked for him to share some of himself with me, and not just in the carnal way. I even woke to find him already inside me on one occasion, so desperate for a release, using me in his perverted fucked-up way. He had no problem talking dirty, it was just talking after sex that he couldn't master.

I held him throughout the night and whispered 'I love you', and he always replied with some variation of 'you're mine'. Maybe that was his way of saying he loved me? Telling me I was exclusively his.

When I woke the next morning, I felt the exertions of the night before in every burning, aching muscle. I stretched out and twisted around in the bed, but Luca had already left. His side was cold and empty. I threw the covers back and plodding into the bathroom to start the shower and brush my teeth. Today, I'd focus on the positive. No more negativity and brooding trips to the beach to wallow. I'd contact my medical school and find out when I could return. Maybe do some catch up sessions for my course. I needed to make sure Teresa was okay too, and think about what to do about our shared apartment. Would I move in here with Luca? Or keep my independence and move back in with Teresa? Things with Sanchez had to have settled down by now.

I stepped into the steaming hot shower and stood under the flow of water. My stress melted away with the warmth, and the massage of the sharp jets helped to ease my sore muscles. I hadn't heard him come in, but my skin prickled as he wrapped both of his strong arms around me, his warm front caressing my back. He nestled into my neck and I turned my head to kiss him. Having him surround me, blanket me like this was pure heaven. He had this uncontrollable magnetic pull that drew me in. He was a force of nature.

"You started without me," he said in his low gruff voice, as he squeezed my waist, nibbling along my neck and down across my shoulder.

"I thought you'd left," I sighed into the air and let his dirty, sexy mouth take me away.

"No. I had some emails to send, but I'm not leaving yet. Still time for a morning shower with my baby." He smiled and caressed my breasts, his other arm heading downwards, skimming over my tummy.

"You think I'd miss this?" He pushed me forward to lean against the shower wall and told me to, "put your arms out...that's it sweetheart...on the wall."

I did as I was told. I always did where he was concerned. He stroked his hand down my neck, all the way down my back to my ass and then back up again.

"I can't seem to leave you alone," he whispered. "It's like I'm addicted to you, Chloe. Addicted to your body. How it tastes, how it flushes pink when I touch you. How it responds to me, squeezes me tight when I fuck you. I can't stop wanting you, Chloe."

"Why do you have to stop?" I replied, breathless and needy.

"I don't, I can't."

He held one arm under my tummy and without warning thrust his cock into me, making me cry out.

"Nothing has ever looked more beautiful than you bent over, just for me. Your mouth open in that silent scream you do before you come. You're like air for me, Chloe. I feel like I can't breathe when I'm away from you," he said, as his hips rocked into me.

I felt my heart flutter as he used his words to give me what I'd been yearning for. He might think he couldn't express himself well, but this morning, in this shower, he was doing a damn good job of putting my earlier fears to rest. He did love me. He just said it with his body.

"Harder," I cried, as he pounded into me. Pushing me to the limit, but not quite getting there. I needed more.

"Fuck, Chloe. I feel like I need to be in you all the time. I crave this...you."

"I know," I gasped. "Me too."

He was working me to a mind-blowing end and I moaned as it built up and up, feeling so fucking good I couldn't cope.

"Yes. Luca, please don't stop." I cried as the first pulse and contraction ripped through me, gripping his cock tight.

"I can't stop," he breathed heavily into my ear. "I can't live without this, Chloe...without you."

With that, he exploded inside me and I gripped him with every last bit of strength I had. I couldn't live without him either. I was his. I'd fallen so hard that all I could do was pray he'd catch me. And after this shower? I didn't doubt him at all.

Once we'd regained some level of energy, we soaped each other down, stepped out of the shower and dried each other off.

"I have a lot of meetings today. I probably won't be home until late baby, I'm sorry." He looked genuinely disappointed as he shrugged his navy blue suit jacket over his broad shoulders. I smoothed it across his back and adjusted his tie.

"You look so handsome. I hope none of those meetings

are with any females." I glared through my eyelashes.

"The only female I'm interested in, is standing in front of me now, making me question my plans for today." He bent down and placed a gentle kiss on my forehead, then held my face in his hands.

"Wait up for me baby, okay?" He asked, looking deep into my eyes with his sparkling greens.

"I will."

He left the bedroom and I took the towel from around my body to dress for the day. I was standing in the walk-in wardrobe deciding what to wear, when I heard the buzz of Luca's mobile on the bedside table. He'd forgotten his phone and I knew he'd need it today. I pulled the large fluffy towel back around my body and secured it tight, then grabbed his phone and headed out to the stairs to find him.

"You know boss, it suits you." An unfamiliar deep voice sounded in the living area downstairs.

"What the fuck are you on about?" Luca growled back.

"Being in love. Since that Chloe came to stay you've been different, more...mellow."

I took the first few steps down slowly, wanting to hear this exchange. Get a glimpse into the world of these men and how they interacted.

I could see Luca with his back to me, his shoulders tense and his muscles taut.

"What the fuck did you just call me?" He marched over

to the guy who must've made the comment, his eyes boring into his as he stood toe to toe with him.

"I didn't mean any offence, boss. I just think she's good for you."

I took two more steps down and stood still. A few of the men noticed me, but didn't say a word.

"You think I'm fucking weak, is that it? You think some pussy can make me weak?" I held my breath as I listened to Luca's response.

"I didn't mean that boss." The guy sounded scared. He was backed up against the wall, his hands flat against the surface. I couldn't see his face, but I bet he looked petrified, he certainly sounded it.

Luca took a gun from behind his back and pointed it at the guy's head, pressing it right between his eyes. I hadn't even seen him with a gun this morning.

"Let's get one thing straight. I'm not weak. I haven't been weakened by some dirty little fuck. Next week I'll have another one, maybe two or three bent over in my bed, screaming my name. I don't do singular pussy. Why tie myself to one, when they're all so...fucking... good." He snarled, ripping my heart out with his vile words.

"If you ever dare to question me again, to question my power in front of my men in my fucking house, I won't hesitate to shoot you in the fucking head. Do you hear me?"

My body went onto automatic pilot, as I took the last steps down into the living area. The other men hung their heads at my entrance. Luca stayed facing the guy he was threatening. Freddie was the only one to address me.

"He didn't mean it, Chloe."

I didn't care what anyone said in that moment. I wouldn't have heard them anyway. He'd stood there in front of all these men, there must've been at least ten of them, standing around like his brainless minions, and he'd called me a *dirty little fuck*. I was done.

"You left your mobile upstairs." I managed to speak without sounding like the loser he'd made me feel.

I turned to go back up to get changed, but on the fifth step I swung back round to face them all. Luca hadn't moved, he couldn't face me. He didn't dare.

"I'll be gone when you get back."

"Don't Chloe," Freddie begged. Luca remained silent.

"Your *dirty little fuck* has had enough. I'm done. I'll be out of your hair for good. So you'll be free to fuck any god damn bitch you like. Take as many as you want to bed with you, I don't care anymore. We are finished. Over. I'm out of here."

I ran up the last few steps, but as I got to the top I jumped as I heard the gun go off. Luca had shot the guy in the foot, and he was lying on the floor crying in agony as Luca and the others just stared at him.

"If I ever see your face again, you're a dead man," Luca growled over him, before storming out of the house and roaring off down the drive in his car.

I raced to the bedroom to get changed and get myself the hell out of there.

Freddie appeared at the door as I was darting about, grabbing things I'd need.

"Chloe, please don't leave."

"No, Fred. I'm done. Don't say another word."

"I'll talk to him. He didn't mean a word of that down there. I know him. I know how much he loves you. He only said it because...well that asshole made him feel weak. I don't know why, but he did. He wouldn't have wanted anyone questioning his power, that's all it was."

I spun round to face Freddie with fury burning my eyes.

"Don't you dare defend him, Freddie. He's a grown man for Christ's sake. He didn't have to call me a dirty little fuck, did he? He didn't have to say he was moving on to another girl next week, but he did, and this is the consequence. I'm leaving. Don't follow me."

I walked away into the bathroom, slamming the door behind me, and slid down to the floor, much like I had that first night I'd been with Luca. Two minutes later, I heard Freddie leave the house and drive away.

'Come on, Chloe. Get up and get going. As one door closes another one opens.' I tried to reason with myself. But right now, as I gathered together what belongings I had, it felt like all the doors were closing. Everything was shutting down.

Chapter Twenty Five
LUCA

"What the fuck are you playing at?" Freddie burst through my office door, nearly taking the damn thing off its hinges, before slamming it shut.

"Get out!" I wasn't in the mood for his shit. I wasn't in the mood to see anybody.

"Like hell I will. What the fuck was that, Luca? Do you have any idea how badly you've fucked things up?"

I wasn't going to discuss this with my brother of all people. "It's none of your God damn business," I shouted. "Don't get involved in shit you know nothing about."

"I know a damn sight more than you, it seems," he snorted angrily, as I knocked papers over and made a complete mess of the organised chaos that was my work today. "She's the best thing that's ever happened to you, and you're gonna throw it all away because some schmuck dared to say you looked happy, mellow or whatever the fuck he said. What the fuck is wrong with you, brother? Do you like being lonely and miserable? Because after today that's all you'll ever be, unless you do some serious damage control."

"I don't need to do shit. She knows I didn't mean it. She'll calm down." I wasn't sure I believed what I was saying, but I didn't think too far into it, I couldn't.

"If you really believe that, then you're more delusional than I thought." Freddie banged his fists down onto my desk and leered down at me from the opposite side.

"Do you know where I found Chloe, yesterday?"

I threw my gold pen across the desk. I wanted to throw it in his smug-ass face, but the desk would have to do.

"No. I don't follow her twenty-four-seven." I gave a fake grin, but inside I felt like my guts were twisting into an unforgiveable knot.

"I found her close to tears, sitting on the beach. She looked miserable as hell."

"And that's supposed to make me feel what?" I shrugged, pretending I didn't give a fuck, when everything in my life was balanced on a knife's edge.

"Well, guilty for one? Sorry maybe? I don't know, how about concerned?"

"Just spit it out, Freddie. Say what you've gotta say, then leave," I snapped, tapping into my emails and staring at the computer screen, hoping to block my sad, sorry life out for a few minutes.

"She told me she felt vulnerable. She said she was scared you'd hurt her."

I glared back at him, my teeth clenched and my jaw

aching with the force of tension I was using to keep from exploding.

"I've never laid a finger on her, not like that."

"That isn't what she meant, dumbass. She said she thought you didn't love her. She thinks it even more now though, doesn't she? After you gave her a whole heap of reasons to doubt you. Christ, brother, for a successful business man you really are as clueless as they come, aren't you?"

I couldn't speak, I had no idea what to say.

"So was she right? Don't you want her? Is that why you acted like a dick this morning?"

I banged my fists down onto the table, then put my head into my hands.

"For fucks sake, this is all such a fucking mess," I growled. I had the urge to break things. Lots and lots of things. I wanted to hurt someone and take my anger out on them until I had no energy left to even think.

"Do you love her?" Freddie asked me.

"Of course I do. What sort of stupid question is that? Why would she ever think that I didn't?"

I had no idea this was how Chloe had felt. I was so confused and messed up. I shook my head in frustration. Even I didn't know what was going on with me right now.

"Maybe because you never told her?" His self-righteous voice mocked me.

"I told her every fucking day," I shouted back.

"You showed her. You might've even said something like it, but you never actually said those three damn words. She told me as much."

I sat back in my chair, racking my brains. Maybe she was right? Maybe I hadn't said it? But surely all the other things I'd said had made it obvious. How could she think I didn't love her, after what we'd shared? I had her in my bed every night. Why would I do that if I didn't love her?

"I know what you're thinking," Freddie said more calmly now, as he sank into the chair opposite mine across the desk. "But even showing it, saying all the things you've said, sometimes that's just not enough. She still needed to hear it. To have it spelt out for her. We all do. Why couldn't you say it, brother?"

I cast my gaze to the floor, thinking about the last woman I'd said those words to. My Mother. I hadn't said it since, and although I hadn't thought about the coincidence before, it started to dawn on me that maybe I had held back. The last thing I'd said to my Mother was, 'I love you', and she'd said the exact same back to me. In some deep, subconscious way, did I see that as a goodbye? Was that why I couldn't bring myself to say it to Chloe? Because I didn't want to tempt fate and lose her?

I shared my thoughts with Freddie, opening up to him in a way I'd never done before. He didn't judge me, just sat and listened, taking it all on board.

"I think you're right," he said finally, after I'd offloaded all of my fears onto him. "I think you love her, but your past is weighing you down, brother. What you need to do, is ask yourself this. Do you want the past to destroy your future too? Or are you willing to do the one thing you've never really done before, for her...put yourself out there...tell her what she means to you and bloody fight for her."

I couldn't lose her. I'd meant what I said that morning, I was addicted to her. I couldn't live without her.

"She's everything to me." I admitted. "If I lose her, I don't know how I'll get over it."

"Well, the way I see it you have three choices. You could call her, but I doubt she'd pick up, and a phone call is so impersonal, so I don't think you should take option one."

"And the other two?" I searched his eyes looking for an answer.

"Option two, you wait for her to calm down. Hope to God she stays put, and then talk to her tonight. Tell her how you feel. Or three, you get your ass back to that house right now, where I know she's busy packing her bags. You beg her to hear you out. Get on your God damn knees and tell her how you feel. Then hopefully, she'll give you a second chance."

"What do you think my odds are?" I asked, knowing already what option I'd choose.

"If you wait? I'd say slim to none. If you haul ass now? I'd say fair."

I shot up out of my chair and grabbed my jacket. I had to make this work. There was no way I was screwing this up.

"Tell Rosa to hold all my calls and cancel all my meetings. I'm gonna be busy for the rest of the day."

"Tell her yourself," Freddie snapped back. "I'm coming with you to make sure you don't fuck this up."

"Fine."

We flew down the back stairs and out into the underground carpark, where my car, which was haphazardly parked over two spaces, had been abandoned a few hours earlier. I started the engine and spun the wheels, as I threw the car into gear, and propelled us forward. I called Rosa on speaker phone and told her I was out all day. She assured me all my meetings and calls would be dealt with. I had some serious damage control to take care of. I needed to get my house into order, literally.

-

When we pulled up to the driveway, we found the gates wide open. We exchanged a cautious, unnerved glance at each other and made our way up to the house. When we got to the front door it was unlocked. My senses told me everything was wrong. I felt bile rise from my stomach as I stepped into the house. What I eventually saw, sent me into a spiral of panic and fury.

Chairs were overturned, tables knocked on their sides and glass smashed on the floor. Two cups of what looked like coffee had fallen onto the cream rug by the sofas. I walked over and bent down to touch the beige splatters, but they weren't hot, not even warm. They'd been there at least an hour or two.

"What the hell happened here? Do you think she trashed the place before leaving?" Freddie asked, picking up a table and setting it back in place.

"No. It wouldn't matter how pissed off she was, she'd never do this," I replied, looking around me at the devastation.

"What's that?" Freddie pointed over to the glass doors leading to the pool.

On the glass there was some kind of picture taped up. I walked over to take a closer look and I knew straight away what'd happened. Every inch of my body shook violently as I ripped the picture off the glass and looked at the image.

I was lying on one of the sun beds by the pool, and Chloe was straddling me. It'd been taken days ago, when we'd had sex by the pool. Chloe was riding me and whoever took this photo had been in my yard, standing just metres away from us. Watching. Waiting, like a predator.

I flipped the photo over and on the back, in thick black letters, was written-

'I've taken back what's mine. S'

He'd got her. God knows how he'd got in, but he'd taken her. Eduardo Sanchez. Filthy trafficker and scum of the earth. He'd come into my home and taken my Chloe. God knows what he was doing with her now, but he wouldn't have her for long.

I was coming for him.

LUCA

I was going to kill him.

Chapter Twenty Six
CHLOE

Two hours earlier…

I dragged the overstuffed suitcase I'd borrowed from Luca's collection down the staircase, bumping it roughly along each step, before it finally hit the ground and toppled over with the effort of being moved so forcefully. I hadn't been entirely sure that I should take the outfits and things Gina had bought for me. I felt like I wanted to just leave, but then, why should I leave behind good clothes meant only for me? Toiletries and products that'd go to waste if they were left behind. Plus, Luca Marquez owed me. He owed me big time. So I crammed every damn thing I could into that case, and didn't give it a second thought.

I cast my gaze around the living area, day dreaming of all the things that'd happened to me since I'd been taken from the strip club that night. The hustle on Marco and Vinnie that first night playing poker, the parties and nights under the blanket with Freddie watching films and T.V, and the countless arguments and make-up sessions Luca and I had. It felt like the end of an era. After today, I wouldn't ever see any of them again. Not if I could help it anyway.

The buzzer from the main gate outside broke my reverie, pulling me into the now so fast I gave a startled yelp. My first thought was that Luca had come back to apologise, but why would he buzz his own gate to gain entry? I went over to the computerised keypad, monitor and security hub on the wall. Standing, looking up at the camera mounted above the gate outside, was Teresa's daft, grinning face. She was wearing a tracksuit and trainers, and pulling a suitcase, with a massive pair of sunglasses perched on the top of her head, as if she was off on her holidays. The sight of her made my heart jolt. It was as if the Gods had seen I needed a friend, and sent their angel to me in my hour of need. An angel to whisk me away from all the drama and heartache.

I pressed the intercom to speak.

"T! Oh my God. What are you doing here?"

"I'm here to see you, Clo." She gave a little jump and giggle as she spoke. It looked like she was going to take me away from all this, Thelma and Louise style, only without the cliff-hanger ending.

"You are one hell of a sight for sore eyes today, I can tell you," I sighed. "Hold on, I'll open the gate and leave the front door unlocked, okay? Just head on up."

"Get the kettle on princess," she sang, putting her thumb up to the camera at me. "I'm in need of a decent caffeine fix."

I laughed and activated the release button for the gate, then unlocked the door. I headed into the kitchen and turned the fancy coffee machine on. A visit from my bestie definitely warranted the best latte and cappuccino Luca had to offer, especially after my shitty morning.

I held the two steaming mugs in either hand, and pushed the kitchen door open with my elbow, as I cinched my way out of the doorway and into the living room to greet my best friend.

"My little Kiki. Looks like the break from me has been good for you. You look radiant."

The mugs slipped out of my hand and crashed to the floor, spilling coffee all over the cream rug, and splattering boiling droplets onto my bare legs. But I didn't flinch. I felt numb.

Standing in the doorway, surrounded by about eight muscle mountains, was my old boss, Eduardo Sanchez. He had his black hair slicked back, and a scar ran from his lip across his left cheek, giving him a menacing edge. A reminder that he lived in hell, and had faced demons just for the fun of it. Where Luca was beautiful and deadly, Sanchez was the epitome of evil in every way. Standing there in his designer suit, he made my skin crawl.

"How the hell did you get in here? Where's Teresa? What've you done to her?"

"Now, Kiki, that's not the way to greet an old friend, is it? Didn't your Mother teach you anything about good manners?"

"My Mother taught me to always look after number one and never trust anyone."

"Pity you weren't listening when she told you about trusting best friends then, isn't it? Your little friend, Teresa, she's probably halfway to the airport by now."

He looked down at his expensive gold watch, as if it held the answer.

"She was way too easy to buy off you know. She gave you up straight away. It was a bargain, really. I'd have paid double what I did to get to you, little Kiki."

I knew I had to act fast. This was an ambush, and time was not on my side. I scanned the room to look for something I could use as a weapon to help me.

"Luca will be back any minute. If I were you, I'd get out of here before he kills every last one of you."

He laughed back at me and took a few more steps into the living area, prowling like a panther about to strike.

"Oh Kiki, you think I don't know exactly where he is? I've known his daily schedule for weeks now. I know exactly what meetings he's in today and where he's going to be. He isn't coming home to you, little girl, until much later tonight. Or rather, let me rephrase that... he won't be finding out you're *missing* until later tonight."

I didn't stop to think, I just darted towards the backdoor in a blind attempt to make a run for it. But a dark shadow stood on the other side of the door, waiting for me.

"There's no point trying to get away. My men are at every door and window. Your days of hiding from me are over."

He stalked right up to me, his grin showcasing the gold tooth he had hidden in the right-side of his mouth. The stench of stale coffee and cigarettes hit me as he leered over me. I was the fly caught in the spider's web, and he was just about to devour me.

I tried to push past him and run up the stairs, but my tiny frame was no match for him and his men. Two of which came to stand either side of me, hemming me in.

"Don't grab her too hard, we can't afford to send her off covered in bruises." Sanchez ordered, as the men held the tops of my arms to keep me from escaping.

"You won't get away with this, you know," I spat out. "He'll find me, and when he does, you're a dead man."

Sanchez pressed his nose against mine and looked me dead in the eyes.

"I've no doubt about the last part, Kiki. But as for saving you? He won't have time. You see, I sold you weeks ago, and now times up. My client wants delivery of his merchandise. You'll be on a plane to Colombia in the next few hours, before Marquez even knows you're gone. So, little Kiki, I suggest you come with us now, without making a fuss. Trust me, it'll be better for you in the long run if you do."

I wasn't going without a fight. I'd never done anything in my life without fighting, and I wasn't about to stop now.

"Fuck you!" I said and spat right in his face.

The fucker just smiled and licked his lips.

"You know, it's a shame I have to ship you off so fast. I'd have loved to taste you myself first. I like it when girls fight, and you look like a feisty little fighter." He bent forward and licked my cheek, making me gag and pull away. The henchman's grip only tightened, so I kicked out with all my might and let the weight of my body drop. If they weren't allowed to hold my arms tightly, in case of bruising, then I guessed they'd have to let me go if I was falling to the floor.

Sure enough, they loosened their grip on my arms, as I reached out to put my hands on anything that could double as a weapon. My arms and legs flayed wildly to keep them at bay.

"We can do this the easy way or the hard way, Kiki," Sanchez huffed, and another thug came to stand at the side of him, a needle containing God knows what in his hand. My stomach churned as I thought about all the things they could do to me if they managed to use that needle. I couldn't bear to think about it. I didn't do 'helpless'.

So I fought those men with everything I had. I kicked them in the legs, the torso, I even got a lucky kick in the face of one of them, but it was all pointless. Eventually, my energy levels depleted, and the thug with the needle straddled me, holding my arms in place with his massive frame as he jammed the needle into my neck.

Within seconds the drugs were dragging me into the darkness. The last thing I heard was Sanchez telling his men it was a shame such a pretty little thing had been sold to a monster, and that I wouldn't see the week out in his opinion.

I'd no idea who'd bought me, or what lay ahead in my future, but I wasn't broken. I wouldn't ever be broken. I'd fight with my very last breath before I ever let the likes of Sanchez or anyone else defeat me.

Chapter Twenty Seven
LUCA

"She put up a decent fight, I'll give her that," Leo said, as we poured over the CCTV footage from the house and grounds. We checked every minute detail, from every available angle, for a hint or a clue as to where they might've taken her.

"Didn't really stand much of a chance though, did she?" Dan replied.

I could barely contain my fury, watching those bastards put their hands on her. How dare they think they could walk into my home, touch my girl, and then take her away from me? All with a smug as fuck grin on their sadistic faces. Their own Mothers wouldn't be able to identify them when I'd finished with them. A special place in hell would be reserved just for them, and I was going to make sure they got there sooner rather than later.

I glanced over to my brother, and he looked as venomous as I felt. His jaw was tense and he wasn't normally a teeth grinder like me. His hands were balled into fists by his side and he was breathing deep and fast. Every time one of the men went anywhere near her, he sucked in his breath as if he was in pain. I think he actually *was* hurting to be honest, we both were.

I made the necessary calls to round-up my men. I needed a strong team to face off with Sanchez. I didn't like it, but I decided to include Vinnie. I knew how he felt about Chloe, and although it pissed me off, I knew he'd stop at nothing to protect her. I needed my best men beside me when I went to get her back. I couldn't afford to fuck this up. Sanchez had crossed a line and made a bold statement coming into my home. I had to respond with as much force as I could, otherwise my whole network would collapse around my ears. Sharks were always circling, and I couldn't afford for any cracks to appear in my organisation, or someone would come along and take advantage. The fact that Sanchez had taken Chloe, was the worst fucking statement he could've made. If I couldn't even keep my woman safe, what did that say about me as a boss? It needed sorting now. And I couldn't wait to get our team together and head over to the warehouse, where I knew Sanchez would be hiding, like the vermin he was.

I was going to burn the place to the ground. I'd tear down every last building in this God forsaken city until I found her. No man was going to stand in my way. Not unless they wanted to be taken down, permanently.

-

LUCA

I split my men into groups. One to secure the perimeter of the warehouse. Three groups to secure the main building. And my team, who were coming into Sanchez's office. I needed to interrogate him in my own way, find out where he'd taken Chloe. I knew she wouldn't be at the warehouse, he wasn't that stupid, but we needed to act fast. Time wasn't on our side.

We checked our weapons, guns, knives and protection. Sanchez had no idea what was heading his way. I was a man on the edge, with nothing to lose. That made me his deadliest enemy and worst fucking nightmare.

We headed out to his compound on the other side of the city in a convoy of blacked out trucks, vans and SUVs, ready to drive straight through the steel gates and into their territory. As the first van charged through the suspiciously opened gates, the men around the building stood back. I'd no idea why they weren't firing. I guessed they were expecting our arrival, and had been told to let us through. Marco asked me if I thought it was an ambush, whether we were being set up. But I just shrugged and said I couldn't give a fuck. We were going in regardless. This was the only way we could reach Sanchez. It was our only link to Chloe.

The first team assigned with securing the outside perimeter exited their vehicles and approached Sanchez's men. After a few minutes, two of them came over to our vehicle, to let us know that Sanchez was expecting us. The three teams securing the building led the way into the compound, and we followed, heading towards the office where Sanchez and his top men would be hiding out.

As we walked through the warehouse, we could see drugs being packaged, cut, weighed and processed in one far corner. A strange indoor caravan park, with approximately fifteen or twenty old, dilapidated caravans, was on the right-side of the warehouse. Holding bays for the people they trafficked, I guessed.

Was Chloe being held in one of those?

I'd figured Sanchez would be a fool to keep his 'merchandise' in the same place that he worked. But maybe he wasn't as smart as I thought.

The place stunk of death, misery, violence and deceit. It was damp, with zero natural light. Old rainwater dripped from the ceiling as you walked through, and the dirty hard floor was covered in filth and shit, probably from the rats who shared the building. Looking at the men who worked for him, I wouldn't have trusted them as far as I could throw them. They all wore shifty expressions on their surly faces, and the whole outfit screamed of corruption. Business dealings were being conducted in shady corners, everyone looking like they were out for themselves. There was no camaraderie whatsoever. I never claimed to be the best boss, or control the best operation, but at least I knew with true conviction I could trust every last one of my men to support me and have my back.

When we got to the back area of the compound, and the

steel door that stood between us and Sanchez, we each braced ourselves for what lay ahead, standing a little taller and flexing our muscles ready to do battle. Ready for whatever onslaught Sanchez had planned for us.

One of the men outside the door insisted we surrender our weapons to him before entering, so Dan agreed to stay outside and hold our guns and ammo. We weren't about to hand over our protection. Freddie, Vinnie, Marco, Leo and myself entered the office to find Sanchez, sat behind his desk. He had a smug, satisfied smile on his face, and three men stood around him with guns hung over their shoulders.

"Marquez. You came sooner than I expected."

He leant back in his chair and put his feet up on his desk, like this was some cosy social visit.

"Where...the fuck...is she?" I snarled, putting both of my hands flat on his desk, and leaning over to stare him dead in the eyes.

He chuckled to himself, making my back go up and my instinct to attack him across the desk grew out of control as he grinned, mocking me.

"You're too late." He shook his head and smirked at the man stood to the right of him.

"Fucking tell me!" I snapped. "Where is she? I'm not here to play your fucking games, Sanchez."

He took his feet off the desk and leant forward, his eyes ablaze as if I'd offended him.

"I don't play games." He took a deep breath in, then

pointed over at Freddie. "Your brother on the other hand...he seems to think it's all a fucking game, coming into my clubs and taking what belongs to me. Now that...that is a dangerous fucking game to play, Marquez."

Freddie stepped forward, his hackles raised, but he wouldn't stand a chance going toe to toe with a snake like Sanchez

I leant forward myself, fighting the urge to punch his scarred, ugly face, and teach him a lesson in manners when addressing my family. "She was never yours."

"She worked for me. She was mine. And now, I've sold her." He laced his fingers together to rest his chin, false bravado oozing from him as he attempted to rile me up.

"I'm not gonna waste another minute arguing with you, Sanchez. Give me a name and an address and we'll be on our way."

Obviously, I would annihilated him, his men and his whole damn setup, before leaving, but that was by the by.

"Sorry, no can do. Anyway, it'd be pointless. She's already halfway across the ocean as we speak. By the time you get airborne, she'll be in transit, on the way to meet her new and dare-I-say extremely excited owner."

He shook his head and tutted over at Freddie, before turning back to me.

"Your brother nearly cost me a hell of a lot of money, not to mention my impeccable reputation for supplying the best girls in the business, and I don't mean for stripping." He chuckled at his own weak attempt at humour. "I sold her months ago, Marquez. She wasn't mine or yours. She belonged to someone else all along."

"You better start talking, Sanchez. I'm losing my patience and I don't take kindly to being fucked around." I was losing my shit fast.

"You'll get nothing from me." He smirked and I lost it completely.

I stamped my left foot hard, to release the knife that I'd had specially made and stowed into the back heel of my shoe. It was perfect for situations like this. Within seconds, I had his wrist in my hand, and I slammed the blade through his palm, sticking it firmly into the wood of his desk, as he screamed in agony. His men drew their guns and pointed them all at me, as I shouted in his goddamn face.

"Tell me now...where the fuck is she?"

I pushed away from the desk, leaving the blade in his hand, and enjoying the weak whimpers he was making.

"Try it. I fucking dare you," I said to the guy standing to his right, and bumped him out of the way, as I stood behind Sanchez, and lent down to talk into his ear.

"I hear you like doing things the easy way, not the hard way. So I suggest you use your free hand to write down a name and an address, before I try the hard way, and destroy every one of your fucking men in this room."

I reached forward and twisted the knife, making him squeal like the dirty pig he was. His men moved forward, but he held his hand up to stop them.

"I'll give you a name and an address, but you won't see her again. This guy is a fucking maniac, and that's coming from me." He turned to look at me and I could've sworn I saw a hint of some remorse in his eyes. Jesus, who was this guy?

"I've done a lot of business with him over the years, and he never keeps a girl for longer than a few weeks. He has very specific... tastes. He practises the more extreme pleasures of BDSM. I hear he has a real lust for knife play."

I wanted to throw up. I'd dealt with some mean motherfuckers myself, but the thought of her, my innocent little Chloe, being subjected to someone like that, filled me with pure vengeance. She liked to think she was badass and could handle herself, but she didn't really know how fucked-up the world could be. I needed to go after her, now.

I grabbed a pen and paper and slammed it down in front of him, holding it still so he could get on with it.

"Get writing, now!"

He began to write the details down as he shook his head, moaning in pain and muttering about it being a pointless rescue mission.

'Alfredo Gomez Diaz'.

The address was some village outside of Cartagena in Colombia.

"I would wish you luck, but it'd be pointless. He's throwing one of his special parties tomorrow night, and she's his prize for the guests. Although, I think he'll be sampling her himself before then."

He sat back in his chair, still grimacing and moaning about the knife in his hand.

I nodded over to my men. They knew my next move, and they knew what they had to do. I ripped the blade out of his hand, and with my other hand I grabbed his head. Then I dragged that bloody blade heavily across his neck, putting him down like the animal he was. Blood sprayed out across the desk, but the gurgle of his last breath didn't fill me with the satisfaction I usually felt, ridding the world of one more evil fucker.

Marco had grabbed the man closest to him, and used his classic headlock and twist to break the fucker's neck. Vinnie was strangling another with his own AK 47, and Leo had stabbed the last guy in the side of the neck with a knife he had stashed in his boot.

Seconds later, I swung the door open and ordered my men to shoot to kill. No man would walk free from this warehouse, and the building would be burnt to the ground. After today, nothing would remain of Sanchez, and his vile, dirty business. Any women or children found in the caravans would be taken to a safe house and dealt with accordingly.

"I need a plane and I need to be in the air now," I shouted, as my men got to work destroying every last inch of this evil.

Marco rang an associate, who had access to a private jet for us to use. I was about to embark on the most important mission of my life, and failure was not an option.

Chapter Twenty Eight
LUCA

The last time I went up against pure evil, things didn't quite work out the way I'd wanted them to. That wouldn't happen again.

-

Fourteen years ago...

"Please, Al. I didn't mean to do it. It was an accident. I just-"

Bang.

Thump.

Thud.

I could hear my Mother and Father arguing downstairs. I should've figured things wouldn't change after moving into this new house. I spent most nights covering my ears to block out their rows, or rather my Father's shouting, followed by my Mother's cries. I usually ended up in Freddie's bed, hugging him and trying to distract him by reading a story, or talking to him about his day.

Tonight sounded particularly brutal, and hearing those crashing noises coming from downstairs, I guessed things had gone from verbal to physical pretty quickly. I looked across at Freddie. Luckily, he was spark out. Fast asleep and oblivious to world war three breaking out downstairs.

I heard a woman's cry, followed by a whimper. I was so sick and tired of my Dad bullying my Mum and beating her. He was at least twice her size, it just didn't seem fair. I threw back the bed covers, crept out of the bedroom and down the stairs.

The whimpers were growing quieter now, but I could hear my Father grunting and huffing. I tip-toed off the last step and walked over to the kitchen door, and what I saw would stay with me until the day I died.

My Father was sat astride my Mother, his belt wrapped around her neck as he pulled it tighter and tighter. She was facing me and her eyes were bulging out of her head. Her lips were turning blue and her breathing became a gurgle, then a rattle. Her body started to shake as my Father used every last bit of energy he could to pull on that belt. Then I knew for sure she was gone. The light had left her eyes. Her face took on a mask-like quality. I gasped, and my Father turned to see me watching his evil deeds.

"What the fuck do you think you're looking at boy?" He spat at me like I was the one in the wrong.

I couldn't speak and I couldn't take my eyes off my beautiful Mum, lying lifeless on the floor. I noticed a gash on her forehead where he must've hit her with something. Why did he do that? Why would he want to hurt my Mum? She was the kindest person I knew. Kinder than any of my friend's Mums. But that didn't seem to matter to my Father. The fact an angel had graced his life and stood by him through thick and thin was of no consequence. Once she stepped even an inch out of line; burnt the dinner, forgot the sugar in his coffee or rearranged the living room in a way he didn't like, she'd be for it. He'd beaten her so badly before now, she'd had to use sunglasses whenever she went out. She never visited the doctor or the hospital, but I know he broke her bones too. My Father was the worst of all mankind, and I hated him.

"Don't just stand there like an idiot, even though you are one." He smirked. "Help me clean up this goddamn mess."

The Goddamn mess he referred to was my Mother's fragile body. The man who called himself my Father expected me to cover her with a tablecloth, help him pick up her dead body, and carry it to his pick-up truck. The only positive thing I could hang on to was that Freddie was still asleep. He hadn't been touched by the evil that was our Father tonight.

Once he'd thrown her into the back of his truck, like a piece of garbage, he stalked back towards the house and then emerged holding a spade.

"Get in," he barked, and I jumped into the passenger side of the truck, never daring to look at my Father. I feared I might be his next victim.

-

We drove for about an hour into thick woodland. My Father turned the truck off the road and drove across wasteland, until he came to a clearing. He kept the headlights on to illuminate the area, but shut off the engine.

I jumped out at the same time as he did. He grabbed the spade and threw it at me. I caught it, but my hands were shaking so badly I could barely grip the handle. My palms were sweaty and my mind was racing from the fear and rush of adrenaline. My Father reached behind him and pulled out a handgun. He pointed it at me, as if I was a wild animal he was hunting.

"Now dig, and make it fast. I need to be out of here before sunrise."

He sat down on the hood of the truck, as I started to dig up the cold, hard ground.

"Put your back into it boy. We haven't got all night," he called out to me irritably.

All I could think was, *Am I next?* Was this grave that I was digging going to house my Mother and me? If it did, what'd happen to Freddie? Who'd look out for my little brother if I was gone?

I got blisters on my blisters that night, digging the hardened ground. Eventually, my Father seemed satisfied with my work, and ordered me to climb out of the shallow grave. He dragged my Mother's body off the back of his truck, banging her head on the bumper as he did, then laughed like a mad man.

"She was a dirty whore. Don't feel sorry for your Mother," he snarled. "Never could get anything right. She got what she deserved."

He rolled her body so it fell into the muddy hole I'd dug for her. The tablecloth offered no protection, and she landed face down in the dirt. The final image I had of my Mother was the way her chocolate brown waves fell over the dirt like silk. Her skin, now paler, reflecting the moonlight. She didn't belong in this ditch. She didn't deserve to be treated so inhumanely by my Father. I knew she was a good woman, and I vowed right there, over her shallow grave, that I'd grow up to be a better man than him. I'd look out for my brother and give us a good life. I'd honour my Mother in any way I could. She always told me I was the love of her life. She told me she loved me every single day and I always said it back. It was our thing. Freddie had his own childish ways of showing her how he felt, but for us it was always plain and simple. I loved her and she loved me. Unconditionally.

Now, that love was gone. And I felt angry that I hadn't saved her. Why hadn't she fought harder? Why wasn't love enough?

I wanted to be strong and fierce when I grew up. A man that was feared but respected too, not like my Father, but like the men in suits I saw sometimes on my way to school. They didn't need to hit women like my Mother to be powerful.

I took a deep breath in as I shovelled the last pile of dirt into the hole to cover her. I'd never say those three special words again. What was the point? Love only led to heartbreak, and I could feel it in my chest already; cracking, splintering and making it difficult for me to breathe.

My Father never did use the gun on me that night. Instead, he drove back to our house, humming like he'd just been out on a day trip. When we got back, he headed straight up to bed. I stayed up to clear the mess in the kitchen. I didn't want Freddie to wake up and see the chaos that the night had witnessed. There were specks of blood on the linoleum, so I wiped it up, and when I was sure everything was back in its rightful place, I crept back into bed.

The next morning we both headed downstairs to find my Father burning my Mother's clothes and belongings in the backyard. He told Freddie that Mum had left him for another man. Freddie cried. He cried buckets and got mad at Mum for leaving us behind. I hugged him and told him to be thankful that our Mum was in a better place. *He* couldn't hurt her anymore. After using up every last tear he could muster, he agreed that she was better off away from our Father and his tyrannical ways.

I told Freddie that I'd always protect him, no matter what. I vowed that when we were old enough, and had more money, we would leave too, and find a place of our own.

To this day, I've never told my brother what happened that night. I never told anyone. I killed my Father and buried my own Mother. I'd spent a life time living in the dark with my demons. My only ray of sunshine was her. Chloe. Now she'd been taken from me by demons just like my Father, maybe even worse, if that was possible. It was my time again to fight for those that...well, that I loved. Only this time, I wasn't twelve-years-old. I had an army with me, and I would stop at nothing to get her back, and bring justice the way I wanted to. I would be this evil motherfucker's judge, jury and fucking executioner.

Chapter Twenty Nine
CHLOE

Present Day

My arms were tied tightly around my back with some sort of plastic, or cable ties maybe? They made my wrists sore as I twisted and pulled at them to see if there was any give. There wasn't. My arms ached beyond anything I'd ever felt before, as if they'd been forced into this unnatural position for days. I wondered if they'd ever feel the same again when they were free to fall at my side. Would I ever be untied, or was this my new normal?

I tried to move my legs to feel around me, but they were tied too. I was lying on a cold, hard floor, and any movement was severely restricted. There was a dusty rag of some sort, stuffed into my mouth, and another rag tied around my face to stop me talking or screaming. The smell of oil and rust hung so thick in the air, it made me want to gag. I felt like I'd been hit by a truck. My body was heavy, my head was throbbing and I had such an excruciating thirst, I felt like I'd been in a desert for months.

My eyes slowly refocused, and for some strange reason, I wasn't blindfolded. I could see four men, dressed all in black, sitting not far away from where I lay. *'This must be some type of delivery vehicle'* I thought, as I looked around me. The walls were a dull metal, and where the men were sitting was more a bench than a chair. The hum of an engine sounded over their low chatter. They hadn't realised I was awake, so I closed my eyes, not wanting to alert them to my conscious state just yet.

My mind automatically drifted to Luca. His beautiful rugged face, chiselled jaw and stubble. The smell of his aftershave mixed with his natural scent. The feel of his strong arms around me. I missed him with a pain I'd never felt before, a physical pain that radiated from my chest. What would he think, when he got home and saw the state of the house? Would he think I'd done that? That I'd left and trashed his house as a 'fuck you' parting gift? I hoped not. I needed to hold onto the hope that he would know I'd been taken. That he was going to come for me, maybe. I wasn't going to pin all my hopes on being rescued though. I knew from past experience that I had to rely on myself to escape, but I could always dream. Dreaming of him and the way he touched me, kissed me, it was all I had right now. I wanted to get back to him, even if it was just to call him out for saying those hurtful things about me. Why did he have to do that? Why were the last words we spoke to each other ones of hate?

My eyes started to well up, as a familiar surge to my senses alerted me to the fact that I was on board a plane. It dipped and caused my ears to pop painfully with the change in air pressure. I had to remind myself to stay positive and never give up fighting, despite the fact that I was now heading towards an unknown destination. There was always a way out, I just had to find it.

I thanked my lucky stars that I was brought up by an army loving trickster like my Father. He prepared me for the perils of growing up in a man's world, and I had a feeling I was about to put every last lesson he'd taught me into practise, to try and save me from what lay ahead.

"I think she's coming round," one of the men grunted.

I had no idea how he knew. I was trying to stay as still as I could. Maybe my watery eyes gave me away, damn it.

"It'd be better for her if she was still under," another piped up. "I heard that Diaz is the devil himself. He won't go easy on her. Quite the opposite. He's pissed he's had to wait so long."

"Boss says he's throwing some weird sex party, and she's the star turn."

My tummy turned over as another laughed and said, "I don't think I'd be able to stomach one of his parties. I'm not that way inclined. Don't get me wrong, I'm not into plain old vanilla sex, but what he does is a whole different ball game."

What the fuck was I going to have to go up against? I had zero experience of sex parties and slaves, I didn't want any experience. This all felt horrifically surreal, like I was stuck in my own private horror movie. Well, I wasn't about to be the dumb girl who screams and runs into the arms of the killer, I liked to think I was smarter than that.

I felt a shoe kick me in the ribs, hard enough to make my eyes instinctively fly open.

"Wakey wakey, little girl."

One of the men leered over me grinning, and showed me how rotten and yellow his teeth were.

"Not long left now. We'll be landing soon. Then we'll have you off to your new home."

He patted my cheek like I was a kid, then sat back down.

"Excited?" He smirked as the other men laughed.

I glared at them all, damning them to hell and hoping karma would let me watch their demise when it finally came.

These men obviously thought that they weren't of the same level of evil as the man they were taking me to. But the fact that they dealt with men like that, made them guilty by association. They were his minions, dealers for the devil himself. Their day of reckoning would come.

Once the plane landed with a rough bump and a jolt, they hauled me mercilessly to my feet. They cut the tie from around my legs carelessly, nicking the skin on the back of one of my ankles as they did. Then they pulled me along to exit the plane. I was bundled into the back of a waiting van, thrown into the dark and left to fend for myself, as they sped down uneven roads. My body bumped and jostled around, as

I desperately tried to hang on to the walls. In the end, I found rolling up into a little ball was my best protection.

I guess it must've been about two hours later, when we finally came to a stop, and I heard the doors of the van open and clunk closed. I was covered in a layer of sticky sweat, and my hair stuck to my neck and back. I winced and shut my eyes, as the bright sunshine invaded the darkness of the van. A muscly arm shot forward and dragged me out. I stumbled as I caught my foot on an uneven part of the van's back doors, and I fell onto my knees on the dusty ground.

"She's on her knees for me already, just how I like them. Good job, men." A gruff voice boomed over the hissing and chirping of the insects that were hidden in the thick undergrowth of the dry wasteland that I'd been flung onto.

I raised my chin up in a show of defiance, and stared at the overweight bear of a man stood in front of me. He wore a pair of cream linen trousers that looked ridiculous on his heavy frame, with black flip-flops on his podgy feet. He had a gaudy shirt with splashes of colour all over it, like some kind of grotesque modern art, and he wore three large gold chains of varying lengths around his bulging neck. He had a short, dark, wiry beard on his round face, and his hair was receding, although he still styled it with gel, as if he was years younger. At a guess, I would've put him at about fifty-years-old. The paunch hanging over his trousers, and the jowls around his neck and face made him appear teddy bear like. But the dead look in his grey eyes, and the sneer on his face, showed he was anything but cuddly. This man was heartless, evil and he had just met his match in me.

He walked towards me and ran his chubby little fingers over my face and down my hair. He smelt of stale sweat and tobacco. Each coarse stubby finger had a large gold ring on it, to symbolise his wealth and power, no doubt.

"Beautiful and such soft skin."

I jerked my head away from him in disgust and he laughed.

"I knew I'd like this one, she's feisty. I love a good fight before they submit." He bent down to put his face right in front of mine. "And you will submit to me, bitch."

'Game on motherfucker,' I thought to myself, as I stared unflinching at him.

He folded his arms, then instructed the men to bring me in. He stood back and watched two of them lift me up under the arms and usher me forward. The home they were taking me into looked deceptively pretty, with white plaster and a terracotta roof. Flowers of every colour adorned the garden, and crept up around the walls of the villa style home.

Once I entered the reception hall, they threw me down onto the polished wooden floor, and I pushed myself up onto all fours, before pulling myself to stand.

"You are dead men walking," I sneered over at them. "When Luca finds you, and he will, he'll make sure you suffer for this."

They just laughed at me. "Your boyfriend will never

catch us. He'll never find you, either. So you may as well put that little scenario right out of your pretty little head, sweetheart."

"Fuck you," I spat back.

I glanced around the entrance hall. A skinny young guy, about nineteen or twenty, stood with his head bowed next to the staircase. He wore white shorts, but no top, and he had no shoes on his scrawny feet. He didn't make eye contact with any of us. His greasy blond hair hung over his forehead and almost covered his eyes. Behind him, a girl about the same age with similar blonde hair stood, almost cowering in the corner. A dirty yellow sundress hung off her bony frame. I guessed these two were brother and sister. They certainly looked alike.

Sanchez's men turned and left the villa, and the 'boss' strode in, slamming the large wooden door shut behind him.

"Aren't we just a cosy little family, now we're all finally together?" He grinned.

"Evan, Lyla, this is our new guest, Chloe. She'll be staying with us until...well, until she's not able to anymore," he shrugged. "Say hello and make her feel welcome."

His bored tone showed how unconcerned he really was with how *welcome* I felt.

I turned to face the two quivering wreaks that he called Evan and Lyla.

"Hello," they both said, without looking up from the floor. I didn't answer.

The boss walked over to where I stood, and picked up a handful of my hair to smell it. His close proximity made my skin crawl. He was like a walrus, only less friendly.

"As much as I love your smell, I will need you cleaned and ready for my guests to enjoy later," he snarled, then turned to the other two. "Take her upstairs. Get her cleaned up and ready for the party tonight. I've left her outfit in Lyla's room. Once she's prepared, take her down and secure her for me."

"What the fuck does that even mean? I'm not being *secured* by you or anyone."

Instantly he spun round and stalked over to where I was standing. I hadn't anticipated the swift, harsh blow that struck me, and I fell to the ground, as his hand knocked me on the side of the head. He stooped low over me, as I lay crumpled on the floor.

"Let's get one thing straight, *bitch*. You belong to me now. I own you and I own your fucking body. If I want you secured, tied up or hanging from the fucking ceiling by your hair, I'll do it. You don't get a say anymore. Kiss goodbye to your old life, because you'll never see that again."

As he snarled, spit flew out of his dirty, vile mouth and onto my face, making me lean back. He went to walk away, then stopped and turned to face me again.

"And that's the last time you'll address me in that manner. To you, I am Sir. You only speak when spoken to, and you never look me in the eye. Disobey me? And I'll make sure that's the last thing you ever do." Then he headed down the hallway and out of earshot.

"Asshole," I whispered, and Lyla giggled. Evan shushed her and looked at the doorway, twitching and nervous.

They went to approach me, then froze in fear and put their heads down. I turned around expecting to see the boss, but instead a woman stood behind me, about fifty-years-old, with leathery brown skin. She was dressed up like she was bloody Christmas, head to toe in gold glitter and sequins, and she was scowling right at me. This had to be Mrs Boss.

"So you're his new little fuck toy," she sneered. "Do as you're told and maybe you'll last longer than the last three. God knows I don't want to have to share his bed."

Then she spun round and exited through the door I'd just been dragged through.

How could she? I inwardly seethed. How could she sit by and let that vile excuse of a man use people like he was, and let him get away with it? What sort of woman sat by idly, as her 'husband' screwed around and did God knows what else to innocent, vulnerable people like Evan and Lyla? No way was I putting myself in the same category as them. It was obvious they were slaves. Me? I was still my own warrior. I'd play his game...for now. But I was merely biding my time, until the opportunity came along to take him down, and it would. Everyone had their weakness, and I was going to find his.

Chapter Thirty

Turned out Evan and Lyla were twins, and both were the sweetest, most docile and subservient people I'd ever met. They led me upstairs, all the time bowing and stooping like some kind of hunched over medieval servants, ready to dote on their master.

"Chill out guys," I urged. "No need to keep looking down and creeping around me."

Lyla looked up into my eyes, as if she couldn't quite believe that she was allowed to look at me. But Evan scolded her straight away, and told her to get on with her job, unless she wanted a whipping or worse. He didn't trust me, and I didn't blame him. I had no idea what these two had been through.

"How long have you lived here?" I asked, hoping to gain some insight into their state of mind.

"About three years," Lyla whispered, as Evan shushed her again.

"For fucks sake, Lyla, do you want to make him angry

again after last night?" He threatened.

"What happened last night?"

I looked at both of them, but Evan just shook his head at his sister and they both clammed up. Shit, this was going to be harder than I thought. They were so conditioned into servitude, and whatever their *master* had brainwashed them to do, that I doubted I'd get through to them in the time I had. I just hoped that in time I could help them too, and get them back to their families to live a healthy and more normal life, after all of this was over.

Evan ran a bath, then placed various lotions and potions out for Lyla. Lyla tried to help me take my clothes off, but I pushed her off. I wasn't about to let her paw all over me and make this whole humiliating experience any worse.

"Why do I have to bathe with you here?" I snapped.

Lyla cowered in response to my anger, and Evan swallowed hard and gazed at the floor. "We have to stay in here, the Master told us to. Lyla can help you bathe. I'll just stay here in the corner."

"I don't need help to take a fucking bath," I shouted. "I'm not a child."

Lyla reached forward to touch my arm, then cautiously took it back, like I'd given her an electric shock.

"Don't make so much noise, Chloe. We don't want to hurt you. We're only doing what we've been told to do. Please. If he hears you shouting, he'll come up. Then we'll all be punished."

Her eyes looked petrified, desperate, and so full of sorrow. I actually felt bad for defying them.

"It's only us. We won't hurt you and we'll get this over with as quickly as possible," Lyla said, trying to show me the kindness behind her dead eyes.

"It'd be better for you if you learned to lose the inhibitions you have about showing your body," Evan chipped in. "After tonight, every man within a twenty mile radius will have seen every inch of you, and then some."

He shook as he spoke, and I guessed that both Evan and Lyla had experienced that level of personal intrusion. I felt sick to the stomach for myself and for them.

"Fine," I agreed, speaking in a quieter tone. "Let's get this over with. I have an escape plan to hatch."

Lyla smiled, but Evan just shook his head.

"Don't fill my sister's head with anymore nonsense about freedom. Everyone who comes here does that, but no one leaves here unless it's in a bag or a box, trust me."

Lyla's face dropped, but I ignored Evan's defeatist attitude and squeezed Lyla's hand.

-

Lyla was gentle as she helped to bathe and dry me. She made me use oils on my private area, which I found strange. She also praised me for being so newly waxed. Apparently I'd saved her another tricky job. I rolled my eyes at that one. Like anyone was going to get anywhere near there anyway.

She wrapped a red silk robe around me, then walked me

into a bedroom, where she sat me down in front of a mirror and blow-dried my hair into the biggest, softest curls ever.

"Damn girl, you should open your own beauty salon," I joked and she grinned.

"I was training to be a hairdresser before we were taken." She averted her gaze, so I wouldn't see the pain that she held within. "I'm also doing your make up. Do you have any colours you like to use?"

"This isn't a spa, Lyla," Evan snapped at her. "Just get on with it."

"Leave her alone." I couldn't help but jump to her defence. "You both live a pretty shitty life as far as I can see, so why can't she pretend and play around once in a while?"

His cheeks flushed in embarrassment and he slunk back into the corner. He must've realised how unjust he was being to his sister. Lyla went to work, making my face look more glowing than it'd been for a long time. No mean feat in this heat, and with the tiredness I'd felt after the past twenty-four hours.

"Lyla, you're a miracle worker. When we get out of here, I'm definitely coming to you for my hair and make-up."

She giggled as Evan tutted but remained otherwise silent.

"Chloe, I don't think you'll like what he's gonna make you wear."

Lyla looked at me through the mirror we were both facing.

What Evan brought over couldn't be described as an outfit. It was a disgusting, leather studded, bondage style bra with strange hooks, and a tiny leather thong which was crotchless. Like it needed the extra, empty space in the middle. The two thin pieces of leather, that'd sit either side of my private area, wouldn't have been much of a covering anyway. I was going to be open for all the world to see.

"What the fuck? I'm not wearing that! No way, never ever." I stood firm with my hands folded over my chest.

"You have to, Chloe. He'll do terrible things to all of us if you don't," Lyla pleaded.

"He can try, but I still won't wear it," I shouted.

"Please." Lyla held the strips of material forward.

"No!"

The fat-ass boss must've been listening, or worse still, watching us on some hidden camera, as he flung the door open with brute force and marched right up to me. He grabbed a handful of my hair and yanked my head back, so I was bent backward at an unforgiving angle, and forcefully cowering below him.

"I've had about enough of your shit, *bitch*." He held up a hunting knife with a serrated blade, then threw me down to the floor and stalked over to where Lyla stood wide-eyed.

"Put that on, or I'll cut her throat."

He held the knife up to Lyla's neck and pushed it into her skin, causing a red trickle to pour down her front and stain her yellow dress. Lyla's eyes bugged huge and she whimpered like an injured animal, caught by the prey.

"You're next, bitch. Put it on, or you'll both be cut up real bad." He was loving the fear he was projecting onto Lyla and Evan.

I just felt furious that he'd hurt a girl half his size and not given a damn. He was a coward and a bully. Why hadn't he hurt me first? I was the one being difficult, but I guessed I was more valuable to him than the scrawny, blonde slip of a girl. He already had plans for me.

"Fine, but I won't be wearing it for long." I kept my eyes fixed on him to show him I wasn't frightened. "And I'll enjoy slitting your throat later. I might even use that same knife."

He threw his head back and laughed. "Oh sweetheart, you're going to be my favourite project. I'm gonna break you so badly, you'll be begging me to kill you and put you out of your misery."

He took the blade from Lyla's neck and stalked over to whisper in my ear, the blade now resting against my legs as if to reinforce what he was saying.

"The things I'm going to use to fuck you...you have no idea. It's going to be...beautiful...and I'm gonna invite every single one of my friends to join in too. I'm really gonna go to town on your little pussy and tight ass. Get ready for it. The fun begins tonight."

He wiggled his eyebrows and left the room. I had to stop myself from spitting or hitting out at him before he left. He really was born from the depths of hell, and he deserved to go back there as soon as possible.

"If you can shut your mind down and drift off to another place away from here, it helps," Lyla said, to try and offer me some comfort. "That's what I do, when he uses my body. I go back to the beach we used to holiday at when we were children."

I wanted to reach forward and hug her, she was so fragile and broken down. But I could tell from her body language that she wouldn't want me touching her. In this private moment, with myself and Evan, she had control over her own body, something she obviously didn't experience very often, and I didn't want to intrude upon that.

"I'm sorry, Lyla. I didn't mean for you to get hurt."

"It's okay." She smiled weakly. "I've had worse."

Once I was trussed up in the ridiculous outfit, Evan took my arm and led me out of the room.

"Don't make a fuss once you're down there," he said cryptically. "He'll like the fight and it'll go worse for you if you do. He usually spends time before the party drinking and getting ready. You should take the time to mentally prepare yourself. You'll need it. The last thing you want is him coming to you all angry because you disturbed him. Trust me."

I did. I knew now that whatever Evan was saying was to help me.

"Where will you be?" I asked, turning to look at them both.

"We're serving drinks and snacks," Lyla said sadly.

"That doesn't sound so bad." I smiled.

"It is when you're the table, and if you drop one thing, they whip you or worse," she sighed.

Oh. My. God. Was he expecting these two to curl up and crawl around all night like freaks, serving drinks and things from their backs? What kind of fucked-up world had I entered?

"Don't look at us like that, Chloe," Evan said. "We've got the good deal compared to you." And with that, he led me into the room where I would be *secured*.

Chapter Thirty One

This wasn't a room. No. It was a dungeon, a darkened torture chamber. The brick walls were damp and cold, and the smell of mildew filled my nostrils. There were a number of shackles hanging from the wall, one of which was to be my holding place for however long the 'boss' saw fit to keep me here. There weren't any windows to let in natural light, only four strip lights that buzzed, one flickering slightly, as it neared its end. I knew how it felt.

There was a wall full of whips, chains, floggers and what looked like various horse-riding gear hung up from hooks and nails. Another wall held a glass cabinet full of vibrators of every size, shape and colour, along with butt plugs and various other weird and painful looking 'toys'. Opposite that wall was the worst section of this dungeon. Knives, scalpels, saws, drills, and contraptions that looked like whisks or metal sculptures, with spikes and blades. They hung off the wall or sat on the shelves shining brightly, but holding the darkest threats of all.

Whatever was going to happen down here wasn't going to be pleasant, I knew that for sure. I also knew I had very little chance of escape once I was locked into the shackles that Evan held out to me.

"Fuck this shit." I shook my head, determined to defy anyone and everyone right now. "You're not locking me in here and leaving me."

"Oh, but he is."

The gruff voice sounded from the door. He knew I wouldn't play ball, that's why he was lurking around in the shadows like a demon.

"Cuff her," he ordered, but I shrugged Evan off easily. He was so weak and feeble.

"You're bloody useless," he snapped and punched Evan in the face, making him fall to the ground clutching his nose, as fresh red blood oozed between his fingers.

Then a knife was pushed into the side of my neck. I felt the sharp point pierce my skin, and the hot trickle of blood as he increased the pressure.

He breathed menacingly into my ear. "Get your fucking arms and legs into place, or I'll tie you to that table and cut off every last piece of material from your body and fuck you bloody with every last toy from over there." He pointed the blade over to the wall of knives, but it was the table that filled me with dread. It was like a butcher's block for humans, with cuffs at each corner, and blood stains that'd long since dried to a brown pattern in the wood. Tales of the violence that'd taken place before.

I took a deep breath in and thought hard about letting him slit my throat and end this nightmare, but as he pushed himself forward to brush up against my back, and show me how aroused he was because of my resistance, I felt a solid object in the left side of his trousers. A glimmer of hope sprung fresh in my mind. *Don't let him win, Chloe. Don't give up*, my inner voice called out. I was my Father's daughter, and I couldn't go down without a fight. I had to give myself a chance to escape, or at least give myself something to fight with. Using my Father's legacy, an expert sleight of hand, I gently slipped two fingers undetected into his pocket, and eased out what felt like a small knife. I held it close to my wrist, hidden from view behind my back. My heart fluttered with renewed hope. He hadn't felt a damn thing.

He stepped away from me and pulled Evan up off the floor, propelling him forward into my direction to carry on with his task.

"You'll regret ever meeting me." I smiled at him as I put my feet next to the cuffs on the floor, standing with my legs astride like a prisoner. "I'll kill you before the nights over."

I tucked the knife into the material at the back of the g-string I was wearing, and reached my hands up to be cuffed above my head.

"No. I'll break you before the nights over, and then I'll enjoy doing it all over again the next day, the next day, and the day after that." He smirked.

Evan secured the cuffs, then stepped back sheepishly as the boss moved forward. He planted a wet kiss on my cheek and reached in-between my legs to run his coarse, calloused fingers along the seam of my pussy, then forced them roughly inside me.

"It doesn't matter if you're not wet. The blood will give us all the lubrication we need."

Then he walked away chuckling, with Lyla and Evan following behind, locked the door, and left me in total darkness.

I gagged and wished to God that I wasn't tied up, so I could wipe away the feeling of his hands on me. I felt grossly violated already and he hadn't properly penetrated me yet, well not in the way he wanted. What would I do if he did?

'No, Chloe, don't think like that. He won't get that far. You won't let him,' I told myself, but I was starting to doubt my own skills and ability. I'd never been so utterly helpless in all my life, including the time I'd fought off my Mother's grabby boyfriends, and fended for myself on the streets. No, I'd never been in a situation quite as helpless as this. This was a do or die scenario, and the longer I stayed here, the less hope I had of Luca or anyone else coming to save me. My freedom was mine alone to win.

I decided I couldn't focus on my old life. It distracted me too much to think about Luca and Freddie, to pin my hopes on anyone else. No, I had to use every last brain cell and drop of energy to think of ways to better my situation. Whether that was talking myself out of this hellhole, or fighting off any would be attackers.

It was dark, so I used the opportunity to focus my other senses, listening to any noises from around or above. The cuffs were sturdy and unforgiving, so I had no chance of breaking free of those. I would have to use other means to secure the upper hand.

Eventually, my arms began to ache from being forced into a raised position for so long, so I tried to let them hang limp to ease the stress on my muscles. It helped for a short while, until cramp became my next enemy. God, how had I got myself into this mess? Why was I here?

I started to think about all the things that'd happened to me over the course of my life, and no matter how positive I tried to be, everything went back to that night when Luca and Freddie left me. That, and the day my Father died. Three men, who were the keystones of my life, and all three had left me. I'd harboured anger for years towards my Father for dying so young. Why hadn't he sought better medical care? Why did he have to die?

My anger towards Luca and Freddie? That was beginning to surface again with a vengeance. If they hadn't left, or if they'd taken me with them, I wouldn't have wound up in a strip club run by a sex trafficker. If we hadn't argued that day, maybe I wouldn't have been so foolish as to let Teresa trick me into opening the doors. Maybe I'd have gone to the club with them, and spent the day with Rosa or Stacey.

What ifs. That was all I was left with. That, and the reality that at some point tonight, I was going to have to fight for my body and my life.

–

I'm not sure how long I stood, chained up against that cold, unforgiving brick wall, before I started to hear the low mumble of male voices, chattering and laughing above me. It might've been a few hours, although judging from the strain on my limbs, it felt like a hell of a lot longer. Music played much like it would at any other party, but this wasn't any party. This was the kind of party you didn't want an invite to, not unless you were seriously fucked-up in the head.

I heard the booming shouts of the boss, as he called over the music to his so-called friends. Probably warming them up for the main event. Then a few moments later, I heard footsteps and voices on the stairs outside this chamber. The clank of metal, the click of the lock, and then light filtered through as the door creaked open.

"There she is."

The boss held the door open as another older guy, not as fat as the boss, but still with that evil glint in his eyes, stepped into the room.

"I'll leave the door open. Enjoy yourself...and her. Leave something for the rest of us, though. It's gonna be a long night."

He chuckled as he pulled the door to and left me and the old guy standing staring at each other, as the strip lights buzzed in the background.

"You're a pretty one aren't you? Al said he had something special for tonight, but you're a nice surprise. How old are you treasure?"

He grinned, showing tobacco stained teeth.

"Fuck you."

He smirked and slunk over to me like the reptile he was.

"I do like them young, and you look nice and fresh to me, petal."

He licked my cheek and ran his hands down my front, from neck to groin. Ugh, his cold rough hands felt gross against my skin.

"Such soft skin," he chuckled, as I shivered and turned my head away. "I love the ones who fight, it makes the pussy so much sweeter. I'm hard already and we haven't even started yet. I'm gonna enjoy tasting you."

He licked down my neck, then breathed into my ear. "Will you squeal like a pig when I cut you?"

I flinched as he pushed his whole body up against mine, pinning me to the wall and letting me feel his hard cock in his trousers. He tried to kiss me and stick his slimy tongue in my mouth. His left hand started to fumble with my breasts under the ridiculous bra, as his right hand rubbed hard between my legs. I felt like telling him there wasn't any chance of a genie appearing no matter how hard he rubbed, but he seemed to think that was the key to getting me 'ready' for him. I braced myself, and decided I had to play smart with this guy, if I had any chance of escape.

"An older guy like you must go for ages." I had to stop myself from gagging at the thought and the taste of him on my lips. "Maybe it'd be more comfortable for you if I'm on the table?"

He leaned away, looking at me with suspicion in his eyes, before he bit his lip and nodded.

"I gotta admit, the thought of bending or holding you up against this wall isn't great. I suffer with my back. I would turn you round, but looks like Al trussed you up really good."

He walked over to the glass cabinet and opened it, picking up what must've been the keys to unlock the shackles, and came to stand in front of me.

"I like a fight as much as any guy here tonight, but I swear, if you try anything, I will fuck you up really bad little girl, okay?"

I nodded and kept my head down as he bent to unlock the ankle cuffs first. I shook my legs as they were set free, and then held my breath as he reached up to unlock my wrists. As my arms fell to my sides I sighed, and shrugged the knots out as best I could.

"Such a sexy sigh. I hope to hear that again soon. I bet you scream and moan like a dirty angel, don't you?"

He looked me up and down, as if I was a prize piece of meat and he was about to carve himself a generous helping.

"Oh, I can moan really good, listen-" I pushed my head towards him to whisper in his ear, and as he leaned into me,

I swung round and stabbed the knife, from behind my back, hard into the side of his neck.

The gurgle sound he made, as he tried to curse me, felt so fucking satisfying. He tried to grab the knife from my hands, but he was too weak from the blow, and I managed to keep it pressed into him, twisting it as hard as I could. I wasn't some sicko into hurting people. I didn't get off on other people's pain. But knowing I was putting down a pervert like him, spurred me on even more. He fell to the floor with a thud and bled out onto the dusty concrete, the life draining quicker from him than I'd expected.

I stepped over him and went to the wall of terror, stashing as many knives and weapons as I could into the leather straps of my outfit. Then I held the largest knife in my hand, ready to attack. I was unshackled. I was heading into the warzone, and I would be killing for my freedom.

I headed over to the door, opening it just a touch to see what lay on the other side. The voices were further away. There didn't appear to be anyone at the top of the stairs, so with extreme caution I went up, being careful to place pressure on each step slowly in case of any creaks. The last thing I wanted to do was alert anyone to my whereabouts. I had the gift of surprise on my side, and it was all I had right now. Well that, and a shit load of blades.

Once I reached the top step, I peered around the corner into what looked like a utility area. I could hear glasses chinking, and murmurs from the other side of the wall, but this area looked safe enough. There weren't any outside doors or windows, just one internal door leading into the kitchen area. I knew it would probably be occupied by a few men, in search of extra drinks and snacks that Lyla and Evan weren't offering. As I crept over to the door, it swung open, and a guy stepped in. He was facing the opposite way to where I was stood, so he didn't see me until he spun back around. By luck, I'd already shut the door behind him, to block out the view from the kitchen. I held my knife up against his neck. He looked petrified, and took a huge gulp before stuttering, "I don't want any trouble. I thought this was the way to the wine cellar."

He was a lot younger than the last two men I'd encountered tonight. He also looked shocked to find me here. I couldn't afford to stop and feel anything though. I had to stay focused and intent on my end goal.

"Shirt," I snapped.

He frowned, so I made it clearer.

"Take off your shirt."

He relented and took off his white dress shirt, then held it out to me. He was shaking and his breathing was unsteady.

I grabbed the shirt from him and threw it to the side, out of the line of fire, then channelling my inner soldier I sliced that blade as hard as I could across his neck. The splatter that followed shocked me. Thank God I'd moved the shirt, I didn't fancy covering myself up in blood-soaked material. My hands were red enough.

I watched him slump to the floor, and his eyes glazed over. Then I wiped my filthy hands on his trousers, to get off what stains I could, and put the dress shirt over my disgusting outfit, securing two or three buttons in the middle to keep me somewhat decent. I pulled his body away from the door and stepped over the second sacrifice I'd made that night, all in the name of my own emancipation.

I pressed my ear to the door and listened. No sound came from the other side, so I pushed the door open gently and peered around. Two men stood against the kitchen island with their backs to me, each holding a leash for the sickly thin girls they had crawling around behind them. These girls couldn't have been older than sixteen, and looked malnourished and broken. Their hair was limp and lifeless, their skin a deathly shade of white, and they were completely naked. One was rested on all fours like a dog. The other was sitting on her knees, as her owner petted her and stroked her hair.

I drifted silently over the tiled floor, pulling two more knives from my leather bindings, and holding my finger up to my lips to tell the quivering wreaks on leashes to stay quiet. The shorter guy moved to the left, so I pushed the knife into the side of his neck, determined to hit hard and with force. The second guy spun round to face him, then me, his eyes showed shock then rage as he lunged at me. Quick as a flash, I managed to thrust the second blade into his stomach. Unlike the shorter guy, who was now on the floor, this one wasn't going down without a fight.

"You fucking bitch," he seethed and grabbed out at me, catching my hair and pulling me into him.

I didn't stop to think, just reached forward and pulled the knife out of his stomach and pushed it into the front of his neck. The sounds I heard would surely haunt me until the day I died. Gurgles, rattles, whimpers and whines, they all added to the ugliness that was death. I couldn't even begin to describe the putrid smells that permeated the air. I was going to need a million baths and showers to rid my body of the filth now seeping through my pores.

The two slave girls scrambled into a corner underneath the counter tops of the kitchen, and cowered away like little children hiding from the bogie man. I didn't have time to help them, or put them at ease. I needed to think about myself first and plan my own escape. I was blinkered, so focused and full of tunnel vision I could only concentrate on getting myself out of this hellhole and to the authorities to report these evil, sadistic fuckers.

I had no idea how the next part would play out. I figured I had two choices. One, try to make a run for the front door and hope I made it without being stopped, shot down or dragged back. Or two, I could make my way into the main living area, which was next to the kitchen, take a hostage maybe and barter for my freedom. I had no chance going up against the number of men in that room with just my blades.

I figured, from the volume of noise I could hear, there had to be about a dozen men in there at least. So which one would it be? Run and hide, or face off and fight?

I heard some type of heated commotion erupting in the living area and decided if I was going that route, now was the time to strike. I was never a run and hide kind of girl anyway. I always chose the more challenging options in life, so it was a real no brainer for me. I took a deep breath, held my knife firmly in my hand and pushed my way into the devil's playground.

Chapter Thirty Two

"No! Fuck no!" I couldn't believe what I was seeing.

I stood there stunned in my bloodstained shirt that barely covered my ass. My palms were sticky from the blood of the collateral damage I'd unleashed, and my hands quivered as I held my knife out. Circled around the room, surrounding the devil and his disciples, stood Luca, Freddie and his men, all dressed in black and pointing their guns at their targets.

"Hell no." I shook my head, as every man looked in my direction. Luca and Freddie seemed to be both relieved and puzzled by my response.

"You don't get to do this." I gritted my teeth, feeling anger surge through my body. "You don't get to show up here and just shoot your way out. Not after what I've been through. Not after what I've done."

I walked further into the room to stand in the middle. "This is mine, my victory. I killed to get out of that death dungeon torture chamber from hell. I fought to be able to stand here in this room. This is my win. Mine. Not yours or anyone else's. I freed me. I made it happen. I'm not gonna let you storm in at the last minute and take all the glory."

Luca and Freddie turned to look at each other. I noticed Vinnie standing to the left his mouth wide open catching flies.

"Give me a gun," I snapped at him, holding out my hand. "And not that stupid big one that you're holding. Something *I* can actually hold and use."

He reached back behind him and pulled out a handgun and passed it to me, looking over at Luca as he did as if to say, 'sorry man, but I'm not arguing with this girl'.

I dropped my knife on the beige rug, next to where Evan was hunched over with shot glasses balanced on his back. Nearby, another slave was curled up at her owner's feet like a loyal lap dog. I held the gun in both hands, checking there were bullets in the chamber and that the safety was unlocked.

I glared into the eyes of the boss, as he stood there with a shit eating grin on his face. He wasn't fazed by any of this. He knew what sort of world he inhabited and he looked relaxed, at ease with how things were playing out. Around him were over half a dozen feeble excuses for men, most of which had slaves with them. Some naked, some dressed in similar barbaric outfits like mine. It was degrading, perverted and now, it was going to be over.

I walked over to him and held the gun up, pointing it at his head.

"I told you that you'd regret ever meeting me." I nodded

at him. His smile grew wider, more sinister. "And I told you that I'd kill you tonight." He had the nerve to actually laugh at me.

I took one step closer, lowering the gun as Luca and his men cocked theirs ready to fire. Then I leant forward, and in a quieter voice said, "but what I didn't tell you was that I'd blow your cock first."

I grinned and held the gun firm with one hand over the handle and trigger, the other securing it underneath and I aimed at his rancid cock and pulled. The kick back made me jump, but I still hit my target in spectacular fashion.

Boss man dropped to the ground, howling and cursing me to hell, but I was the one laughing now.

"That's for every girl and boy you've taken, locked up, abused, raped and killed. You deserve much worse than what I'm about to serve up for you, but you'll get what you truly deserve, when you arrive in hell tonight. Remember, when they ask who sent you, it was me. Chloe Ellis. You see, I'm not a weak little girl. I'm no one's fuck toy and I definitely wasn't made to be anyone's *dirty little fuck*." I said with such conviction, I could feel the prickle of shame coming from a certain dark-haired mercenary behind me.

I aimed the gun at his head, and without a second thought, I shot that evil fucker between the eyes and smiled as he flew backwards into the wall, his head splattering against the pristine white plaster.

"Lyla, Evan, get up and go. You're free to leave this shit

hole. And the rest of you. If you need anything, I'm sure these men here will help you."

I threw the gun at the dead boss's feet and turned, holding my head high and proud.

"Don't follow me. I'm leaving, and I'm in control of where I go. I don't want to see any of you again. Ever." With that I pushed past Freddie and Marco, and walked out of the door of that villa and into the cool evening air.

Chapter Thirty Three
LUCA

(Earlier that night)

Our convoy wound down a dirt track, the overgrown bushes either side of us made me nauseas. What if Sanchez had given us the wrong address? Duped us in some way as a final fuck you. We were minutes away from our final destination and there wasn't a building in sight. Where the hell were they keeping her?

As we rounded a sharp bend, a low, white building came into focus, partially covered by the trees, bushes and flowers that spiralled up the walls. I breathed a sigh of relief. This had to be the place.

We pulled our vehicles to a halt further down from the building, not wanting to alert the inhabitants inside to our arrival with the sound of our engines. I wanted to go in first. I didn't care how risky it was. I wanted to be the one to save her. I felt like it was my duty, my right after doing her so many wrongs.

A few of my men headed down first to check out the area around the villa style home, and gather intel on the doors, windows, escape routes and number of people in there. We needed to know what we were dealing with before we stormed in. We couldn't go in blind, this was a rescue not a suicide mission.

Once we'd established the layout of the building, I sent my men to cover the windows and doors. Determined not to let a single motherfucker out of that building. They all needed to pay the price for the fucked up things they'd done. I was going in through the front door to storm the living room, where I'd been informed the main 'party' was happening. I'd be taking Freddie, Marco, Leo, Vinnie and a few other top shooters with me.

"Are you sure you don't wanna go in ahead and find her? We can take out the trash in the living room," Marco suggested, but he knew me better than that.

"I'll be pulling the trigger on that bastard, Diaz. No one else," I ordered, as we went through our plan and headed down to the target.

Once I knew everyone was in place, I shot out the lock and kicked the door in. Then we charged, storming into that house like a tsunami wave, ready to wash out the filth. We held our guns up and surrounded the sick fucks, outnumbering them three to one. What we saw made our stomachs turn over. Men with young girls and boys chained up, leashed or just bowing at their feet like fucking dogs.

"Time's up you sick freaks," Freddie snapped, as we trained our guns on them.

"Where the fuck is she?" I glared around the room, to see if I could work out which one was Diaz, and then my heart jumped into my mouth, as I heard a familiar voice.

"No! Fuck no!" She shouted from the other side of the room.

The sheer relief I felt in that moment was something I'll never forget. She was alive. She was still as feisty as hell, but god damn it, was she pissed off with *us* right now? Really? All the sick fuckers in the room and she chose us to throw a shit fit at.

I couldn't help my heart from constricting when I looked at her, saw her as she stood there in a bloodstained shirt. She was so tiny and fragile, and yet she just oozed confidence. She was formidable. I fucking loved this woman, and I had to hold myself back from stalking over to her and taking her into my arms. Kissing her hard and throwing her over my shoulder. She always brought out the caveman in me. I think it was her wildness that turned me on the most.

"Hell, no," she snapped, shaking her head.

I glanced over at Freddie, trying to gauge his reaction to all this. I was in a fucking hostage takedown situation, ready to murder the sickest individuals in our society, and I was fucking turned on. What the hell was that about?

"You don't get to do this." She was mad as hell. Under her white shirt I could just about make out some kind of black leather get up. Her hair was a mass of wild chocolate curls falling around her face and shoulders. But her face, damn that face looked fucking beautiful. She was glowing, on fire. Her eyes raged, her jaw clenched tight, her soft pout so kissable, so fuckable. I had to take a deep breath to sort myself out. This wasn't the time to be having the thoughts that I was. I was so horny and so fucking proud of my girl. She kicked ass, and even though I knew it would be mine she'd kick before the day was over, I didn't care. I loved her ballsy attitude, and I'd take any crap she threw my way, because she was mine. She wasn't going anywhere again, not if it was away from me. That was non-negotiable.

She started raging about it being her win, her glory and I had to give it to her. I could see from her clothing, and the knife she threw down, that my girl had fought tooth and nail to get to this room. I hated that she'd had to do that. It was my job to protect her, my responsibility. The realisation that one of these fuckers had touched her, or worse, hit me, and I felt every muscle in my body tense; hatred and thirst for revenge flowing through my veins. But no sooner was I lifting my gun to shoot, I was being verbally shot down by my angel.

She ordered Vinnie to give her a gun. I knew he would. That snake would do anything for her. He looked over at me as if in search of some kind of approval. I just glared at him. He was still on my shit list, and bowing to my woman like that didn't help his cause.

I watched with a sense of pride as she went over to her

target, Diaz. As she talked to him, I raised my gun to aim it at his head and my men followed suit. If he moved even an inch towards her, I'd blow his brains out. If he dared to touch her, I'd fill his body so full of bullets, they wouldn't even know his carcass was human by the time I'd finished. He was lucky he was still alive and sharing the same air as her. I felt beyond murderous right now. I was deadly.

She whispered something to him, then shot the sick fuck in the cock and I smiled. Nice touch angel, I liked her style. No one fucked with my woman, and now we all knew it.

She stood back and started to deliver a little speech to the room, telling Diaz her bullet was for all the girls and boys he'd fucked up. Then the blood in my veins ran cold as she turned her tirade on me, telling the room that she wasn't weak, and she was no one's dirty little fuck. I felt ashamed. I felt like calling out to her that I was a liar, a dumb fuck for saying that and making her feel worthless. She was everything, everything I wanted and everything to me. She was my world. I loved her. But this room wasn't the place to say it. I couldn't show weakness in front of the enemy. Damn, I couldn't even show it in front of my own men.

Freddie looked sideways at me, as she lifted the gun to aim at Diaz's head.

"Not now," I muttered quietly, so that he'd know I heard her but I'd deal with it later.

The shot rang out through the room, and slaves jumped and whimpered as masters braced themselves for their fate, their skin becoming ashen.

Chloe mentioned two names, and said something about us helping them out, but I couldn't focus. I was mesmerised by my beautiful girl and how sexy she looked taking charge, being the boss I always knew she was. My equal, my reflection, my perfect angel and other half. I would make her my wife. She had the title already in my heart. All I needed was the paper. And for her to agree of course.

She held her head high and told us she was leaving, alone, and that she didn't want to see us again. But I knew that was bull shit. She was mine. She'd have no choice but to see me. I wasn't letting her go, not again.

She pushed past Freddie as he turned to me.

"I think now is the perfect time, hell the only time you've got left to get her back, brother. Time to go and make this shit right." Freddie eye-balled me, but he was right. I couldn't let her walk out of my life. I wouldn't let that happen.

"We'll clean up in here boss. The house will be burnt to the ground in a few hours," Marco chipped in. "We'll make sure the innocent are safe."

My body was out of the door, chasing her down, before my brain or mouth could even engage in a response.

Chapter Thirty Four
CHLOE

I really hadn't thought through the whole, 'storming out with nothing on my feet and stomping down the gravelly footpath onto the dusty road', plan at all. My soles felt like they were going through their own personal hell. But I didn't let it stop me or look back as I strode forward. I was shaking like a leaf but determined to escape. I had no clue if there was anything nearby, not even a neighbouring house. All I knew was that I was free and it felt good, terrifying, but good. Those poor souls I'd left behind would be looked after, and I was about to take my life onto an unknown path, yet again. I had to breathe deeply, to stop myself from totally hyperventilating at what had just happened. I couldn't think about it too much, otherwise I was liable to totally lose my shit and free fall into crippling guilt.

I heard the crunching sound of his feet as he ran behind me, and then slowed down to call out my name.

"Chloe, please wait. Just stop and talk to me."

I didn't turn around, just held up my hand and called

back, "I'm not interested. Tell someone who gives a shit."

He didn't give up though. He sprinted forward and grabbed my arm to spin me around. His face showed no hint of the horrors we'd just walked away from. It was just a regular day at the office for him.

"Don't fucking touch me!" I hissed. "You don't get to touch me anymore."

He held both of his hands up, as if to signal his surrender, then put both hands behind his head and sighed up at the sky, before piercing me with his regretful green eyes.

"I'm sorry, Chloe. I'm just so, so sorry."

I shrugged, as if his apologies were useless to me.

"I'm sorry you were ever mixed up in...that," he said, glancing towards the villa behind him. "I'm sorry for anything and everything that bastard put you through. But most of all, I'm sorry I didn't tell you how I feel. I should never have spoken about you like that to my men. It was thoughtless. What can I say? I'm an idiot. A bloody idiot. But I won't let you just walk away from me, Chloe. Not ever. I might be an idiot, but I'm your idiot, if you'll still have me? I love you, Chloe."

His eyes looked desperate now, as if he'd shatter if I turned away. And even though my heart jolted at his words, I still couldn't get the whole 'dirty little fuck' comment out of my mind. I needed more than a weak apology. I wanted action, something more real.

"I'm done," I stated clearly. "I don't want to be your little woman. I deserve better than that. I don't need anyone else. I can cope just fine on my own."

For a split second, I saw the heartbreak behind his eyes, but then the shutters went up and he dropped his head. He was giving up already. I knew I'd made the right decision. Any guy who gave up that easily wasn't worth my time.

I started waging a war with myself in my mind, cursing myself for playing games and not telling him I felt the same. Then reminding myself how crappy he'd treated me over the years. I was all over the place, and my mind was like a fucking kaleidoscope of feelings. Bright then dark, positive then negative. I couldn't make up my mind what I wanted, but I knew I needed to be taken more seriously, by everyone.

Suddenly, a dark SUV pulled up beside us, as we stood silently staring at each other in some weird standoff of power and battle of wills. The blacked-out window wound down and Freddie's concerned face looked between Luca and I.

"Get in you two. I'll take you to a hotel. You won't get far on foot, we're miles away from anywhere."

Luca walked forward to jump in the front seat, but I stood firm.

"I'm not going anywhere with you." I turned and started to walk, as Freddie put the car into gear and rolled along next to me.

"Cut the stubborn bullshit, Chloe. Get in. You don't have to talk to us, but at least let us take you somewhere safe before some other trafficking motherfucker drives along and steals you for a second time."

"Fuck you!" I snapped back, then I stopped, huffed, and pulled open the back door with such force, Freddie yelled for me not to take it out on his ride.

"If anyone speaks to me, I'll jump out of the car. Even if it's moving." I folded my arms over my chest, grimacing at how the leather was starting to cut into my skin. "When we get to a hotel, I'm checking in, then checking out of your fucked-up lives for good, understand?"

"Yep!" Freddie grinned, as if he knew something I didn't, and then we were off. I had to admit, the blow of the air conditioning, and the feel of the luxurious fabric seat was heaven to me.

I reached underneath my shirt and started peeling the grotesque leather bonds from my body and flinging them out the window. The freedom from its tight restraints felt amazing, and the soft cotton of the shirt was the only thing to touch my skin now. I couldn't help smiling, then a quiet laugh escaped my lips.

"You know Freddie, it's becoming a bit of a habit, you rescuing me in my underwear," I joked. "What a shame that fucker had such gross taste in lingerie."

Freddie smiled and looked at me in the rear view mirror.

"Do you want me to turn the air con off? Only you look kinda cold."

He smiled as I looked down at my bullet like nipples protruding from the cotton shirt. I crossed my arms over as

Luca spat out. "You might be gay, but I can still kick your ass for looking. Keep your fucking eyes on the road, brother."

"I'm glad your mirror only catches the top view." I smiled, leaning forward between the two seats. "You don't want to see the view down below." I sat back again. I was sure I heard Luca growl, as Freddie threw his head back and laughed.

"Maybe you two should get into your underwear, make me feel more comfortable," I went on.

"I haven't got any on," Luca replied, and I had to hold my tongue as I looked in the driver's rear view mirror and saw Freddie raising his eyebrows at me.

The sooner we got to this damn hotel the better. I couldn't trust myself in a car with these two. Two minutes in and I'd already broken my no talking rule. Now, I was taunting them and enjoying it. They knew me too well. I needed to get away before I started forgiving and forgetting. I had to stay true to myself.

Chapter Thirty Five

An hour or so later, we were pulling up in front of an exclusive looking Spanish hacienda style hotel, with terracotta walls and rustic looking marble pillars leading to a sumptuous courtyard style lobby. The staff were all dressed in cool cream cotton outfits, ready to wait on their clientele's every whim. I took a seat behind some tropical looking plants. My scantily clad frame stood out in this place, and I didn't want to draw any more attention to myself. The soothing trickle of the water in the central water feature stood in stark contrast to the last building I'd entered. All peace and tranquillity, as opposed to violence and torture.

Luca approached the desk to book our rooms, as Freddie fussed around me, telling me he'd sort out everything I needed and not to worry about a thing. I wasn't worried. I just wanted a hot shower, food and a flight back home.

"You know, you can talk to me about anything," he ventured, as if he expected me to burst into tears at any moment.

"Thanks," I replied, trying to make myself sound bored. "I'll bear that in mind."

Luca approached us and held out a room card to Freddie, then turned to walk away.

"Hey, where's my room card?" I called after him.

He sighed, then looked between Freddie and I.

"They're fully booked. Its some special weekend or something, I wasn't listening. Anyway, all they have is the Presidential suite. I took it." He shrugged and went to walk away.

"Hold on for just one second here," I said slightly louder than I'd expected, as people around us turned to look at me.

"I'm not sharing a room with you two, never mind a fricking bed," I half whispered, trying to take the attention away from us.

Luca came back over to where I sat, stubbornly folding my arms over my still erect nipples and glaring daggers at him.

"You can take the bed. I'm sure we'll manage just fine with the sofa. Come on, it's on the third floor and apparently the views of the Caribbean Sea are *exquisite*." He rolled his eyes sarcastically. As if we were going to be spending our time looking at the bloody views.

I huffed out in annoyance, then stood and followed him, as a smiling concierge showed us to the room and frowned at our lack of luggage and dishevelled state.

When I walked through the door of the room, I stopped

dead in my tracks to take it all in. It was all pure white furniture, with polished wooden flooring and stone washed beams. It was stunning. I could see the private balcony off the main living area. It was huge and spanned the entire room, with heavy cream curtains hanging elegantly in front of the wooden doors that led outside. The lady at the desk was right, these views were something else. I'd never been in such an awesome hotel room before. It was more like an apartment than a room, and it was a million times better than any apartment I'd ever rented.

The guy who showed us to this 'room' mentioned something about a butler, and reeled off information about the Wi-Fi, VIP treatments and other things he thought we'd be making use of during our stay. I didn't listen. I don't think Luca or Freddie did either. Freddie was too busy looking around at the suite, showing his appreciation at the Bose equipment in the room and the Hermes products he'd found as he explored. Luca's eyes stayed fixed on me, trying to gauge how pissed off I still was.

Once we were alone, I made my way through the living area to the bedroom, where a king-sized bed, covered in a ridiculous amount of scatter cushions, was begging for me to dive onto it. The décor from the living area extended into the bedroom, with the same curtains framing the doors that led to another private balcony. For a hotel, it had a real homely feel. I felt Luca behind me at the door, his hot breath touching the skin on my neck and sending shivers down my back.

"You don't have to be alone, Chloe. Don't play the martyr," he whispered.

"I find it easier being alone. Less chance of disappointment," I replied and turned to face him.

He looked from my eyes to my lips then back again. I knew he wanted to kiss me, so I took control and pushed him back gently, then closed the door on him to shut him out.

I crawled into the bed, throwing the scatter cushions around the room carelessly, and within minutes I'd fallen into a deep sleep.

-

I woke with a blood curdling scream, sweat coating my whole body and plastering my hair to my head.

"What the fuck?" I gasped, as I recalled my nightmare. A sweaty, fat trafficker, with a strap-on knife ready to fuck me to death. I couldn't stop shaking.

"Chloe? Can I come in? Please." Freddie couldn't hide the pain in his voice.

"Yeah," I responded, pulling my hair off my face and neck and twisting it into a loose ponytail.

I pulled my knees up to rest under my chin, and held the covers over me for protection.

"You were screaming." Freddie looked tired, as he closed the bedroom door gently and walked over to sit on the edge of the bed. "Do you wanna talk about it?"

I shook my head, but my mouth was on a different wave length to the rest of my body.

"He was gonna hurt me," I blurted out. "He had so many knives and...other things. I was so scared, Freddie. I thought I was gonna die." I couldn't stop the tears from trickling down my cheeks and making the top of the bedcovers wet. Freddie moved further up the bed and gave me a big soft bear hug, the kind we'd always shared as kids.

I sniffed and hiccupped like a child, as I told him about the torture chamber I was chained up in. The blood soaked table, the different walls and the threats of sexual violence they held. All promised for me on this very night. I shook as I spoke and I desperately tried to reconcile myself to the fact that I was safe now. I wasn't going to wake up shackled to that wall again with men coming to *use* me.

"Did anyone...touch you?" He asked, his face going paler as I nodded yes.

"I'm not gonna get a doll out and show you where, Freddie. I'm sure you can already guess, without me spelling it out for you."

That's when I heard Luca curse a string of profanities and threats behind the door. He was listening. Freddie started to cry. He'd always been so in touch with his emotions, even more so than me.

"It's okay." I reached forward to hold his hand and offer him some comfort. "They didn't get any further than...touching...with their hands...and fingers."

I shivered, remembering their fat fingers pressing inside me. He must've picked up on my reaction, as his face turned red with anger.

"I wouldn't let them go further. I'd rather have died than give in to them like that." I tried my best to plaster on a smile. "I'm still as virtuous as I was before they took me." I joked, and heard what I guessed was a fist hit something hard outside the room.

"You promise? You would tell me if they had, wouldn't you?" Freddie looked me in the eyes to make sure I'd told him the truth.

"Yes. I would." I met his gaze with my own and he nodded.

"I know this is probably the last thing you're thinking about, but are you hungry? We were gonna order up some food. The restaurant here serves the best French food ever," he grinned.

"As long as there's French fries I'm in." I grinned back. "And maybe a burger? Thanks, Fred. That sounds good. I'm starving. I'll take a shower first though."

Freddie left the room to sort out some food, whilst I headed off to the bathroom in desperate need of a shower. When I entered the luxurious bathroom, I decided right away I had to have a bath instead. The huge tub, which was sunken into the floor, was right in front of the floor to ceiling windows, offering the most amazing sea views. It took ages to fill, but it looked so inviting, with the rose petals and various products left for our use tipped into it. I was going to enjoy this soak. I felt slightly sad that I'd be alone. There was room for company. But I wasn't in the mood to share really, not now.

I cleaned myself up, washed my hair, and bathed for what felt like an age. Then I started to drift off into a very dangerous sleep in the water, when a gentle knock sounded on the door.

"Are you okay in there, Chloe? Foods here."

I jolted awake. 'Shit, I could've drowned,' I thought, as I hauled myself up from the fragrant water and wrapped a huge, fluffy white towel around me. Once I'd dried off, I put my wet hair up in a messy bun, draped a white robe around me, and headed out into the living area.

"You look all cuddly and soft. Can I sit by you?" Freddie asked cautiously. Normally he wouldn't even ask, but I think after the events of the last few days, he wasn't quite sure where our relationship stood.

The tension radiating from Luca was palpable.

"Of course you can." I smiled at Freddie as he made himself comfortable next to me, pulling me into him, then handing me a plate of very fancy looking burger and fries.

Luca's phone started buzzing and he took the call, snarling down the phone at whoever had dared to interrupt him.

"His phone has been ringing off the hook all day," Freddie said, as Luca whispered and hissed down the phone in-between bites of food.

"When can I go home?" I asked Freddie.

He nodded over to a table, where I saw three passports, along with other official looking documents.

"Is that mine?"

"Yeah. We found it in the suitcase you'd packed before you were...taken."

I gulped down my mouthful of burger, my mouth suddenly going dry.

"I just want to go home." I looked down at my feet, and tried not to let the tears that were brimming in my eyes fall down my cheeks.

"It won't be long now." He gestured over to Luca, who had his back to us and was standing out on the balcony. "He needs to make sure all of the loose ends are tied up. No fingerprints or anything that could tie you or us to all of this. He's looking out for you, Chloe."

"It's a bit too late for that." I bit my lip as I instantly regretted saying it, but I couldn't take it back and Luca had heard me. He was standing in the doorway of the balcony looking worn out.

"I took every precaution I could to protect you, Chloe, but I'm not God. I can't see everything that's gonna happen. Not when you go against me and let strangers into our home."

I saw red. "What the fuck does that mean?" I stood up throwing the burger down on the plate and feeling my appetite disappear.

"One, Teresa wasn't a stranger. How was I to know she'd been compromised? Two, it's not *our* home, it's yours. I'm just the unpaid whore, remember?"

I stomped out of the living area, ignoring Luca and Freddie's calls for me to stop and listen. How dare he put this one on me. I never invited a trafficker into my life to sell me. I never wanted any of this to happen. All I'd done was take a job with the wrong person, to pay my way through medical school.

I slammed the bedroom door shut, then threw a scatter cushion at the door, wishing it was something heavier.

"Fuck you," I spat out through clenched teeth. "Tomorrow, I'm outta here."

Chapter Thirty Six

I jolted myself awake, a pool of sweat surrounded me, and the echo of my screams still rung in my ears. My body was shaking, and my mind racing with the last image I saw in my nightmare. A knife pressing into me, as chubby fingers closed over my mouth to muffle the screams. I felt a strong arm pull me into a warm, hard chest, and heard the hush in my ears as Luca held me close.

"It's okay, baby. You're safe now. I've got you." He soothed me with his deep rich velvet voice and rocked me against him.

I couldn't stop myself, even if I tried. I needed the comfort he was giving me. I needed to feel safe and loved. In his arms, it felt like home. I ran my arms around his back as he covered my face and neck in delicate kisses.

"I don't want to feel scared anymore. I want the nightmares to stop."

I wanted him to take them away, and he was making a pretty good start already.

"Let me help you, Chloe." He rolled me onto my back and loomed over me. "Let me love you."

He kissed my lips slowly at first, tender but apprehensive. I moved my hands up to cup the back of his neck and his head, then pulled him further into me. I didn't want sweet and slow. I wanted him to tear the memories from me and obliterate them. Destroy the touch of evil put upon me by those bastards and replace them with his own mark.

Sensing my urgency he thrust his tongue into my mouth, tasting me, showing me that he was in control now.

"I can take it away" he said, as he ran his tongue down the side of my neck. His hands roamed over my body, caressing my curves. "I can make you forget."

I nodded, then gasped as he yanked me down the bed and snaked his hand under my waist to pull me into him.

"I'm gonna make love to you baby. I'll make you remember who you belong to, and it's not them, it's me."

As turned on as I was, I couldn't stop myself from fighting him.

"I don't belong to anyone," I said, as I writhed underneath him, desperate to feel him inside me. I wanted it so bad.

"Yes, you do." He slid his thick, hard cock into me, making me gasp out loud and then groan in appreciation.

"You're mine and I'll never let you go."

He rocked into me with deep, delicious thrusts and then he lent down to my ear.

"I'll kill anyone who touches you. I'd die for you, Chloe."

I was falling over the edge so fast I couldn't focus anymore. My brain was drowning in lust.

"I love you, Chloe." He thrust harder into me, making my body move up the bed. I had to reach my hand up to stop my head banging on the wooden bed frame. He was hitting the spot perfectly.

"Please...please don't stop," I begged.

The force with which he took me made me scream out my first orgasm. My inner muscles clamped down hard on his cock and my body turned to jelly. I was so weak with ecstasy. Luca's body pinned me to the bed, his hips pistoning faster and making the bed bang against the wall with the strength he was using.

"Baby, you feel fucking amazing. I love...this...us...fuck. Chloe, I'm so close." His fingers dug hard into my hips. He worked himself up to climax, making me come a second time with the delicious friction he created.

Having him inside me felt so right, so perfect, it was just meant to be.

"It's too good," I cried, as my orgasm went on and on pulsing and throbbing, bringing Luca to his own release, as he grunted and shouted my name, and emptied his hot cum inside me.

"We were made for each other," he replied, as he lay down heavily on the bed, half over me and half on the mattress, panting and covered in our joint sweat.

He pulled me to him, as close as he could get me, and kissed my neck whispering his love for me. I closed my eyes and got lost in his smell, his warmth. I loved him. I truly did. But could I go back to being the little woman? I wanted Luca to take me as his equal. I wanted his men to see me in the same light. I'd always wanted to be his queen, not his little princess. As right as it felt being in his arms, my head was telling me it was wrong to just fall back into bad habits. I had won my freedom, I needed to win back my respect.

That's the reason I walked out of that hotel room two hours later. Alone, and with only my passport, enough money to get me home and the clothes on my back. I left behind the two most important men in my life, sleeping peacefully and blissfully unaware that I was leaving them.

Chapter Thirty Seven
LUCA

The minute I woke up I knew something wasn't right. My instincts were always spot on, whether the truth I discovered was something I wanted to know or not. It didn't take long for me to discover my instincts were right yet again. She wasn't lying next to me, or showering in the bathroom. I could still smell her scent on the sheets around me, on me, but she was nowhere to be seen.

Seconds later, Freddie burst through the bedroom door to tell me what I already knew.

"She's gone. Her passports missing and she took money from my wallet. Not all my money, but enough to see her out of here."

He rubbed his hand over his forehead. "What do we do? Do we go after her?"

"No. Let her go."

Freddie didn't looked pleased with my response. He always liked to play the knight in shining armour. Me, I had armour but it was dirty, banged up and well worn, and I needed it for other things right now.

I had a million and one things swirling around in my brain. Had the trafficking ring been shut down? Were all finger prints and DNA taken care of? How would we rehouse or reunite all the slaves we'd saved with their families? The list went on and on. If Chloe needed time to get her head together then so be it, but I didn't like it. I didn't like any of it. I'd travelled here to save her, protect her, but she didn't want it. That much was clear. After this morning, it was pretty obvious she didn't want me either.

I sat up and rested my back against the bed frame, trying to get my head around what I should do. What did she want me to do? I couldn't answer. Chloe had always been a head-fuck to me. I could never second guess her. I had no idea what she was thinking. She was a wildcard, a free spirit, a risk. I couldn't afford to take any more risks. Maybe it *was* time to take a step back.

Chapter Thirty Eight
CHLOE

I knocked on the door and got my best puppy dog eyes ready as the door flew open.

"Chloe! Oh my God, I'm so pleased to see you. I've been worried sick." Gina pulled me forward into a bear hug and squeezed me tight on her doorstep.

"Hey, Gina. I'm pleased to see you too. It hasn't been the best few days," I sighed, looking down at the floor.

She beckoned me in, taking my suitcase from my hand and rolling it into her living room.

"Coffee?"

"Yes please. The crap they serve on the plane doesn't deserve the label of coffee," I moaned but with a smile.

Gina's place was the opposite of Luca's, full of photos and plush fabrics to give it that homely feel. She lived alone, and ran her business from a building round the corner. Looking at the feminine décor of her place, you'd never have guessed what she did for a living.

We sat sipping coffee and catching up on the events of

the past few days. The normality made me feel more relaxed.

"Gina, can I ask a huge favour?"

"You need a place to stay, am I right? Listen, as long as it's okay with Luca, its fine with me. Stay here as long as you like. I'd enjoy the company." She smiled warmly at me.

I couldn't care less what Luca thought about my living arrangements. I didn't need to run anything by him. I decided on my future, not him.

"It's cool, and thanks, Gina. You're a good friend."

"Chloe, you need to tell me the name of that friend of yours who stitched you up. She needs reminding what a real friend does for her girl."

Gina folded her arms and waited.

"Forget it, Gina. It's not worth it."

"It is to me. I wanna know. Call it pay back for the rent I'm not gonna be charging you." She wasn't letting this one go any time soon.

"I'll pay rent. You don't have to put me up for free." I tried to reason with her, but it was no good.

"No way. You're a friend and I don't take rent from friends. Besides, it'll be fun to have a roomie for a bit. So...a name?"

"Fine." I relented. "Teresa Burman, and no, I don't know where she is now. Only that she left town with a nice pay check from Sanchez for ratting me out."

"Don't worry, Chloe. Karma has a way of making a bitch pay." She grinned and I shook my head.

"Whatever, as long as you don't get your hands dirty over it. Believe me, she's not worth it."

-

Staying with Gina turned out to be way more fun than I thought. She was so laid back and chilled, she made my shredded nerves disappear and my nightmares began to wane. We bonded over movie nights and wine, pizza and sharing our dirty little secrets. It felt good to have a female to confide in again, and one I knew I could trust whole-heartedly.

She told me, during one of our late night chats, that Luca had been messaging her to check up on me.

"He can't even find the balls to ask me himself," I responded, expecting her to agree with me, but to my surprise she jumped to his defence.

"He's giving you space, Chloe. He loves you, but it's not his way to come round here or crowd you. You know that already though."

I shrugged. "Maybe that's the reason I'm so mad at him."

"You're mad at *him*? Jeez Chloe, give the guy a break. I know he fucked-up with the way he talked about you that day, but don't you think after everything he's done since then, he deserves to be forgiven? What do you want? Blood?"

I couldn't answer that without sounding like a crazy female with weird standards, so I said what I felt in my heart.

"All my life I've chased that man. Put my heart on the line and had it broken more times than I care to remember.

I'm not doing it anymore, Gina. If he wants me, it's his turn to put himself out there. Me? I'm done. My chasing days are over." I sat back trying to look confident in my reasoning.

"Okay, Miss Independent. You could be waiting for a long time if I know Luca. Putting himself out there is the last thing he'd do. Hell, I don't think he's ever done anything remotely *risky* in that way in all the time I've known him. He's always so...so...guarded."

"Yep, he is. That's why he's gotta do it my way. I'm not the little woman. He wouldn't want me if I was. So...it's my way or the highway." I poured us both another glass of wine from our second bottle of the night.

"Chloe, you are an enigma, wrapped in a puzzle and coated in a riddle. Even I struggle to work you out and I'm a woman. Luca? He's got no chance." Gina sipped her wine as she frowned over at me.

"Gina, even I can't work me out most of the time."

I decided that finishing the second bottle was the most I could manage that night. Everything always looked better after the second bottle of wine. Life became less complicated. Me? I was as complicated as they come when it came to my feelings and the whole love thing. I blamed my Mum. She was a hard woman and never really wanted me. I was her bargaining chip, that's all. A threat to hang over my Father's head. I wasn't loved by her. She couldn't wait to get rid of me once my Father died. No, I'd spent enough of my life being used and now it was my turn to take back control.

Chapter Thirty Nine

I'd been back in the land of the living for a few weeks now, and things had fallen into a happy routine. Medical school had turned down my request to re-join my classes and play catch up. Instead, they'd deferred me for another year and told me to *'come back ready to take it more seriously.'* I felt pissed that they wouldn't budge, but then nothing worthwhile every came easy in life, I knew that. So I kept myself busy helping Gina with her accounts and keeping the business side of things ticking over for her. We made a good team. I'd no idea what Luca thought of me joining forces with Gina, but then I hadn't heard a thing from him or Freddie since I'd left them at the hotel in Colombia.

We'd started going out more too, partying at some local night clubs and bars. We'd invited Stacey from Luca's club along with us a few times, and she seemed really cool and chilled. She gave nothing away about her employer though, she really was loyal to the end. As well as Stacey, I'd been introduced to Gina's best friend, Tate, another red-head who was as ballsy as they come. She didn't take any crap from anyone. I liked our little foursome. On a night out we were formidable and we always had each other's backs. It was during one of these nights out that things changed dramatically for me, and I got the mother of all wake-up calls.

"Ladies, tequila shots then Mojitos!" Gina sang as she passed out the drinks to us at our tall table. "Don't forget lick, sip and suck!" She winked as she put a plate of limes in the middle of the table and passed round the salt.

We each licked the back of our hand and sprinkled the salt, licked it up and took the shot, followed by the suck of the lime. To be honest, I'd have been happy enough to knock the Tequila back in one go and forgo the extras, but Gina loved this ritual to start our evenings off. We did it every time without fail.

The club we were in tonight was on the other side of town, run by some guy called Jackson Caine. I'd never heard of him, but Tate and Gina assured me he was big news. A guy you wouldn't want to mess with, and his club was the best, apparently. So I danced on the spot as I sipped my mojito and glanced around the club at all the pretty people, feeling content with my life in that exact moment.

We were all dressed to kill in our barely there outfits and towering heels. I'd chosen a black corset dress with thin straps to keep the girls in check up front, and criss-crossed corset style bindings at the back. My hair tumbled in curls all down my back and over my shoulders. I felt sexy as hell.

A group of guys next to us started trying to chat us up. Their chat-up lines were so terrible we couldn't help but warm to them.

"Can you touch me just there on my arm?" The tallest blond guy said to me, as he squeezed himself in between Stacey and I. "I want to tell my friends over there that I've been touched by an angel."

The girls laughed and I rolled my eyes at him. "Is that the best you can do?"

I sipped my drink as his eyes sparkled at me. He called his friends over and then gave me the full impact of his chat.

"Oh I have a whole catalogue of lines for you, baby. If you were a transformer, you'd be Optimus Fine!"

That one had me laughing for real. This guy was a fun distraction. If I was in the market for a guy, he'd have stood a good chance, but I wasn't.

"Do any of those lines actually work out for you?" I frowned cheekily at him in the darkness of the club.

"I have a very good track record with my chat-up lines. By the way, is your name Wi-Fi? Because we seem to have a great connection." He wiggled his eyebrows and I groaned and turned to Stacey, to see if her guy was as cheesy as this dude.

It was as the blond guy leant down to whisper, "Do you believe in love at first sight or should I walk past again?" That I noticed a familiar face across the dancefloor.

My heart dropped to the floor and my body went rigid. Luca was dressed to perfection in dark jeans, a white shirt and a dark suit jacket, looking like sex on legs. His beautiful face was tanned, and a hint of stubble covered his square jaw. The sight of him made me go nervous and weak. He stood next to a man I'd never met before, who was also ripped and hot as hell, but he wasn't the companion I was focusing on. No, it was the leggy brunette hanging off Luca's arm that made me want to throw up and throw myself across the room to challenge them at the same time.

"Are you okay, Chloe?" Tate asked, seeing my face frozen in horror.

"Oh come on, my lines can't be that bad?" The blond dude said, but I just ignored him.

"What the actual fuck is that?" I managed to spit out, nodding my head and pointing in Luca's direction. He hadn't seen me yet. He was totally oblivious to our little group watching him.

"Oh shit," Gina said and looked down with a guilty expression on her face.

"Did you know he was coming tonight?" I asked her.

She shook her head no, but then reluctantly she told me what I hadn't wanted to hear.

"I knew he'd started dating again, but I didn't want to tell you."

I didn't know how to react. I felt like crying. I wanted to smash things, throw them round the room and have a childish tantrum. Most of all, I wanted to get away. But running away just wasn't my style.

"Chloe, he's just moving on. As far as he's concerned you don't want a relationship. I'm sorry, babe. I don't know what to say...to either of you. To be honest, Hun, I love you both, so I kinda want to stay out of it. I don't want to lose either of you as a friend."

My fury was bubbling up nicely beneath my calm exterior.

"You could've told me, Gina. I thought we were friends." I felt deceived, it wasn't a good feeling for me.

"I wanted to tell you, but he told me not to. Everyone did." She held her head down and I looked around at Stacey and Tate. Jesus, they knew too?

"This is fucking great!" I spat out. "Now you're all lying to me. I guess you can't trust anyone really, can you?"

I went to walk away, but Tate grabbed my arm, yanking me back into the group.

"We didn't lie to you, Chloe. We wanted to protect you from the truth." She didn't let my arm go, as if she was afraid if she did, I'd disappear forever.

"I'd rather you'd told me than I found out like this."

I pointed over to where Luca stood and as he turned, scanning across the club, his eyes met mine, and the look of horror that met my fury was palpable.

The brunette next to him ran her hands across his chest, then curled herself against him, holding him around his waist. I couldn't stand there and watch, so I did what I always do best. I downed my drink, slammed it on the table, grabbed the blond dude by the hand and headed for the dancefloor.

"Shits about to go off," Gina groaned behind me.

The erotic beat of the music pulsed through my body as I danced up against anyone and everyone on that dancefloor, letting the music take me away. I couldn't believe I'd been playing this game, the hard-to-get-so-fight-for-me game, and I was the only player. He'd folded ages ago. Cashed in his chips and moved onto another girl. I was so bloody self-assured it hadn't even occurred to me that that could've been a possibility. I needed to get over myself and him, fast.

"I guess my chat up lines aren't so bad after all." The blond guy wrapped an arm around my waist and pulled me closer to him.

"Dude, you have the worst chat I've ever heard, but your moves are good enough," I whispered back into his ear as we bumped and ground along to the beat.

My heart was still beating frantically in my chest and I was shaking, but I tried to clear my mind as best I could with the help of the music and the man with his arms around me. The wrong man.

"You know, I think I lost my teddy bear." His mouth was so close to my ear, I had to fight the urge to push him away.

"What the hell are you talking about now?" I closed my eyes to block the world out.

"I lost my teddy...so... can I take you to bed tonight instead?"

I hung my head down groaning, and was about to reply with some sarcastic comment, when a reply came on my behalf.

"Over my dead body."

Luca stood behind us with his arms folded and violence radiating off him. My face fell and I gritted my teeth in anger.

"I think you've already forfeited the right to have a say in who I choose as my bedtime companion," I spat out, turning my back on him.

"Like hell I did." He pulled the blond dude off me, faster than I could form a coherent response.

The blond guy didn't put up a fight. He was here for a fun time. He was a lover not a fighter. Well a one-night-stand kind of lover, but a lover all the same.

"What is your problem?" I pushed Luca in the chest with both of my hands, as blond dude started dancing up against a girl next to us. Luca just stood his ground and glared at me. "Go back to your girlfriend and leave me alone."

"She isn't my girlfriend," he replied through gritted teeth.

"Go back to your fuck buddy then or whatever she is...the new dirty little fuck, I guess?"

He yanked me closer to him and breathed hot, lusty breaths down my neck.

"Trust me, if I could walk away I would, but a little bird

told me we need to talk."

"A little bird called Gina?" I shook my head and bit my lip. "Forget it. I have nothing to say to you. Just go."

He grabbed my arm more forcefully then, and dragged me off the dancefloor and towards a door marked private, pushing it with so much power it ricocheted off the wall as it burst open. Then he released me as he stood to block the doorway.

We stared each other down as we stood in the dark corridor, the vibrations of the music and our heavy breaths the only sounds that could be heard.

"Why do you have to be so fucking...difficult? I don't know what you want me to do." He ran his hands through his hair and then leant against the wall, both palms flat against the plaster as he hung his head down.

"You're an asshole." Was all I could come up with, I didn't know what to say. I was numb, hurt, confused and just so, so tired of always fighting.

"Tell me something I don't know." He turned his head to look at me.

"How long have you been seeing her?"

He looked back down at the floor, as if he was too ashamed to meet my gaze.

"We've only been on a few dates."

"I hate you," I seethed, fighting down the urge to hit things.

"I don't like myself much at the moment either, but hey

what's new?" He pinned me with his dark brooding stare.

"Do you love her?" I swallowed the lump in my throat. I didn't know if I wanted to hear the reply.

He pushed away from the wall and took a deep breath, looking up to the ceiling. Not a good sign in my book.

"What do you think?"

"I don't know, that's why I'm asking you." It really was none of my business, but I had to know.

"No!" He lurched forward, making me stumble and step back against the wall. "I love you, God damn it, but you don't want me. You hate me, right?"

He put both hands on the wall next to my head, pinning me into place.

"You. Don't. Want. Me." He said it like it was a fact, then he softened slightly. "Do you? Do you want me?" This time it was a question.

My whole world, my whole life rested on this answer, this moment. I took a breath in and jumped blindly down the rabbit's hole.

"Yes." I looked at the ground as I opened my heart ready to have it crushed yet again. "Yes, I want you. I'll always want you."

A tear rolled down my left cheek, despite my best efforts at keeping a lid on my emotions.

"You're mine. I don't want you with anyone else. It hurts to see you with someone else."

He took a deep breath, then bent down slightly to meet

my gaze.

"I love you, Chloe. I always will. I want you, no one else."
He cupped my face with both of his hands and used his thumb
to wipe the tear away.

"But you're with her now," I whispered on a sob.

"No, I'm not. I'm here, right now with you...where I
belong. Where we both belong." He leant down and kissed me
softly, and I burst into tears as he pulled me into his chest and
hugged me close. I felt my heart bleed and my tears began to
soak through his shirt as I let it all go. I didn't want to fight
him or my own feelings anymore. I was done with the
bullshit. I just wanted my happily ever after.

"We're so fucked up, so broken." I didn't know if we
could ever get it back.

"No, we're not. We're us, Chloe. This is us. Maybe to
other people we seem broken or fucked-up. But to me? We're
perfect. You're perfect, and I want to be able to love you. To
show you what you mean to me, not just say it. Always. We're
not broken, Chloe. We just need to find our way back to each
other again."

I nodded, warmth seeping into my thawing heart.

"Come on, angel. Let me take you home, please? We
need to make friends."

He gave me a crooked smile and I smiled back up at him.

"What about your other friend?"

"I already told her I was leaving with you."

"That confident, huh?"

"No. I just didn't want to leave with her. I was hopeful that I could get you to leave with me, but whatever happened, I wasn't taking her anywhere tonight."

I had one last thing I needed to know.

"Did you? Did you and her... you know?" I couldn't bring myself to say the words.

"No, Chloe. I haven't had sex with anyone but you since the day you walked into my office in that sexy, black underwear, with the little red roses and fuck-me heels."

"You remember what I wore?"

"Like I could forget that outfit?" he sighed. "I remember everything about you. It's all burned into my brain...for those times when all I have are my memories."

"Hmmm, sounds hot," I hummed, as he ran his lips over my neck and along my shoulder.

"Oh it is," he growled.

"Take me home," I begged.

"Gladly."

Chapter Forty

The drive over to Luca's was the most sexually charged journey I'd ever taken. He was gripping my thigh or holding my hand the whole time. I had thought going back to the place where I was stolen from would be traumatic, but I didn't give it a second thought as I willed the car to go faster.

Once we pulled up to the gate, I could tell instantly that security had been bumped up. There were more cameras, different systems in place, and the butterflies I felt had nothing to do with my safety. I was more interested in the dark-haired Adonis that sat next to me.

He pulled into his parking space and turned the engine off, then reached over to caress my face and kiss me slowly and tenderly. When he pulled back I could see raw desperation in his eyes.

"I need you to give me what's mine," he said in that husky low voice of his. "I need *you*. Every soft, beautiful inch of you."

"You know I crave your touch," I replied, meeting his hot

gaze with my own.

"I know what you've been craving, and I'm the only one who can give it to you."

We got out of the car and he walked us to the house. Once inside he picked me up and I wrapped my legs around his waist as he carried us to his bedroom.

"We could cut the waiting time and make friends down here." I grinned.

He shook his head. "I want to savour every inch of your body, your curves and taste. The softness of your skin, the curls in your hair. All of it. I want it, it's mine. There's no way I'm rushing anything tonight."

He pushed his way through the bedroom door, kissing my lips with an urgency we both felt. Then he threw me down onto the bed and ripped his jacket off and his shirt over his head. I sat up and licked my lips, pulling on his belt to release the buckle and then popping each one of the buttons on his jeans. I dipped my fingertips into the waistband and pulled them over his ass and his muscly thighs. His cock sprang loose, begging to be sucked. I ran my tongue over the tip and down his length as I held him tight. He gave a low moan, and his lingering eyes held promises of the heavenly places he would touch and take me to very soon.

"Fuck, Chloe. That mouth of yours....your tongue. I fucking love it. I love you."

He sighed and moaned as I sucked him, licking the tip and palming his cock, then taking him in my throat as deep as I could. His balls brushed against my chin as I ran my nails across them and then behind; his exquisite musky scent swirling around me. I pulled back and licked his balls, sucking gently and making him whimper and moan. I loved teasing him this way.

He ran his fingers through my hair and stroked my face whilst I tasted him, swirling my tongue along and around him. Then he pulled back and kneeled on the bed, pushing me back. His hands roamed over my legs, up my thighs and under the fabric of my dress to palm my ass. He pushed my dress over my hips and squeezed my ass hard, then rubbed and squeezed again.

"This ass," he growled. Then he rolled me over and bit my ass cheek, sucking the skin into his mouth. "This ass drives me crazy."

He pulled at my hips, forcing me onto all fours on the bed and ran the palm of his hand over my lower back. Then he stroked down my ass, his fingers tracing along the seam of my knickers, feeling the wetness within. I was so ready for him. I couldn't hide it. It was clear from my panting, breathy moans that his touches set me on fire. His hands made me wriggle and groan. My pussy was pulsing, wet and sensitive as hell, all because of him.

"I swear to God, you annihilate my senses. I'm addicted to you, Chloe."

He pulled me upright against his chest and yanked my dress over my head, flinging it across the room. Then his hands were on my breasts, caressing, squeezing, hard then soft, gentle then rough. I loved how he could work me up so well, make me want him more than ever each time he had me like this. I was totally at his disposal. I always wanted control in my life, but when I was with Luca, I could submit to him so easily. I wanted to. He made me come undone and I loved it.

"I'm a mess," I sighed. "I'm totally lost in you, Luca."

"Good."

He nipped on my earlobe, then unhooked my bra and slipped my panties down my leg.

"I want you so turned on, so lost in me, you forget your own name because you're too busy screaming out mine."

He spun me round roughly and I fell back onto the bed. I was facing him now and he stood over my body like some kind of sexual conqueror. His magnificent cock still glistening from where I'd sucked him hard. His eyes bored into mine, twinkling with all the dirty little thoughts going on in his head of what he was going to do to me now he had me here.

His fingers glided tantalisingly slowly down my skin, over my belly and between my legs to feel my swollen clit, just begging to be rubbed, for that pressure he always used on me so fucking well. He pushed a finger into me and stroked me with delicious, long strokes across my most sensitive spot. I was tremoring and pulsating as he brought me so close, I couldn't take any more. All the time his eyes, those dark, lingering, seductive eyes never left mine. I was so desperate for release I moaned out.

"Please, Luca."

I needed him to give it to me. He pulled his finger out slowly and put it into his mouth, groaning as if it was the sweetest thing he'd ever tasted.

"I need you," I begged.

He grabbed both of my legs to balance them over his shoulders. Then he pushed hard into me. No warning, just straight into it, making me cry out with the exquisite stretch I felt as his cock entered me.

"I want to drown in you. I can't get close enough, deep enough," he grunted as he pounded hard into me.

His eyes held mine as he used long, hard strokes, then thrusts into me, making me cry out in ecstasy each time, our hips smashing hard against each other. The animalistic way he was taking me only turned me on more. I wanted this base, raw fucking. I needed it to feel that connection with him. We'd been apart too long, we were too desperate for each other. Nothing but this would satisfy us. We were both on fire, burning for each other and loving the heat. This was what I loved about us. He loved me. I knew he did. And I felt ready to submit to him totally. To give my all in such a debased way and not feel dirty or used. It was fucking delicious.

The first orgasm tore out of me so fast I screamed out, and bucked my hips up into his. When I felt the pulsing for the second and third time it was more intense, and made my eyes roll into the back of my head. All I could focus on was chasing that fall. That burst of fireworks that sent my pussy into overload, and had me contracting and squeezing his cock in appreciation. I didn't have to wait long. My head rested against his forearm as he thrust deeper and deeper, making me feel like I was on another plain, halfway between this world and the next.

"You...fucking...own me," he growled, as his cock started to swell and throb inside. "So good," he cried, and then he was coming too. His hot seed coating me inside and trickling down my ass and thighs as he lost control completely.

His whole body fell over mine as he panted and finished with erratic, hard thrusts, forcing out his release. Then he kissed my neck and my shoulder, as we both came down from the high he'd just taken us to. I ran my fingers up and down his back. Our sweat-soaked bodies entwined between the sheets and each other. This, right here, was what I wanted. Forever.

We lay blissfully tangled together for a few minutes before either one of us could speak. Luca was the one to break the silence.

"I've always wanted you, always fantasised about you, Chloe. I did most days when we were growing up. I couldn't stop it. Back then I hated all the things that stood in my way and stopped me from being with you. All the obstacles from other people, and myself. But you know? After the journey we've both been on, the way we've fought to find our way back to each other? It makes me realise that you and I were always meant to be. No one and nothing could've ever kept us apart.

You're my forever, Chloe. You always will be. I'll love you till the day I die."

He stroked my hair as he planted a delicate kiss on my lips. I couldn't hold back my tears and buried my face in his neck.

"Nothing feels right when I'm not with you," I replied. "It's like I'm only half of who I'm meant to be. But with you, being with you like this makes me feel whole. You make me feel complete."

I could feel him smiling, feel his lips curl as he ran them over my shoulders and into my neck.

"This is gonna sound so cheesy, but I'm gonna say it anyway, because it's how I feel." He held my chin and turned me to look at him. "Freddie might've showed you the stars, but I'll give it all to you. The sun, the moon and every fucking star to make you happy."

"That's not cheesy, I love it." I reached up to plant a kiss on his nose as he chuckled at me. "I love that you love me with all that you are. You don't need to say it, Luca, I can feel it."

We spent the rest of the night drifting from satisfied, sated sleep, to making friends in so many different ways, positions and degrees of intensity that I felt like I'd never want to leave his bed ever again. Finally, I'd found my forever home.

Chapter Forty One
LUCA

I couldn't really pinpoint the exact time when my feelings for Chloe changed from that of an over-protective surrogate brother, to something more. It was so gradual over time. What I could recall though, was the moment I realised exactly how hard I'd fallen. She was fifteen and I was weeks away from my nineteenth birthday. So as we lay together, content in our future, I reminded her of our past, and the day I knew I was in love with Chloe Ellis, the girl next door.

Seven years ago…

I could see Stan's car in the driveway, but no one had answered the door when I'd knocked. I went down the side of the house and tried the door to the backyard, and found that it was unlocked. When I walked through, I froze at the scene that was playing out in front of me. Chloe was sunbathing, lying back on a sun lounger, with her brown curls falling wildly all over her shoulders. She wore a yellow string bikini that barely covered her body and she was looking up, smiling at some blond dude with his shirt off, who was wearing some crazy patterned shorts.

"Who the fuck are you?"

I couldn't hide the fact that I was seriously pissed from my tone of voice. Who did this guy think he was, standing over her like that? His eyes roaming leisurely all over her body. I was a guy and I knew exactly what was going through his dirty mind. I felt murderous at the thought of it.

"Luca, this is Danny. It's okay, he's not some crazy psycho killer. We're in the same class at school."

I didn't take my eyes off him for a second as I spoke.

"What's he doing back here with you? Does your Dad know he's here?"

I was hoping to play the father card, and get this dude running scared at the prospect of Stan doing a job for me and whooping his ass.

"Dad's paying him to mow the lawn." She sounded all flirty and it set my teeth on edge.

"Yeah, paying him to mow the lawn, not stand around ogling you," I snapped, then inwardly cursed myself for showing a hint of jealousy. Why was I feeling so jealous? He was closer to her age than I was. I was jealous though. So jealous it hurt.

"Chill out, Luca. Dad's popped out to get some stuff to fix his car. He won't be back for an hour at least. That's *plenty of time to get the grass cut."*

Danny the douche bag sat down in a chair next to Chloe and started talking in whispers so I couldn't hear. She giggled back at him and I suddenly felt like the outsider. I didn't like it.

Chloe rolled over onto her front, her pert little ass wiggling as she got comfortable. I watched him rake his eyes down her back, salivating over her ass and legs. Then she committed a cardinal sin and reached back to unhook the top of her bikini, leaving her back totally bare. He sucked in a breath through his teeth as I scowled over at him in warning.

"Can you do my back? I can't reach." She held a bottle of sun tan lotion out to him and I sprang into action.

"No you don't, pretty boy. You're being paid to cut grass, so get to it."

I grabbed the bottle out of her hand as she turned her head to look at me. She was a little minx. She knew exactly what she was doing. Douche bag scowled at me, then slopped off and started running the mower over the far corner of the yard. I held the bottle at arm's length out towards Chloe.

"Can't you put it on yourself?" I moaned.

It wasn't that I didn't want to put it on, or touch her. More that I couldn't trust myself to do it without making a complete fool of myself.

"No, Luca I can't. You don't want me to burn do you?"

She gave me those damn puppy dog eyes and I huffed and sat on the edge of the sun lounger, groaning as if touching her was the worst thing I'd ever been asked to do. Damn, I'd been hard the minute I'd seen her lying there. This was going to be pure torture for me.

I poured the white lotion into my hand, as she moved her curls to the side and grinned like a fucking Cheshire cat. Then I started at her shoulders, running the lotion over her soft, smooth, creamy skin, and desperately trying to hide my arousal, which would be obvious to anyone if I stood up. I ran my hands down her back and along her sides. She felt so warm, like velvet under my fingertips. When I got to her lower back, I had to take a breath in when I saw the little ties that were either side of her bikini bottoms. Images of me pulling on those ties, and seeing her pert little ass raised in the air and ready for me, drove me insane. I had to get away from her, before I did something I regretted.

"Is that enough?" I tried to sound as bored and unaffected as I could. She had her eyes closed and looked totally relaxed, like I'd just given her the best massage ever.

"I suppose," she sighed.

I threw the bottle onto the grass and stood with my back to them both, then stalked over to the gate. I couldn't turn around, I was so full of lust for her. So I shouted over my shoulder. "Tell your Dad I called round...and get the grass done before he's back, or we'll both kick your ass."

I went straight home and sprinted up the stairs,

heading to the shower. I needed to jerk off so badly, and thinking about that damn yellow bikini with its tempting ties and her bare naked back made me come hard and fast after a few tugs. What the hell was I thinking? Chloe was driving me nuts, and the thought of that guy back there even looking at her made me so angry. I punched the tiles and cursed myself for being so fucked-up. She wasn't his to stare at and fantasise over. She was mine. I wanted her. I dreamt about her. God I fucking loved her, but I couldn't tell her. I couldn't tell anyone. They'd cart me off to jail if they knew what went through my head on a daily basis about that girl. My girl. The girl next door. My Chloe.

"I thought you hated me that day," she said, her eyes as wide as saucers after my little confession.

"Are you kidding? I was so hot for you, but I couldn't tell anyone, least of all you. I thought I'd get arrested if I acted on my feelings. But that day, I realised I loved you so badly. I wanted you for myself. The thought of that guy even being near you made me wild with jealousy."

She smiled to herself and looked up at me through her sexy long lashes.

"I didn't even like Danny, he was an idiot. He'd called round earlier that day to ask my Dad if he could mow our lawn for a few bucks. He was saving up to buy his first car he said, and you know what a sucker my Dad was for boys and their cars. I saw you knocking on the front door later that day, so I went out back to carry on sunbathing. When Danny had started mowing, I'd gone inside to hide from him. But I knew you'd try the side gate and I wanted to make you jealous. Sorry."

I smacked her ass, then licked my way along her neck to whisper in her ear.

"You've always been a little tease. I wouldn't have you any other way."

I nibbled her ear, making her moan and bend her head to the side to give me better access. Then I rolled her onto her front and pulled her hips back, so her ass was up and ready for me.

"Do you still have that yellow bikini? Because I'd really love to undo those ties at the side and fuck you on the sun beds outside."

She giggled again and wiggled her ass at me.

"I'm sure I can sort something out," she teased back, as I sunk deep into her from behind and smacked her ass at the same time.

"Damn right you will."

-

We spent the day fucking, laughing, and fucking some more. It was what we both needed to put the past behind us. We both craved that connection with each other. After a while, I told her about my father, then I opened up for the first time ever and told her what'd really happened to my Mother. She held me, listened and understood why I'd always found it difficult to trust others, especially women. But I trusted her with my life, and she knew now, without a doubt, that she was my everything.

She asked me why I'd never told Freddie about that night, and I explained that I'd wanted him to keep his hope alive. To believe that like us, she too had escaped to find freedom. She nodded. She might not have agreed, but she understood.

Chloe told me what her father had already alluded to, and shared memories of her Mother's manipulation and emotional abuse. She felt like it'd contributed to her need to be loved, but I reminded her that she'd grown up with at least one loving parent who would've never let her down.

"He knew you know."

She frowned up at me. "Knew what?"

"He knew I was in love with you. He knew you loved me too. He told me once, when we were working together on his car."

She bit her lip and asked, "What did he say about it?"

"He told me to take care of you. Not to hurt you. I gave him my word I would." I rubbed my nose against hers. "And I intend to keep my promise."

Chapter Forty Two
CHLOE

I woke up feeling on top of the world. Everything was right, and I couldn't wipe the smile off my face. I could hear the shower running, so I pushed the covers off and headed into the bathroom to see Luca, standing under the water looking totally fuckable and gorgeous. The rivers of water were trickling over his muscles. I wanted to trace their path with my tongue.

"Morning, beautiful girl." He smiled at me and I melted.

"Why didn't you wake me? I like showering with you." I tried to show him an angry expression but failed miserably.

"You looked so peaceful sleeping. I didn't want to disturb you."

"Always disturb me." I chastised him, then snaked my arms around his waist as I squeezed round to his front to hold him.

Within less than a minute he had me balanced in his arms and pressed against the wet tiles as he pounded into me hard and fast, both of his hands positioned under my ass. My legs were wound tightly around his hips, my arms around his neck, as I lifted and brushed against him to get the friction and pressure I needed. The grunting sounds we were making were such a turn on, it wasn't long before we were both screaming out our release.

When we were both panting out with the exertion, he put his forehead against mine.

"I want to shower with you every day."

"Me too."

Reluctantly, I let him pull out of me and we soaped each other as we kissed and stroked our way through the rest of the shower.

"Shower time is my new favourite part of the day," I laughed.

"I think we need to shower a few times a day. We do get very, *very* dirty."

"You really think you could bring it like that every time?" I joked. "Then damn, I'm in."

He slapped my ass and shoved me out of the shower, then wrapped me in a huge fluffy towel and kissed my forehead.

"I think I need to up my workouts to keep up with your demands." He winked then rubbed me dry before drying himself and walking me to the closet.

We both dressed, me in one of his dress shirts and him in a suit ready for work. Then we headed downstairs for something to eat. His hand never left mine, and as we walked through the kitchen door, we saw Freddie sat at the table wearing the biggest shit-eating grin.

"Don't you have any food at your own place?" Luca scowled at him.

"Yeah, but I prefer eating with you guys. Chloe, I love seeing you here again. Everything is as it should be."

I was expecting Luca to say something sarcastic or give a moody grunt, but he didn't. He squeezed my hand and smiled a panty-melting smile at me.

"It is as it should be." I smiled back and reached up on my tip toes to kiss him.

Luca handed me my favourite caramel latte and leaned back against the kitchen counter as he sipped his strong black coffee.

"I hate leaving you, but I have to go into work today."

"It's okay. You don't need to watch me all day, I'll be fine."

I knew he was being overly protective of me after the whole Sanchez incident. I hadn't been alone in his house since that day. To be honest, I wasn't sure how I felt about being alone, but I needn't have worried.

"I've got a few men staying behind to check the house. They won't get in your way. They've been told to stay outside unless it's absolutely necessary for them to come in. I've also texted Gina to come over and visit. Not to babysit you just to...you know, keep you company."

He looked nervous, like I was about to go off and pull my

usual independent crap. But I held back, because I knew this meant a lot to him, to have me comfortable in his home.

"That's sweet and I'd love to have lunch and a girlie day with Gina. I promise I'll stay here and behave."

He shook his head in amusement.

"You never behave, but I'm used to it."

-

When Luca and Freddie left, I couldn't deny that my nerves became slightly frayed. I looked around and told myself over and over again that I was safe. There was a new security system in place, more cameras, and a few panic buttons that'd been placed strategically around the house for my piece of mind. Luca couldn't have done anymore to put me at ease. I walked to the backdoor to check the locks and squealed when I saw a darkly dressed shadow.

"Sorry, Miss Ellis. I'm just checking the yard. I didn't mean to scare you," a deep voice said, as one of Luca's men bowed at me and moved away from the house.

"That's okay," I shouted through the glass of the door, and made my way to the living area to get lost in a Netflix box set.

It didn't take long for Gina to come over and join me. We spent the rest of the day eating junk food and getting lost in our TV marathon. Before we knew it the sun had set and it was time for Gina to head off to work and me to do....well, what was I going to do? Maybe check in with Luca and see when he'd be home, but I felt kinda useless. I needed to get a job, or keep doing the books for Gina at the very least. I had to do something productive or I'd go insane.

I waved Gina off and picked up my phone to call Luca. He answered on the second ring.

"Angel, are you okay?"

"Yeah, I'm just bored. I think I need a job."

"You can always help me here if you like?" he offered, but I felt like I needed something else that was just mine, something outside of his world.

"Hmm, I'll think about it. Are you working late?"

"No. I'll be home in an hour or two, okay. Do you want me to pick up something to eat on my way home?"

We really were heading towards domesticated bliss. Who'd have thought it?

"Chinese sounds good."

I smiled at the thought of him coming home and feeding me, and how much I wanted to curl up next to him and feel all warm and fuzzy inside.

"Okay, I'll get your favourite," he said, then in a slightly lower tone he added. "I love you."

The warm and fuzzy came earlier than I thought.

"I love you too."

-

I warmed the plates ready, then created a comfy nest on the sofa and made a start on a bottle of Chablis that was chilling in the wine fridge. One glass turned into two, then three. By the end of the bottle I was starting to get antsy. It'd been over three hours since I'd spoken to Luca, and he still wasn't home. Oh well, maybe things had got busy and he'd been held up at the club. I didn't give it a second thought and settled back into the mountain of cushions.

—

I woke up on a jolt in complete darkness on the sofa. The blue light of the clock on the TV told me it was 4:21am, but the house felt eerily empty. I ran upstairs to double check and then outside, but the car Luca had used this morning wasn't there and he was nowhere to be seen. I checked the phones, but no missed calls or messages, something definitely felt off.

I pressed Luca's number on my speed dial, but it went straight to voicemail; it'd been switched off. I tried Freddie's next and he answered my call straight away.

"Hey, sis. What's up? Can't sleep?"

I could hear music and voices behind him and it sounded like he was still at the club or some club anyway.

"Is Luca with you?" I snapped, cutting through the polite chit-chat to get to the point.

"Big bro headed home hours ago. Is everything okay?"

I could hear him start panting as he moved away from the noise to somewhere quieter to talk. My anxiety was growing by the second, my nerves slowly fraying as he huffed and puffed his way to a less busy area.

"Freddie, he hasn't come home yet."

I closed my eyes and prayed that he'd remember some last minute urgent appointment Luca had that he'd forgot to tell me about, or he'd spot Luca across the bar. The line went quiet and I could hear men's voices, then Freddie came back on.

"Marco's going to check the car park to see if his car is still here."

"Great. Can you ring me back, Freddie? I'm starting to freak out here."

That was an understatement. I'd bypassed freak out and was heading into full meltdown territory.

"Sure. It'll be okay, Chloe. I think Luca is big enough and ugly enough to take care of himself. He's probably bumped into an old friend and lost track of time. I'll call you back in a few minutes."

With that Freddie hung up and my stomach went into knots of barbed wire. Luca didn't do chats with old friends. He never wasted a minute of his time on anything unless he really had to. No, this was all wrong and I started to pace the living area, holding my tummy to stop the nausea bubbling up inside me like an active volcano about to erupt.

I decided to try Gina and see if she knew where he might've gone to. Three minutes later I was putting the phone down feeling even more clueless and extremely nervous. She had no idea either, and agreed it was totally out of character for him to be missing for so long.

The minute I hung up on Gina, the lights on my phone flashed Freddie's name and I pressed accept.

"Chloe, his car is still here. We're gonna check the CCTV

to see if we can find out what's going on."

"Bring the CCTV here. I want to see it."

I wasn't being left in the dark over anything. If something was going down, I wanted to know every detail.

"It'll take us another twenty minutes to get to you. We need to get on top of this now."

"I don't care how long it takes. You'll bring it here or I'll come there. Okay?"

"Fine, see you in fifteen." Freddie hung up and I headed into Luca's office to fire up his computer and pour myself a whisky to settle my nerves. Now was not the time to let my meltdown mode take over. I needed to stay focused and get to the bottom of this. I needed to get Luca home. I tried ringing Luca's phone repeatedly whilst I waited for Freddie, but every time it clicked straight onto his damn voicemail.

Minutes later, Freddie and a group of Luca's men strode purposely into his office and gathered around the desk where I sat anxiously waiting, biting my nails and twisting my hair around my fingers.

"Have you seen it yet? The footage?" I asked, looking between all the men in front of me.

"No. Let's get it all fired up," Marco said, reaching over me to set it all up.

We sat and watched the black and white footage and saw Luca leave the club and head towards his car. Then we saw a blacked-out SUV speeding out of the car park moments later, but the camera that would've given us the information we needed, to tell us exactly what happened between the moment Luca walked through that exit and the van speeding off, was out of action. It didn't take a genius to know that Luca was inside that SUV when it left the car park.

"How long has that camera been down?" I turned to Marco for the answer. He didn't do bullshit and I needed quick answers.

"It hasn't. It was working fine when we did security checks earlier in the evening."

"So someone broke it. They didn't want us to see what happened." I could see where all of this was heading and I didn't like it one little bit.

"Who would want to cause trouble like this?" I asked, my mouth was going dry and my body was on automatic pilot.

"Who wouldn't want to cause trouble, would be an easier question to answer," Leo replied, then thought better of his response, judging from the redness creeping up his neck into his face.

"Well don't just stand around here with your dicks in your hands, get back out there and get answers for me. I need to know where he is and what we're up against. I need to decide what we do next." I glared at each and every one of them, so they'd know how deadly serious I was.

"Sure thing, boss," Vinnie said and patted Marco on the back as they turned to the others and started to agree on a plan of action.

My phone started to vibrate across the desk, announcing an incoming call from Gina.

"Hey," I answered with a raw throat and feeling ready to burst into tears, but desperately fighting it down in front of my all male audience.

"Chloe, one of my girls said she had a punter in earlier. Some South American or Mexican dude, she wasn't sure. Anyway, he got kinda chatty and mentioned something about a boss of his being in town to tie up some loose ends. She made pointless chat with him, as we do, and he mentioned a long standing business deal that'd been fucked-up by a local down here. He said they were in town to 'put it to bed'. She didn't mention it before because she just thought it was some guy sprouting pointless shit, but it sounds fishy to me. I think this guy could be linked to Luca going missing."

"Can we speak to her? Will she talk to me or Freddie?" I looked over to Freddie to let him know he needed to stay with me and he nodded in acknowledgement.

"Yeah, I don't see why not, but I'll bring her over to you. I don't want more people than is really necessary being involved in all of this if that's okay. My girls are easily spooked."

"Of course. Head over now."

Gina agreed and I hung up the phone. Luca's men headed off to do their thing and Freddie stayed behind with me. Being alone with Freddie, I could let my walls down.

"Why is this happening, Fred? Why me? Why us?"

He shrugged and gave me a sympathetic smile.

"I don't know, Chloe. It doesn't seem fair."

"It's not, it's so unfair. We've only just found our way back to each other and now someone's stepped right back in to fuck things up for us yet again. I can't lose him, Freddie." The tears silently rolled down my cheeks as I spoke. "I can't let this be the end. We deserved more than this. I swear to God, I'm not letting this be the way it ends for us."

"It won't," he said, but he knew as well as I did what Luca's world was like. I'd only had a small taste of it and it was brutal, nasty, violent and unforgiving. You got your name on someone's shit list and it didn't end well for you. These guys didn't carry guns because it made them look good. It was a necessity, part of the job.

"Let's try and get a better hold on things, find out what the score is before we jump to conclusions. For all we know, it's just someone trying to scare Luca, scare us all."

"You don't believe that any more than I do," I sighed, but neither one of us had the energy to think about the alternatives. We had to focus on formulating a plan of action. Anything to keep our minds from wandering to all the other more realistic alternative outcomes to what'd happened to Luca tonight.

Chapter Forty Three

Gina's girl couldn't tell us much more than we already knew. Some guy, who couldn't keep his mouth shut, had bragged about being in town to sort someone out for fucking up a long standing business deal. The only useful information she added was that he had a tattoo of a snake on his left hand. Not a cobra, but a gunmetal grey snake with an inky black mouth. She thought nothing of the dull colours, until she saw his chest was an array of bright, colourful tattoos. Then she realised it was odd that the one on his hand was so dark.

I heard Freddie take a deep breath, but before he could convey his reaction to this information his phone lit up with an incoming call.

"Yep, give it to me," he shot down the line as he listened intently and nodded. "I already know. It's the black mambas...I know, but we should've seen this coming. We were naïve to think the buck stopped with Sanchez."

I gasped at the name. What the hell was going on? And who was black mamba?

Freddie gave a few more orders, then threw his phone down onto the desk and looked over at me.

"What's going on, Fred? And don't sugar coat this shit. How is Sanchez linked to this? And who the hell is black mamba?"

"Not who, Chloe, what."

"Don't talk in fucking riddles, Freddie, just tell me."

He sank down onto the leather sofa in the corner of Luca's office and ran his hands over his face, before leaning forward to speak.

"The black mambas are an organisation you don't want to mess with. They're involved in all sorts of organised crime, drugs, money laundering, *trafficking*." He gave me a knowing look as he said the last part. "They took the name black mambas, because like the black mamba snake, they're highly aggressive, deadly in fact. They move fast, strike with speed and precision. They can move faster than most humans. They're toxic, Chloe, and if they're the ones we're chasing, we've got our work cut out for us. I don't even know where they operate from or who their top guy is. All I do know is, they always work in pairs or groups. Like the snake, they attack their prey, then stand back and watch it die, before they slither back to devour it whole. And when I say devour, I mean dump the body somewhere public for the family to find. The last guy who fucked with the black mambas ended up being returned to his wife, a body part a day."

I couldn't comprehend that level of depravity. That

extent of violence was something I wanted to block out completely, pretend it didn't exist. But it seemed life had other plans for us.

"If it is them, we all need to watch our backs. When a black mamba strikes, it strikes repeatedly. We could lose a few more men before this is over."

"No." I shook my head. "If it is them, then we need to find their weakness. Even snakes have a soft underbelly. We can beat them at their own game." I'd no idea what I was saying, but I wasn't about to give up hope. Defeat wasn't in my vocabulary, especially when it came to Luca.

"We'd be the first ones to ever succeed," he replied grimly.

"Women," Gina piped up.

"Come again?" Freddie looked up frowning.

"Women. That's their weakness. I bet if I went back and questioned my other girls, I'd find out a few more men with snake tattoos on their left hands had been on my premises these past few days. Then there's the local clubs. Maybe not Luca's, but if we asked around, we could find out where they've been hanging out."

"They do tend to stick together." Freddie nodded to himself. "Where one black mamba is, there's always at least one more close-by."

"So that's what we do then. We get out there and find their hunting ground."

"Then what, Chloe? We go in guns blazing and shoot at

each other until we're all dead?"

"No, Fred. I go in and use their weakness to my advantage. They like women. I'll give them me and I'll get them to trust me. Hell, I'll lay it on a fucking plate if it saves his life," I argued.

"We don't even know if this is them." Freddie tried to reason with me, but my mind was made up.

"I'll do it," Gina jumped in. "I know what these kind of men are like and I'd rather they used me than you. Luca wouldn't want you anywhere near this."

"She's right, Chloe."

"No, I'm doing it and that's final. It's non-negotiable. If you want to come along to support me, Gina, then I'll happily work with you. But I'm not sitting at home on my ass, waiting for news like some little wifey. I'm involved in this whether you like it or not. So come on, Freddie, tell me the rest. What does Sanchez have to do with all this?"

Freddie got us up to speed on what he believed was happening with the black mamba. Word on the street was, they were heavily involved in the trafficking ring which Sanchez was a part of, and didn't take too kindly to Luca shutting it down. The ring had made them a lot of money, and now it'd folded, their boss was baying for blood. Luca's blood to be exact. Turned out the Colombian, Diaz, was their biggest paying customer. That's what the other men told us when they came back to us early the next morning, to debrief Freddie and I.

I informed them of my plans, which didn't go down well with any one of them, Vinnie and Marco especially, but I wasn't to be swayed. No, I wanted to do everything I could to get Luca back, and I'd stop at nothing. I wasn't about to stand around twiddling my thumbs, whilst some out of town low lives robbed me of my happily ever after.

It was agreed that Gina and I would do a tour of the local clubs that night, to see what we could find out. We both agreed to be fitted with trackers, injected just under the skin, so we could follow any clues that could potentially lead us to Luca, and keep the guys on the outside updated on where we were. I refused to wear a wire though. I couldn't take the chance that one of them might frisk us if we were to track their outfit down. No, this whole operation needed to be flawless. No wires, no listening devices and none of Luca's men could follow us into any of the clubs. If any of the black mamba suspected we were planted there to catch them out, it wasn't just Luca's life that was endangered, it was ours too.

-

That night, Gina and I dressed in the sluttiest outfits she could find in her work wardrobe and headed to the first club, weaving our way through the crowds like a pair of lionesses out on the prowl. A few groups caught our eye, but when we got close enough to chat with them, none of them sported the tell-tale snake tattoo on their hands. We spent about an hour pacing the floor, before we decided it was pointless to stay any longer, and moved on to try the next night spot.

We headed into Euphoria, a newly opened club, and made our way to the bar to give ourselves some Dutch courage. After downing a few shots, we sipped our cosmos and glanced around the room. Everyone here looked stylish, well-bred and snake tattoo free. The club itself had a cool, futuristic vibe. With chrome, metal and blue lighting flashing across the room and dancing off the mirrored tables and white leather seating.

"I think this might be a bit too classy for the likes of the black mamba," Gina said in a low voice.

"Maybe we're looking in the wrong type of places. If you wanted to find women in this town, where would you go? And don't say your place, because I know your girls are already on red alert for any snake tattoos that might call in."

"You know exactly where men go, Chloe. You worked there, remember?"

I rolled my eyes and felt the twist in my stomach as I thought about going back to that place again, but I'd do it. I'd do anything to get Luca back.

"Looks like we're heading for a night at Jack's Kitty Kat club then," I sighed.

It was ironic really, the place where Freddie had saved me could possibly be the place where I could save Luca. It seemed as if we'd done a whole 360 and come right back to where it'd all started.

We downed our cosmos and left the trendy clientele in Euphoria behind to enjoy their classy night out, and headed to my least favourite club.

"Kiki? Is that you? Damn girl, I never thought I'd see you walk back in here."

Ron was on door duty tonight. He still had that older uncle vibe going on, and I had to fight the urge to give him a big old bear hug. I was too tense and too wound up about Luca to act naturally. Where was he? Would we get to him in time? The thought of going on without him made me catch my breath on a hiccup.

"You okay, girl? You looked like you were about to blart all over me." Ron gave my shoulders a friendly squeeze and unhooked the red rope for us, so we could walk in ahead of the queue winding around the front of the building.

"Go and see Terry at the bar. Tell him Ron sent you and he'll get you a drink on the house, okay Kiki? It's good to see you again. You had us all worried you know."

I guessed Ron had no idea why Freddie had taken me that day, and I also guessed he was clueless about Sanchez and the whole trafficking ring. When we entered the main room, I could see that Sanchez's death hadn't harmed business. The place was packed, and groups of men cheered and whistled like packs of hungry wolves as Jackie, one of the bitchier dancers I'd had the displeasure to work with, finished her set.

We did as Ron suggested and headed to the bar, where Terry poured us both a glass of champagne on the house. We lifted ourselves onto two high stools to survey the area, and that's when I noticed the guy standing next to Gina, ordering a round of drinks. His grey snake tattoo was visible under his cuffs as he paid Terry for the drinks. I discreetly tapped Gina with my foot to alert her to the guy. We both eye-balled him and gave our sweetest smiles as he picked up the tray loaded down with drinks and turned to leave.

"Evening ladies."

He winked at us and walked over to a table in the far right corner of the room. The best table in the house, as it gave the customer a perfect view of the stage and a free flow to the bar, without having to fight their way through the crowds. Of course Jack's also provided table service, but sometimes it was easier to go up yourself, and most guys liked to work the room as a lot of the dancers mingled with the customers after their set.

We watched him set the tray down and join the other men at the table. There were six of them altogether, every one of them branded with the same snake tattoo on their left hand, and every one of them looked like they'd been spawned from the depths of hell. As covertly as we could we watched how they interacted with each other, saw them pawing women as they walked past the table, and heard their calls and chants as each new dancer took to the stage.

I soon figured out that the main guy was sat in the middle of them all. He was taller than the rest, lean but muscular, with his greasy black hair tied back from his face in a ponytail. He looked like he belonged back in the 1980s. He had a black leather jacket on and his jeans were skinny and ripped at the knee. The other guys seemed to follow his lead and hang off his every word.

Their table started attracting the attention of a few of the dancers, and Jackie was draping herself across one of the guys sitting on the edge, as Ruby her best mate worked her stuff.

"I'm going in," I said quietly to Gina, as I hopped off the stool and picked up my glass. I was going to walk past their table and try to catch one of their eyes. Maybe then I could join them too, and get myself invited back to wherever they were hiding out tonight. It wouldn't hurt to piss Jackie and Ruby off either. Not to mention, time was of the essence here. Black mambas worked fast. I needed to do everything I could to get to Luca.

Gina followed me as we both pushed our tits out and swayed our hips, giving it everything we had. It worked better than I thought it would, and I felt a strong arm wrap around my waist and pull me down onto a guy's lap at the table.

"Come and sit on my lap, sexy." This guy stunk of tobacco, it made me want to gag. "Maybe later you can ride on my cock like a good little cowgirl," he laughed and smacked the side of my ass.

"Depends how big your cock is." I bit my lower lip trying to appear seductive, but feeling like kneeing this asshole in the balls, and hard.

The guy laughed again, but as I looked up through my eyelashes, I noticed the boss guy licking his lips and looking me up and down.

"I think she'd prefer my lap," he grunted, his voice all gravelly and full of promises of violence. "And my cock." My guy was still laughing, but this boss guy wasn't. Soon the atmosphere at the table changed and I was passed down the line of men like some kind of pass the parcel.

"Woah, steady," I said, as they manhandled me over to their boss and he yanked me forcefully onto him, then stuck his hand up the skirt of my dress to grab my ass.

"Nice." He breathed down my neck as he squeezed my ass hard with his rough calloused fingers. "I bet your pussy will be the sweetest thing I'll eat tonight. I can't wait to taste it later."

He ran his rancid tongue along the side of my neck and then bit my earlobe. I kept Luca in my thoughts as I gave a false grin, and ran my hands over his greasy, dirty hair. This was for him. This was to save him, I reminded myself, as the dirt-bag pawed at my body, staking his claim for the evening.

Gina had caught the eye of a blond guy with a goatee beard who sat opposite the boss. She seemed so much more at ease with playing this game than I was. I was terrified that they'd find me out at any minute and kill me for being a fake. I felt like they'd smell the scent of a traitor on me.

"You're coming home with me," boss guy grunted at me. The club started to play dance music as the acts took a longer break, and the men discussed taking the girls they'd managed to hook back to their place to carry on with their own private party. Seems they weren't here for the disco and drinks.

Suddenly, they all started to move, getting themselves ready to leave.

"You ride with me," the guy said, pulling me from the booth and dragging me out of the club ahead of all the others.

"You're a bossy one, aren't you?" I purred, trying to sound sexy.

"That's because I'm the boss. You'll do whatever I want tonight."

"Will I?" I said, challenging him.

"You play nice and I'll treat you good," he whispered in my ear. "Play dirty and things will get a hell of a lot dirtier for you."

I didn't like the deadness behind his eyes as he leaned back after saying that. I knew he meant what he said. If I didn't do what he wanted tonight, I'd probably be used in the dirtiest ways, and not just by him. What the hell had I got us into? *It's for Luca'*, I kept reminding myself. It's the only way to find him.

Chapter Forty Four

My guy, the boss with the greasy ponytail, rode a huge motorbike. I spent the entire ride to their mystery place hanging on the back for dear life. He sped down roads and curved round corners with no regard for my safety. When we finally pulled up to their hide out in the middle of nowhere, I could see from the lights streaming through the old farmhouse that they'd commandeered for their mission, that there were another dozen or so men inside.

As the rest of the party from Jack's began to pull up next to us, I glanced around to scope out the area. There were stables to the left of the main house, and I could hear the sound of the horses. Next to them were a few out-houses, but nothing that could lead me to Luca's whereabouts yet.

"Come on, let's keep this party going." The boss guy pulled me against his side and strode into the house. "I think things are gonna be hotting up real fast between you and me."

He smiled, showing a gold tooth at the side of his mouth and tobacco stained teeth. The stench of cigarettes and beer made my stomach turn, but I managed a coy smile and fluttered my eyelashes at him.

"I'm not usually such a naughty girl, but for you, I'll make an exception." I purred and a low growl came from deep within him. This guy would tear me apart if I let him. He petrified me.

I managed to catch a glimpse of Gina as she walked past with her arms around the blond guy. She gave me a questioning look, but I smiled back sweetly to try and put her mind at ease. I could tell she was concerned about how far I'd go tonight to get the information I needed for us to find out if and where they were holding Luca. I didn't even know myself. All I did know was that this was the best, hell probably the only chance we had of getting to him alive. I couldn't fuck this up.

We went into the house, which was filthy and smelt of animals. The floor was covered in mud, straw and all manner of dirt. Every surface was littered with beer bottles, cans and ashtrays full of cigarette butts.

"Cleaners day off?" I couldn't help commenting, brushing an old newspaper from the threadbare sofa and perching on the edge. Then I thought better of it, as images of mice and fleas living inside the frame of the couch freaked me out.

"Drink." Boss guy ordered, and he held a beer out to me. I took it from him and pretended to sip, but I wasn't about to take it down. It could be drugged for all I knew.

I watched the other girls start dancing to the music playing through the downstairs speakers, rubbing up against the guys like stray cats. The boss didn't take his eyes off me for a second though, and I began to feel the pressure as he moved closer towards me.

"I need to use the bathroom. Where is it?" I asked, trying to buy myself some time.

"Down the hall, second door on the right." He pointed to the door with his beer bottle, then leant down to my ear to add, "Don't be long little girl. I'm taking you for a private party in my room and my cock won't wait much longer to be inside of you." He grabbed my hand and held it against the front of his jeans to show me how serious he was about our private party.

I smiled sweetly and turned away to walk seductively out of the door. Once I was out of his sight, I started to push doors open frantically, to see if I could find anything to help me. I guessed I had about two, maybe three minutes, before he came looking for me. The first door led to a cupboard full of cleaning stuff covered in a thick layer of dust and cobwebs. How ironic, the cleaning stuff was the filthiest shit in the house.

Sure enough, the second door was the bathroom, if you could call it that. The toilet was stained brown from years of zero cleaning and it smelt like a farmyard. Well it was a farm house, so I suppose before the black mamba had taken over the house the animals had ruled this place. They'd certainly put their stamp on it. I bet if I looked closer, I'd find horse manure and other animal shit ground into the floor or hidden behind the furniture.

I tried the third door and stumbled into a kitchen, where two guys stood chatting and drinking beer. Both looked up as I fell through the door and then grinned as their eyes went from my feet up to my head and back down again.

"You lost?" one of them said, taking a step over to me.

"She's with me." I recognised the greasy boss's rancid stale smell before I felt him behind me. He snaked an arm around my waist and pulled me back against his vile body. "But I'll let you know when I'm finished with her. If there's anything left by then. I'll let you pick up my left overs." I gave a sexy giggle, but he was being deadly serious. This was how they treated women, used them then cast them aside for the next one to try out. I felt disgusted.

"It's party time," he grunted into my neck and led me to the stairs like a freaking lamb to the slaughter. I followed, my legs feeling like dead weights and my mind screaming *get the fuck out of here Chloe, this isn't gonna end well for you'*. But I kept Luca's face in my mind and tried to recall why I had to do this. I couldn't let them win. This would be pay back.

At the top of the stairs were four doors. I assumed each one led to a bedroom, maybe one was another bathroom. The boss pushed his way through the first door on the left and pulled me into a cold and sparse bedroom. There was a musty, old bed in the middle, one bedside cabinet with two small drawers next to it and a yellow stained velvet armchair in the corner next to the window. An off-white sheet hung up at the window as a makeshift pair of curtains, but the light of the moon still shone through the gaps.

He slammed the door behind him and looked at me with eyes that told me exactly what he had planned for me. He was going to devour me like a wild animal. He took a handgun out of the back of his jeans and laid it down on the bedside cabinet, then shrugged the leather jacket from his shoulders and threw it onto the chair.

"Strip," he ordered and when I hesitated, he picked up his gun and pointed it at my face.

"You hard of hearing bitch? I said strip."

I gulped, my eyes following the gun as he waved it up and down my body. Then he placed it back on the cabinet as I started to unzip my dress.

"That's it. Nice and slow. Give me a good show."

He got onto the bed and lay back with his hands behind his head. I wriggled the dress down my shoulders and pushed it to my waist, then wiggled my hips from side to side as I peeled it slowly over my hips. So slowly, that I was surprised he didn't cuss at me for taking my time, but from the heat in his eyes he was enjoying his private show.

"Do you do anything else here other than party and hang out?" I asked in a husky voice, hoping to get him talking.

"Shut up. Time for talking's over," he snapped back.

So much for my information gathering, this wasn't going

how I wanted it to at all. I took a deep breath in as I stood in front of him in my black lace strapless bra and panties. Watching as he unbuttoned his jeans and started palming his vile cock.

"Come here," he demanded, but I couldn't get my legs to move. I knew the minute he got me close I was done for. This was my last chance to run.

"I said... Get. That. Tight. Ass. Over. Here. Now," he said through gritted teeth, emphasizing each word. I knew it was now or never, run or face ruin, fight or flight. You never know what you'll do in a moment like this, until you're standing with the decision right in front of you. I did what I always did, I stayed and I fought.

I got onto the bed and crawled up over him. At least this way I had some control. I could still reach across to his gun. I could try to overpower him, straddle him and shoot him in the head. Jeez, who was I kidding? I didn't stand a chance.

He ran his hands over my ass and pulled me down to his lap to rub me over his cock. He lay there, his eyes hooded and his body ready to pounce. I didn't even have chance to react, he just threw me onto the mattress on my back and rolled on top of me. He stuck his tongue down my throat and squeezed my ass so hard I yelped in pain. He was really hurting me and we hadn't even started. I felt sick.

After a few seconds of choking me with his tongue, he sat back on his knees, straddling me, and pulled my bra down to expose my breasts.

"That's a nice pair of tits you got there. I'm gonna find it hard not to bite those pretty pink nipples clean off." He grinned, but the bile washing around in my stomach told me he probably would bite them off. He was a savage, and I was his prey.

He pinned my arms above my head, his body caging me to the bed. Then he leant his head down to take one of my nipples into his mouth and he sucked so hard I screamed and started panicking. My chest panting and sweat forming all over me.

"You like that? You like it rough, huh?" He bit the side of my neck before moving to the other nipple. "I have a lot more where that came from." Just as he put his dirty mouth over me the door pounded and a voice from the other side shouted. "Raul, its time."

"The fuck?" the grease ball hissed quietly before shouting back. "Fuck off, I'm busy."

I closed my eyes, begging them not to fuck off and please disturb him again. I was trapped here and I had no way out. This guy at the door was my last chance.

"He's close. I thought you wanted to do the last round?" the angel from hell on the other side of the door called out.

The boss or Raul as I now knew he was called, pushed off me and stalked over to the door, grabbing his gun as he did.

"Talk." He pointed the gun at the guy and listened, as he told Raul that someone was close, and that if he wanted the last round, it had to be now. I had no idea what that meant, but I watched as he nodded along, then turned to me on the bed, pointed his gun at me and said, "You don't move from that spot. I have business to take care of. Then I'll take care of you." And with that, he walked out and left me lying there, thanking my lucky stars for whoever was close and had saved me.

Chapter Forty Five

I grabbed my dress from the floor and squeezed myself back into the tight fabric, thankful for the coverage that I'd originally thought was lacking.

I had to leave this room and find out where they were going. What was going down that was so important? What'd made Raul leave me here unattended? My gut instinct told me I had to follow it up. I scoured the room for something to take with me, some kind of weapon for protection against these guys. I had no intention of ever letting Raul near me ever again. I knew this was my last reprieve, and if I was alone with him one more time he'd destroy me, hurt me, and fuck me up for life forever.

I had a small mobile phone in my bag, which I'd brought into the room with me. I took it out and tucked it into my bra. The idea being, if I found out where Luca was, I would ring or text Freddie to give him the go ahead to come to us. Through the trackers in our body and on the phone, they'd bring the cavalry to the right location.

Through my search of the room I found zilch, zero, nada that could even be considered a weapon I could use. So I decided to bite the bullet and head back to the kitchen to get my hands on whatever I could find in there. Chances were, I'd have to trick my way past the two guys hanging out in there, and use some of my Dad's skills to get my hands on something. But I wasn't afraid of a bit of hustling to blag my way out of things. That was the story of my life.

I crept out of the bedroom and listened for voices, but all I could hear was the music, and a few questionable grunts coming from down the hall. I took each step carefully, so as not to draw attention to myself, and then peaked my head around the kitchen door. Empty.

I yanked the drawers open two at a time and eventually found a hunting knife. Why a serrated hunting knife like this was in a kitchen drawer, nestled amongst the other rusty crap inside was a mystery, but I didn't care. I had something to defend myself with. I guessed the men had used it to skin rabbits or other animals to cook for themselves whilst they stayed here. Even savages used utensil drawers I supposed.

I was heading out of the kitchen to further explore, when I spotted Raul and two other men outside by one of the outhouses. I held the knife steady in my right hand and went towards the back of the farmhouse to find the backdoor and head over to where they were. I wanted to see what business they were involved in that couldn't wait.

-

"I'm done with this shithole. Let's get this job done and get out of here. If I have to spend another night sleeping next to horse shit, I'm gonna kill someone."

I heard some guy grunt in agreement. I crouched down behind the bales of hay that were piled up next to the outhouse, where the three men were smoking and griping about the standard of their accommodation. I personally thought they suited the shithole. It wasn't good enough for the animals, though. In my opinion, they deserved better than to share the black mambas' dirty, shitty living quarters.

"Let's get this over with."

I watched Raul flick his cigarette onto the ground and head into the outhouse, followed by the other two. I held my knife firmly and went to leave my hiding place, but then jumped back as one of the men walked back out and headed towards the main house. Two men were in the outhouse now. I stood more of a chance against two. I stayed against the side of the brick building and crept to the door, listening carefully to the men inside. I could hear muffled voices, the clanking of metal, but not much more. As I stepped over the threshold into the building, I saw one of the men leaning against another doorway that led into a main area inside. Raul's gravelly laugh, more evil than jovial, came from further inside the room.

"Where's the iron bar? I want the fucking iron bar," Raul shouted out.

"Take that piece of shit away and get it now."

The guy leaning up against the wall stood up straight and caught something that Raul had thrown over to him, it looked like some kind of horses' whip. Maybe they were tending to one of the horses from the stables? The guy disappeared out of the back of the building and my curiosity got the better of me. I had to see what Raul was doing in that room.

I saw what looked like old farming machinery against the wall, opposite the doorway the guy had been leaning against, and I stealthily crept over to hide behind it and get a better view of the room Raul occupied. As I crouched down, I clamped my teeth shut to stop myself screaming when I heard the squeak of a mouse or some other small animal dart out from where I'd chosen to hide. It was imperative I didn't give away my presence or my hiding spot at this time. However, when I turned my head to face the doorway in question, I couldn't stop the gasp coming from my mouth.

Chained against the back wall of the outhouse, like some kind of butchers' room or twisted abattoir, hung Luca. His arms were chained above his head as his battered and bloody body hung limply. His feet could barely touch the floor. His head was resting forward, lifeless on his chest, and his eyes were closed as if he'd passed out, but he was still breathing. I could see the rise and fall of his chest and the effort it was taking for him to breathe. His face was barely recognisable, it was so swollen and covered thick with blood; red and fresh as well as brown and dried up. He'd been beaten repeatedly over and over. I couldn't imagine what he'd suffered through, and how much more he could take, or rather couldn't take. His chest was bare and covered in lashes, cuts and bruises. His jeans were stained and dirty and his feet were bare and looked too weak to holdup his strong frame. They were beating him to death. He didn't have long, even I knew that. The thought made me feel sick and terrified all at once.

My hands shook uncontrollably as I slipped the mobile phone out of my bra and tried to text Freddie. I couldn't type properly. I could barely hold the damn thing still, but he would get the gist.

Come quick, he's here and we don't have long.

I watched the guy walk back over to the door and throw a thick metal bar to Raul. I knew then what he planned to do, and the blood in my whole body froze.

No.

They couldn't use that on him, not with how weak he looked. He wouldn't be able to take a single blow. They'd kill him. I had to stop them. I had to move or do something, anything.

I panted and felt the panic rise like bile from my stomach into my throat.

"I need another smoke," the guy at the door said calmly, like it was just another day at the office, and walked over to the external doorway.

I didn't stop to think about the consequences or the prospect that he might overpower me, I followed him outside.

My feet were bare, ensuring I moved quietly across the ground undetected. Then with as much force as I could muster, and not a second thought to what I was actually doing, I rammed my hunting knife into the back of his neck. I pulled it out as he fell to his knees, making a grotesque gurgling sound, and then I plunged it back in again, just as hard. Red spurted out over the gravel in front of us, and he slammed forward onto the floor. One down, one to go. I knelt down and felt his pockets. I got lucky, he had a handgun. A quick check of the chamber and I could see it was fully loaded. I threw the hunting knife onto the ground and stalked back into the outhouse with the gun, ready to put the deadliest black mamba down for good.

-

"I bet you regret fucking with us now, don't cha?" Raul was pacing up and down, dragging out the torture for as long as he could.

"Fuck you!" Luca spat back, using every bit of energy he had to lift his head and reply.

He spat out the blood from his mouth onto the floor, then bared his teeth at Raul. I stood watching from the side of the doorway, waiting patiently to strike.

"Did you really think you could shut us down and walk away? No blow-back? You're gonna pay for what you did to Sanchez and Diaz. And you'll pay for causing us so much shit. I'm gonna enjoy fucking you up for the last time, Marquez. I think your brother will love the way we're gonna send you back to your family. You know...head first."

Luca didn't flinch or show any fear, despite what he'd said. I, on the other hand, wanted to hunch over and throw up. *'Stay focused, Chloe,'* I told myself, *'you can do this'.*

I stepped into the room and stood silently behind Raul. Luca didn't even look at me, he kept his gaze and attention on Raul, as he held the metal bar up ready to strike.

"I've left a prime piece of ass in my bed to come down here and deal with your shit, Marquez." Luca didn't react as Raul moved closer to him.

"Little brunette with the sweetest ass. Sucking on her tits was like sucking on candy and the little moans she made? Man, she's a real keeper. I can't wait to taste her pussy when I'm done taking you out. I'm gonna ruin her for any other guy. After I'm done with you, she'll get the full black mamba experience and then some."

I shook my head in disgust and lifted the gun to point it at Raul's back. I would've gone for the head, but I wasn't the most experienced shooter and the back was a better bet.

"Maybe I'll take a little trip to find your girl, Marquez. Make it a threesome. You'd like that wouldn't you," he cackled and I snapped.

"Get the fuck away from him." I could feel the anger flowing out of me. I had to put this dog down before he ruined anyone else's life.

Raul spun around and grinned at me, his stained, dirty teeth giving him a demonic edge.

"Well, well, well. Looks like we've got ourselves a nice little party going on right here. Couldn't wait for me in the bed sweetheart? Want to put on a show for our guest here too?"

"Move away from him, now," I growled through my clenched jaw. I tried not to show that my arms were shaking as I held the gun in his direction.

"I'm not the bad guy here, babe. Go back upstairs and wait for me like a good little girl. Let me finish up here and then I'll finish you off up there."

I wanted to shiver, even the thought of him made my skin crawl.

"I don't think so." I clenched my jaw ready to strike, but he just laughed at me and then gave me a pitiful look.

"Now, let's not pretend you're actually gonna use that, little girl. Put it down and come stand over here before you hurt yourself."

He was delirious. He actually thought I'd go to him? I shook my head.

"I'd rather die." I said, and pulled the trigger.

"Fuck!" he snarled as he bent over holding his stomach where I'd hit him.

"Finish him, Chloe. Finish him for good," Luca managed to gasp.

Raul gave a pained laugh.

"Is she yours, Marquez? Well, she wasn't a few hours ago when she was sat on my-"

I squeezed the trigger one last time, and this one hit the spot perfectly, right between his eyes. Its amazing what you can do when you put your mind to it.

My arms stayed outstretched, even though I knew he was dead and I had no intention of firing again. I was frozen to the spot, I couldn't move.

"Chloe." Luca's pained, quiet voice pulled me out of my trance, and I altered my gaze from the spot where Raul lay to Luca hanging so helplessly.

"He lied," I spluttered, not knowing what to say or do. "I didn't do anything with him. I didn't...sit on him like that, I wasn't-"

Luca shook his head as it hung down in front of his broken body. "I know," he gasped. "I trust you, Chloe."

I dropped the gun on the floor and ran over to him to hold him. I put my arms around his body and give him the support he needed. He leant forward and rested on me. I felt the weight of him fall upon me as he relaxed his muscles and let go of the tension that'd been building up inside of him. Tension that'd helped him withstand the onslaught of blows that were coming his way mere seconds ago.

"I need to get you out of here." I looked up at the shackles that held him to the wall so mercilessly, and doubted I could use the gun in any effective way to release them.

"Windowsill," he grunted out. "The keys are on the windowsill." He nodded to the only small window that the building had. A small rectangular window that was high up and covered with bars.

I went over to feel along the high sill, and sure enough my dust covered fingers found the small metal keys that'd give my Luca his freedom.

I unchained his ankles first, then moved up to his wrists. As the locks came loose letting his arms fall free, he fell forward and the weight of him almost knocked me to the floor. I'd never seen Luca so weak in all my life. Hell, I'd never seen any man so weak. He could barely move on his own, so I tried my hardest to be the strong, steady support he needed me to be to get him out of this dungeon.

I put both of my arms around his waist to hold him up and he wrapped his arms around my shoulders. Side by side we stumbled through the first doorway and out towards the main door. Luca's breathing was laboured and his body was shaking, but he was fighting like a warrior to stay upright for me.

We tumbled out onto the gravel path outside, and two men ran across the grass towards us. My throat tightened, but Freddie's voice over the distance made my body sag in relief.

"Chloe, you're a fucking star. Are you okay?"

Luca laughed. "Of course she's okay, she's my fucking star." He coughed and the rattling sound coming from his chest made me wince.

"You look like shit, bro." Freddie was trying to be nonchalant, but I could tell he was distressed about seeing his big brother like this.

"Don't worry about me." Luca pushed off me as if to show he wasn't as weak as we all thought. "You took your time coming to get me, didn't you?" He went to walk forward and fell like a ton of bricks to the ground with a thud.

"Shit!" Marco said, as he jerked away from Freddie and ran over to where Luca had fallen.

I knelt down too, taking Luca's face in my hands and calling out to him to check he was okay.

"He's passed out, Chloe. He'll be okay. We just need to get him home." Marco looked over at me, but his eyes told me a different story, he looked panicked.

"Fred, get the car now," he snapped, and Freddie sprinted off in full Olympic mode to get a car to take Luca to safety.

"He needs a hospital." I stroked his hair as he lay lifeless on the grass.

"No hospitals. We don't do hospitals," Marco responded without a second thought.

"You might not do hospitals but I do, and I'm taking him to a hospital now."

"No, Chloe. Luca always says no hospitals. It's not up for discussion."

I gritted my teeth in anger.

"I don't take orders from you, Marco. If I say drive to the hospital, you'll fucking drive to the mother fucking hospital," I spat out with as much venom as I could, which wasn't hard considering how I felt.

A black Range Rover pulled up next to us and Freddie jumped out, leaving the engine running.

"Let's get him in the back and get out of here. The rest of them can clean up the mess." Freddie and Marco started to lift Luca and walk him to the car.

"She wants to take him to the hospital," Marco said with a knowing look to Freddie.

"No hospitals, Chloe. It's Luca's main rule." He looked me right in the eye. "Even I'm going to go against you on this one. He wouldn't want it. He always makes it very clear that we deal with our own. No hospitals, no authorities sticking their noses in our business. Everything stays in-house."

I shook my head and stopped myself from screaming and pulling my hair out in exasperation at their stupidity.

"And if he dies?"

"He won't die," Freddie said with such certainty I felt like slapping him.

"Anyway, you're almost a doctor, Chloe. Can't you take care of him?"

"I'm a student with basic knowledge and experience, Fred. I'm no emergency room doctor. Plus, I don't have the resources even if I could do the job."

"Don't under estimate yourself. Tell us exactly what you need," Marco stated. "We'll get it in for you. Whatever it is, we can get it."

I was still in a state of shock as I watched them settle Luca onto the back seat. I climbed in next to him and lifted his head to rest on my lap.

Marco and Freddie got into the front and we started racing across the grass towards the driveway out of hell.

"You're seriously not gonna take him to a hospital? No matter what I say?"

"No, sorry."

I closed my eyes and started doing a mental checklist of all the things I'd need to help bring Luca around.

"Fine. I'll look after him myself. I'll need drips, antibiotics, pain relief and not the weak shit either. Bandages..." I rubbed my hand over my forehead as I thought about all the possibilities. "I'll make a list for you. When can you get this stuff to me?"

"An hour, maybe two tops." Marco leant forward to open the glove compartment and then passed a pad of paper and a pen to me.

I made a list of the things I thought I might need and passed it back to him.

"We'll drop you both off at home, then I'll head straight out to get this for you." Marco twisted round in his seat to look at me. "If you need any help, we have a few doctors on the pay roll that can come and take a look at him."

"Okay. Thanks. I'll let you know if I need their help," I mumbled and bent down to kiss Luca on the forehead as I carried on stroking his hair. I could feel the warm flow of his breathing which calmed me. Even though he wasn't out of the woods yet as far as his health was concerned, I already felt at peace just to have him near me, and I vowed never to be apart from him ever again.

Chapter Forty Six

The next few days were some of the worst of my life, watching as my unbreakable warrior lay weak and helpless. My whole body ached for him, and I stayed by his side religiously every minute of every day. I daren't take a step away in case he needed me, I had to be there. I gave him medical attention, the best I could manage with my limited expertise. But every once in a while a sob would catch in my throat, as I looked at his bruised and battered body and realised how close I'd come to losing him forever. That thought would cripple me, then I'd bat it away and focus on all the positives. He was alive and back in my arms.

It took a few days for the fluids and other medication to take effect and make Luca slightly more lucid. But once he'd been seen by a private doctor at home, he began his road to recovery. He had broken ribs, cuts and injuries that'd heal over time, and I took pride in taking care of him and nursing him back to health. I wasn't sure if the mental scars would linger, but I needn't have worried. My man was made of strong stuff after the childhood traumas he'd experienced.

Freddie, Marco and the others set Luca up with his own private hospital bed at home, with access to whatever we needed. I still wasn't happy that he hadn't been into hospital to be properly assessed, but this did come a pretty close second.

About a week or so after the nightmare night, Luca was sat up in bed wincing as he tried to get comfortable against the pillows. His cracked and broken ribs caused him pain every time he moved.

"Angel." He wriggled to the side a little to face me, trying to hide the pained look on his face. "I love that you came for me, but promise me you'll *never* put yourself in a position like that ever again." His glare told me he was deadly serious, but he wasn't winning this one.

"Hmm, let me think." I rolled my eyes sarcastically. "Err, that'll be a no." He huffed and went to speak, but I beat him to it. "Don't tell me what to do, Luca. You'll always come through for me and I'll always do what I have to do for you. It's who we are. It's what we do. You can't change us." I folded my arms over my chest.

"I know and you're right. I just hate to think of you in danger."

I knew where he was coming from, but I wasn't about to make any promises that I couldn't keep. I told him as much and he nodded in agreement.

"We're a right pair aren't we?" he laughed, then groaned

as the chuckle turned to a stab of pain, and he clutched his side. I stood up to plump his pillows and give him more stability and comfort.

"You can say that again. I'm hoping we get a few weeks off from all the drama. I'm not sure I can take much more of our brand of excitement," I joked.

I did feel immense relief that the whole trafficking ring was over, and nothing else was lurking in the wings to come and destroy us linked to that. It was well and truly done. Over. Finished.

"There's nothing exciting about what we've been through these last few months." Luca looked down as he said this, guilt playing over his face.

"Hey-" I linked my fingers through his, holding his hand and squeezing so he'd look back at me. "I have plenty of memories that are exciting, don't you worry about that." I leant over him and gave him a delicate kiss, brushing my lips softly over his, then slowly lifting my hand up to stroke his face. I ran my finger nails down his week's old scruff to come to rest on his solid chest.

"Are we keeping the beard?" he asked me, and I moved back to look him in the eyes. He ran his hand over his chin thoughtfully.

"Hmmm, I kinda like you with a bit of stubble." I tugged his beard down smirking. "But not this much. I'll get someone in to tidy it up for you and me." I winked.

"You're the one who's got to live with it. Whatever you

want, angel."

He gave me a warm smile and my heart just burst with sparks of love for what we'd finally found together, in each other. I felt like the luckiest girl in the world. Every one of my dreams was coming true. After so many years of hoping and waiting, wanting and ultimately left hurting, it was all falling into place for us. All the moons and stars were fully aligned in our favour.

"You'll make a fantastic doctor, Chloe. You know I'll support you one hundred percent through your studies."

"I know you will, but I won't be going back to my studies just yet. I've been thinking that maybe I could help out more, help *you* with whatever you need me to do. We're a team. I want to pull my weight."

Luca shook his head, but I wasn't giving up on this one.

"I mean it, Luca. It's us against the world now, so you need to let me do my part."

He was the one rolling his eyes this time.

"Fine. When I'm back at it I'll bring you in, but you're not doing anything in the club during opening hours. I'm not having every low-life in the city ogling what's mine."

"You're such a caveman," I chided.

He didn't disagree, and he didn't apologise either, but then if the shoe was on the other foot, I'd go into full on cavewoman mode myself. We were two peas in a pod and we fiercely defended and protected what was ours. We were a formidable force.

Chapter Forty Seven

Three months later…

"I can't believe you've got me here on a Saturday night watching this garbage," Luca moaned as we sat cuddled together on our sofa.

He lay on his back and I lay next to him, my head resting on his chest as he played with my hair and stroked my neck. I loved his touches. He could send shivers down my spine with the tickles and traces of his magic fingers. I was like a contented little pussy cat rubbing up against him. The latest celebrity dance competition was playing on the T.V, and in true best boyfriend style, he was enduring it just for me on his extremely rare night off.

He'd wanted to go out, even gone so far as to book some swanky restaurant in town, but I didn't want to go out. A night cuddling on the sofa was heaven to me.

"Don't lie, you love it really. Secretly you'd love to wear all that Lycra and sequins," I teased, running my fingers down his chest.

"I reckon I'd be good at the Latin." He smiled to himself.

I threw my head back laughing and hauled myself up to kneel over him.

"Come on then, Fred Astaire. Show me what you've got."

I pulled him up and across the living room, giving him my sexiest dancer eyes as if I knew what I was doing.

He held his arm around my waist and made a frame like the dancers on the TV. I couldn't keep a straight face as he smouldered at me, ready to give the Paso Doble his best shot.

"Hmm, I don't think we'll be dancing with the stars any time soon," I giggled as he spun me round and burst out laughing himself at how awful we were. My feet were tripping over his and I almost fell over more than once.

"We'll have to take lessons, we can't do this at our wedding."

I pulled back and at that exact moment he put his hand into his pocket and fished out a small, black, velvet box. My eyes grew wide as he knelt down on one knee.

"I know this isn't our first proposal, but I'm hoping this one is more successful than the last." I frowned, not entirely sure what he was getting at, but eager for him to get on with it, so I could jump on him and smother him in kisses. "But since you turned down my plans for a private table for two in the best restaurant for miles, I'm kinda stuck doing this here. I can't wait any longer to do this and well...here, with you in my arms, it's the perfect time. I love you, Chloe. Always have, always will. You make my life complete. You make me a better man. Your place is by my side, and my place is by yours. I want to love and protect you for the rest of my life. So my angel-"

"Jesus, Luca, yes! Fuck, yes I'll marry you." I couldn't wait any longer. I flung my arms around his neck and jumped up as he stood, wrapping my legs around his waist like I was his pet monkey.

"Don't you want to see the ring?" he chuckled, holding me up.

"Yeah, but let me breathe you in for a little bit longer," I said, as my face was glued into his neck.

Slowly, I peeled myself off him and looked at the box he'd held open to me. The most stunning emerald cut diamond winked back at me, sparkling in the light and cushioned either side by a cluster of diamonds, to create the perfect frame for what was a real show-stopper of a ring.

"Woah! You didn't get that out of a Christmas cracker," I smirked.

"No, and you know what, Chloe? I bought this ring for you the day after you walked into my club, wearing Freddie's jacket and not much more."

My mouth fell open. That whole time he'd behaved as if my being around was the biggest inconvenience he'd ever encountered.

"I know what you're thinking. I was an asshole back then, but trust me, I was an asshole who was desperately trying to think of a way to win you round. I haven't got the best moves or chat up lines, but there wasn't a chance in hell I was letting you walk out of my life again. I wanted to keep you for good this time."

"Luca, I wouldn't change you for the world. I love you as you are, please don't ever change...and just for the record, I wouldn't have let you go either."

He threaded his long fingers into my hair at the nape of my neck and pulled me into him. His lips brushing against mine in a soft but dominant way. His tongue tasting me with long leisurely strokes that sent my head into a spin. His hands held me still as he made love to my mouth and then his hands drifted down my back to cup my ass firmly.

I pulled back, loving the look of lust and heat in his eyes. He gave a hint of a frown, wondering why I was stopping him.

"I need to ask you, Luca. What other time did you propose?"

He burst out laughing and pushed his forehead against mine.

"Not me, sweetheart, you. Don't you remember?"

"Err no." I bit my lip and gave him a quirky grin. "Should I?"

"You were eight-years-old, angel, so don't beat yourself up for not remembering such an important thing in our lives."

I slapped him playfully, as he pulled me to him again with both his arms wrapped tightly around my chest.

"We're even then. We've both proposed to each other."

LUCA

Fourteen years ago…

"Coming, ready or not!"

I heard her shouting out as I crouched down in my hiding place behind the shrubs at the bottom of our garden. Freddie had taken himself off to the front of the house to hide. He knew she'd never look out there, but I wasn't really up for this game of hide and seek. I'd only agreed to it because it was easier to go with the flow than try to argue with Freddie and Chloe when they got together. So I'd chosen a really rubbish hiding place. One that I knew she'd check first. That'd give me more time to myself, as she went off in search of Freddie. He was bound to have found some obscure corner to squeeze himself into.

"Come out, come out, wherever you are," she teased, and I rolled my eyes and grimaced as my legs started cramping because of the awkward way I was squatting.

I tried to shuffle my weight from one foot to the other, and the rustle of the leaves drew her near.

"That's either a wild animal scurrying around back there or…GOTCHA!" she shouted, propelling herself over the shrubs and landing on me, like a lioness pouncing on her prey, forcing me to fall backwards as I lost my balance.

"Ugh. You win, you got me," I grunted in a bored tone,

trying to roll over and push her off me.

"I have got you," she stated with confidence. "I found you, Luca Marquez, so I get to keep you."

"What are you spouting on about now, Chloe?" I sat up and rubbed the back of my head to get rid of the dead leaves that'd tangled themselves into it.

"You're mine," she said without a shadow of a doubt on her face. "I'll marry you one day, Luca and we'll live in one of those big houses on the other side of town, with a swimming pool and games room and everything else we've ever dreamed of."

"You're crazy. I'm too old for you."

"No, you're not." She folded her tiny arms over her skinny frame and pouted those rosy pink lips at me. "Marry me, Luca. Say yes, go on. I'll buy my own ring or borrow one of my Mum's, she's got loads."

"Chloe, the boy is supposed to ask the girl. This isn't how it's done."

"Says who? Why can't the girl ask? I'm asking you right now, aren't I?"

Chloe never failed to surprise me every single day. I'd never met anyone like her in my whole life. There were hundreds of girls at my new school, and since moving to the area I'd got to know tons of them, but no one was like her. She was special, she stood out in a crowd. She was unique, crazy and infuriating all at once. But she was the only girl I ever enjoyed spending time with. The others were shallow, obsessed with their looks or the latest fashion, but not Chloe. She had depth unlike anyone I'd ever met. She intrigued me and held my attention, even though she was so much younger than me. She wanted to spend time getting to know the real me, not the face I put on for the rest of the world. Chloe had seen me at my worst, and yet she always thought the best of me. I didn't feel worthy of her praise and her attention. I couldn't ever tell her that though, her head would grow way too big.

I liked that she'd always argue the opposite with me. She liked to challenge me and no one ever dared to do that these days. I was the tough guy, with the walls of steel, but she didn't care. She'd broken them down and forced her way into my life. She was a nuisance, a pest, and my reason for getting out of bed each morning. Hell, even I was confusing myself right now.

"So?" She gritted her teeth together and gave me her evil 'I'm not taking your crap Luca' stare. "Is it a yes?"

"I'm not playing your silly games anymore, Chloe."

We both stood up. I towered over her, but she didn't look intimidated.

"I'll take that as a yes then. And Luca? I don't play silly games when it comes to important things like marriage, babies and adulting." She nodded to herself and strode off towards the front of the house, shouting her intentions to find Freddie, and leaving me gawping at her as she stomped away.

What the hell had just happened? Had I agreed to marry Chloe Ellis? I couldn't even remember what I'd said. The girl had tied me up in knots. I crossed my arms over my chest and stalked back into the house. I was twelve, she couldn't hold me to anything. I'd been tricked. If and when I was going to marry anyone, I would be the one doing the asking, not Chloe. She'd have to wait until I was ready.

-

CHLOE

Present day

"I can't believe you've remembered that, I'd completely forgotten."

"I never forget anything about you, Chloe. Every moment, every memory with you is etched into my brain. I think I loved you even back then, but I couldn't admit it to myself, let alone you."

"It all worked out right in the end." I wrapped my arms around his neck and he lifted me up so I was perfectly in line, my body to his.

"Enough chat, time for bed," he whispered in his husky, sexy voice.

"Yes please!" I purred, as he ran his soft lips across my jaw and down my neck. I was more than ready to spend the rest of the night being as close to him as I could get. To feel him inside me and know that without a doubt he was mine, I was his and we were each other's.

"I want you to grab my hair and grab my ass, just like you grabbed my heart. Pull me close and never *ever* let me go. I want to feel you inside me, stretching me, stroking me, making me come because of what you do to me. You always take my breath away, so make me breathless and then bring me back to life, Luca."

He growled his response and carried me up the stairs, throwing me down on the bed ready to take what he needed and give me what only he could give. This right here was everything. This was my happily ever after.

Epilogue

One year later…

I skipped my way through the doors of the club, barely able to contain the excitement bubbling away inside of me.

"Afternoon, Chloe."

I turned to the left to see Dylan, the new guy, casually leaning up against the deserted bar and checking out something on his phone.

"That's Mrs Marquez to you," Marco snapped back at him, then gave me a sly smile.

"Easy tiger," I joked. "Is he in his office?"

"No idea, but head on up. You'll find him eventually."

"Thanks Marco. Oh and one more thing, tell Gina I said thanks when you see her next. She'll know what it's about."

Marco frowned at me, but he didn't argue. I knew Marco and Gina had something going on and they were keeping it on the down low, but in true girlfriend style, she told me everything. I was so pleased that my best friend had found such a great guy to take care of her. Marco was one of the good guys, and I knew that things were getting serious pretty fast. At first I'd thought they were like chalk and cheese, but then, were they really so different? Okay, so Gina had her business, but that didn't define her. When all was said and done, she had a heart of gold and was loyal to the end; traits that could also be used to describe Marco. So actually, they were a match made in heaven.

As to why I wanted to say thank you? Well that was all down to an anonymous envelope I received through the post the day before, containing mug shots of one Teresa Burman. The photocopied documents attached showed she'd been arrested for prostitution, possession of a class A drug and intent to supply. I had to admit the news certainly gave me a lift. It couldn't have happened to a nicer person, but when I saw the name of the arresting officer in amongst the paper work, I had to smile at the helping hand that Karma was given. Officer Anthony DiMarco. Who'd have thought Gina's brother was a cop. Not me. I was grateful for the information nonetheless, and the thought that my ex best friend would be spending time repenting her many, many sins, made it even sweeter.

I crept up the back stairs, listening out for any tell-tale signs that Luca was up there, but it was all quiet. I pushed my way through his office door, but apart from the glow of his screens the room was void of life. Perfect. I took the plastic gift I'd bought especially for him to see and gazed around the room. Where would be a good place to put it for him to find? I wanted to surprise him, but I didn't want to just put it in a box and present it to him. I glanced at the crystal tumblers that he kept near his whisky, and decided that was the best place. Luca always poured himself a few fingers of whisky when he came into his office. So I balanced it across the tumbler closest to the edge.

Just as I was about to head out and see where in the building he was hiding, Luca burst through the door and upon seeing me his face lit up. He walked straight over to me, cupped my face and kissed me like he hadn't seen me for weeks. It had been three hours.

"I've missed you."

"You haven't been gone that long."

"Any time away from you is too long."

Luca had turned extremely soppy and sentimental since we'd got married six months ago. I think he was making up for all the years he'd held his feelings back. I wasn't complaining though, I loved his possessive overprotectiveness. I put my own hands on either side of his ruggedly handsome face and kissed him back with just as much longing.

"I love you, husband of mine."

He smiled and asked if I wanted a drink. I shook my head but bit my lip as he headed for his drinks cabinet and the gift I'd left for him. He looked down at it and froze, a deeply furrowed frown appearing on his forehead. He picked up the white plastic stick and turned to me.

"Is this yours?"

"Well I should hope so, unless there are any other women in the building who'd be leaving random pregnancy tests in your office?"

His eyes bugged out of his head.

"It's got a cross on it. It says pregnant...are you...?"

I nodded, still biting my lip as the reality started to filter into his stunned brain. He gasped, then looked from me to the test and then back to me again. Then his face erupted into the biggest shit-eating grin I'd ever seen.

"We're gonna have a baby? Fuck, Chloe. I'm gonna be a Dad?"

I couldn't hold back my own smile now as I revelled in his excitement. I knew this was what he'd dreamed of. He talked about babies and kids incessantly. One of the older guys who worked for him had recently become a Dad again, and seeing Luca look at the baby when he'd brought her in to show us had melted my heart. He even asked if he could hold her, and I'd never thought in a million years that Luca would be the baby type. But that day, it was glaringly obvious that my husband was broody, and who was I to deny him what he wanted?

"You'll make the best Daddy ever, Luca." I smiled as he peered back down at the test in awe, not quite believing what he was seeing.

Then he was walking over to me, pulling me into the

warmest hug, and lifting me off the ground.

"I fucking love you, Mrs Marquez. You've made me the happiest man alive."

"This is just the start of our new adventure," I said, as he placed me back down like I was made of glass, and stroked his hand over my flat belly.

"We've got a peanut, but soon it'll grow into a brazil nut, then a walnut...and before we know it, there'll be a little Marquez running around driving us all nuts."

He laughed and nuzzled my neck as we held each other close, breathing each other in. Then he stood back and looked me straight in the eye and said, "Thank you."

It was clear from the sincerity in his face, that today I'd given him the world. He deserved it though, because he was my world, and I couldn't wait to share this new chapter in our lives with him. Our story would never end. The happily ever after would just become happy moments in our forever, because for Luca and I there was no beginning and no ending. Our story spanned a lifetime and we'd always be together. Soul mates never part and a love like ours would never die.

I'd met the love of my life, my soul mate, when I was eight-years-old. Some people search a whole lifetime to find what we'd found so early on in our lives. Luca and I were always written in the stars.

Thank you so much for reading. If you enjoyed

following Luca and Chloe on their journey, then please spread the word about their story and leave a review.

Leave a written review if you have the time,
Or just click on those stars that too will be fine!

Other Books
by NIKKI J SUMMERS

RYLEY

Don't trust the fairy tales. They trick you into believing true love will appear on the back of a white horse, in the form of a perfect, handsome Prince Charming. Most of the time, Prince Charming turns out to be even more deceptive and evil than the wolf himself. I thought I'd met my soul mate at high school. Turned out my Mr Wright was so very wrong.

JACKSON

I live in a cruel and unforgiving world. I learnt from an early age how vicious life can be, but I'm a survivor. Life may have dragged me down to the depths of hell, but I know how to dance with the devil. Sometimes bad things happen to good people for no other reason than to remind us that this life is cruel. Sometimes good people are pushed to do very bad things to right the wrongs of another. But when all is said and done, we need to ask ourselves... how far would you go to protect the ones you love?

Ryley thinks she has her whole life mapped out. Her happy ever after with her high school sweetheart, Justin, is already planned down to the very last detail. But life doesn't always work out the way we expect it to, and when demons from Justin's life threaten to destroy everything they've built up, Ryley finds herself thrown into a world of deception, lies and confusion. Truths get twisted, love and hate walk a dubious thin line, and the enemy you think you know isn't always what they seem.

This book serves as a reminder that the first Prince Charming to cross your path isn't always the hero in your happily ever after.

*An enemies to lovers, second chance novel. Although this story isn't a dark read, there are elements of darkness within, so please take note of the trigger warnings. There are cameos from Luca's story in this book. However, you don't have to have read Luca to enjoy this, it can be read as a standalone.

**Warning: 18 years + recommended reader age due to

sexual content. This story also contains scenes of drug abuse, suicide and sexual violence that may be upsetting to readers. Please proceed with caution.

Hurt
TO LOVE

After darkness, always comes the light.

The darkness is where I've lived ever since they took me all those months ago. Dragging me into the shadows to play their sick and twisted games. I don't know why they took me. They talk about an eye for an eye, but I don't know these men. How can I be punished for a sin I know nothing about? A sin I didn't commit.

They love to watch me suffer, they live to make my life hell. I thought my life was over.

Until him.

He blazed through my darkness like a lightning bolt, shining through the void of nothingness. He was a force to be reckoned with.

They thought they'd broken me, that somehow they'd won. But they didn't expect him. I know I never did. And now, my life will never be the same again.